THE EMERALD LIZARD

THE EMERALD LIZARD

CHRIS WILTZ

A Neal Rafferty Mystery

A DUTTON BOOK

DUTTON
Published by the Penguin Group
Penguin Books USA Inc., 375 Hudson Street,
New York, New York 10014, U.S.A.
Penguin Books Ltd, 27 Wrights Lane,
London W8 5TZ, England
Penguin Books Australia Ltd, Ringwood,
Victoria, Australia
Penguin Books Canada Ltd, 2801 John Street,
Markham, Ontario, Canada L3R 1B4
Penguin Books (N.Z.) Ltd, 182-190 Wairau Road,
Auckland 10, New Zealand

Penguin Books Ltd, Registered Offices:
Harmondsworth, Middlesex, England

First published by Dutton, an imprint of New American Library, a
division of Penguin Books USA Inc.
Distributed in Canada by McClelland & Stewart Inc.

First Printing, January, 1991
10 9 8 7 6 5 4 3 2 1

 REGISTERED TRADEMARK—MARCA REGISTRADA

LIBRARY OF CONGRESS CATALOGING IN PUBLICATION DATA:

Wiltz, Chris.
    The Emerald Lizard / Chris Wiltz.
      p.   cm.
    I. Title.
    PS3573.I4783E44   1991
    813'.54—dc20   90–46189
                                                                    CIP

PRINTED IN THE UNITED STATES OF AMERICA
Set in Times Roman
Designed by Leonard Telesca

PUBLISHER'S NOTE
This is a work of fiction. Names, characters, places, and incidents either are the
products of the author's imagination or are used fictitiously, and any resemblance to
actual persons, living or dead, events, or locales is entirely coincidental.

For my daughter, Marigny

Violence today? It's what people pass on to their kids instead of a value system. If it's not already in the home, they bring it in via the TV set. It's replaced work as a way to make money. It's replaced sex as going to get some action.

Detective Lt. Roderick Rankin
Homicide Division
New Orleans Police Department

Contents

THE EMERALD LIZARD

1

Jackie

There were three remarkable things about the night of November tenth: it was the first time a woman ever slapped me in the face, it was the first time a woman ever beat me in a game of pool, and it was the first time I'd heard anything from Jackie Silva in sixteen years.

A couple of hours after Diana DiCarlo slapped me—and after being humiliated at the pool table by a twenty-two-year-old *girl*, if you can believe it—I was reclining in bed, propped up just enough to nurse a Scotch and smoke a bunch of cigarettes. I was wondering what to do about Diana.

The phone rang. I looked at the clock. Five minutes till midnight. I fully expected it to be Diana. Unlike a lot of women who would rather die than be first to call, she was more interested in games that are played in the boudoir, not games that get you there.

"What," I said into the receiver.

"Is this Neal Rafferty?"

I said I was.

The voice was a woman's, low, husky and tense. "Remember me, Neal?" A whiskey voice, talking quickly and right up against the mouthpiece, like maybe she didn't want someone nearby to hear what she was saying. It was a voice that sounded as if it were in trouble. It was also disturbingly familiar. I sat up in bed, listening hard.

"Am I calling too late?" she asked.

"Depends on who you are."

"It's Jackie, Neal. Jackie Silva. You remember, don't you?"

Sure I remembered Jackie. She and my sister were inseparable all through junior high and most of high school. Then Reenie met Michael who became her husband, and Jackie met too many guys in too many places where a high school girl shouldn't meet guys, mostly French Quarter bars and nightclubs.

Jackie had polio when she was eight or nine and had been left with a slight limp. She walked a bit more slowly and a bit more provocatively than she would have otherwise. She'd also fallen behind a couple of grades. So while the other girls were turning sweet sixteen and still decorating the gym for sock hops, Jackie turned eighteen, the legal age at that time to bar hop and drink in New Orleans.

Reenie got married and Jackie came to the wedding, and after that we didn't hear from her again until she called and told us she was getting married, too, to a man named Larry Silva, a deep sea diver she'd met in a joint on Decatur Street, a place called La Casa. Our whole family went to the wedding.

That was sixteen years ago. I still remembered Jackie walking in that oddly sensual way down the aisle of the Mater Dolorosa church on her daddy's arm. She was dressed in white lace from head to foot and smiled radiantly for the wedding guests, who didn't fill the first five pews on either side of the aisle. Jackie's daddy wasn't smiling.

On the Silva side of the church were a bunch of guys looking like thugs in their shiny new suits. The girls they were with had long hair ratted high up off their heads, breasts that pointed straight and sharp ahead, and dresses that clung to each hard curve. Somebody popped her chewing gum. It rang out against the high vaulted ceiling like a pistol shot. A laugh was shushed. From where I was sitting in the third row, I could see that the backs of Larry Silva's hands were tattooed.

When Jackie's father handed her over to Larry, the echo of a stifled sob lingered along the sanctuary walls. It came from Jackie's mother.

The tenor of my phone conversation with Jackie seemed to be anxious and secretive. I matched the tone.

"Where are you, Jackie?"

There was a moment's pause during which I heard the flick of a cigarette lighter, a sharp intake of breath, and then she let go with a loud, raucous laugh.

"Westwego," she said finally.

"Westwego?" I repeated.

Westwego is on the West Bank, the other side of the Mississippi River from New Orleans. If I sounded amazed, I didn't mean to. After all, Larry was a diver and the diving and salvage company he worked for was on the West Bank. I knew they had moved there after they got married. I guess my amazement was because of the way she was laughing.

"Yeah," she said. "Might as well be in China, huh?" She laughed some more. She didn't sound anxious anymore; she sounded as if she were pretty well into tying one on.

But then she got serious again—and anxious. "I'm in trouble, Neal." I heard ice rattle against the side of a glass. "There's a man over here, a stupid man. He's stupid about everything except how to hurt people. And he's cheap. He's stupid and cheap and that's why he's dangerous." She was talking quickly again, not making a whole lot of sense. "And I owe him a lot of money. I owe him for The Emerald Lizard."

As you can imagine, I was concerned, but I had no idea what she was talking about. "Is Larry there with you?" I asked.

"Oh no. Larry's going to die. It's all he thinks about . . ."

"Jackie, you're not making sense."

"Yes I am. Just listen. This man—he's got a contract out on me."

"Who is he?"

"His name is Bubba Brevna, and he says if I don't come up with five thousand dollars by Friday, he's going to have my tongue cut out."

I managed to find out that The Emerald Lizard was a lounge Jackie owned in Westwego. I told her I'd meet her there the next afternoon, figuring she would need most of the morning to sleep off her drunk, and also because I had to be in court.

I had trouble going to sleep. I had stopped thinking about Diana; I was thinking about Jackie, about that provocative walk of hers, the way it could make you want to crawl the walls, and those sloe-eyed looks she could give you, looks that made you suspect she was up to no good. And that crooked smile that ended in two crescent-shaped lines, a smile that could bring a sixteen-year-old boy to his knees.

And I remembered how dangerous it all had been. *She* was danger—the walk, the eyes, the smile, all of her. She could make you do things you'd swear you'd never do again, and then you would do it again, and the more you did it, the bolder she got, until sometimes you thought your sixteen-year-old heart would stop.

I got a whiff of the way Jackie used to smell on those steamy nights, and with that whiff came a taste way on the back of my tongue. My adrenaline kicked in. Sleep was out. It was the taste and smell of danger all grown up now.

* * *

But, in a strange way—strange because this is New Orleans, a tiny town really—the story doesn't exactly start with Jackie or in Westwego, but in the office of my closest friend, Maurice, on the morning of November tenth.

2

Pinkie

Maurice sat behind his desk wearing a black three-piece Western-cut suit, heavy black-frame glasses, and the look of love.

Little did I know that this was the last time I'd ever see him like this, sitting in his law office—the only place where he was completely comfortable except a courtroom —happy, in control of his destiny, single-minded in his pursuit of justice for all. I might have been a bit more sentimental if I'd realized.

"Not only that," he was saying, "she thinks I'm sexy," and blushed to the roots of his shiny brown hair.

Let's see. I'd known Maurice for about fifteen years, since he was a brilliant young assistant district attorney and I was a foot-sore young cop on the beat. In those fifteen years Maurice had seen me go through a lot of changes, including my more or less forced resignation from the New Orleans Police Department. He then persuaded me to do what he'd done—go to work for myself—

and gave me my first case as a private investigator. The biggest change I'd seen Maurice go through was from prosecutor to one of the most respected defense lawyers in town, which was exactly what I'd expected. Otherwise, he still wore the black Western suit and cowboy boots he'd worn ever since I'd known him, and still had those slightly lopsided horn-rims. He carried a black leather schoolboy's satchel instead of a briefcase, and to get him out of the house he had to be held at gunpoint. I'd heard him described as boyish, eccentric, genius, worka-holic, weird . . . but sexy? That one hadn't come up before.

"Sexy is in the eye of the beholder," I said.

He sat forward, his elbows on the desk, and talked to me intently. "We're exactly alike," he said. "How can I explain it to you?" His eyes drifted around the walls of books, then snapped back to me. "She's like a twin, my long-lost twin. We think alike; we like the same things. We read voraciously. We hate TV. We both like to work more than anything else. Well, except being together." He stopped to chuckle. "You won't believe this, Neal, but at two o'clock this morning, Nita realized we'd for-gotten to eat dinner."

Maurice knew I wouldn't be surprised that he could forget to eat.

"Did her remembering do any good?" I asked. Since Maurice rarely remembered to eat, there was rarely any-thing to eat in his house.

"She is so fantastic, Neal. She found a can of red beans and whipped up the most fabulous omelet."

My stomach churned and growled in protest. "And did you get any sleep after that gourmet's delight?"

"Oh, a couple of hours. Nita seems to need a bit more sleep than I do."

"A couple of hours, huh? That could get to be habit-forming."

"She's moving in with me."

I now have to interrupt what Maurice said to impress

upon you how incredible this was. I don't mean to say he'd never had a girlfriend before. He'd had a few and some of them were women he really liked, but none of them could take the fact that Maurice was married to his work, and that she was always going to come second. He was too obvious about it. I'd even heard him admit it once when under direct examination, so to speak. No woman can take hearing that. But this time was different. I'd never heard him this excited over someone, never heard him talk about living with anyone, much less anyone consider living with him. Maurice had an obsessive personality, but even women drawn to obsessive personalities couldn't take him. He was so honest, direct, and open about it that it was almost unbearable to most women. He didn't really need anyone, so I thought, so he didn't try very hard to get anyone. When they started getting unhappy, he let them go. A couple of times when they wouldn't go easily, he refused to see them anymore.

He was saying, "She loves my house. She's going to transform it." He added, "She's very artistic," as if I should already know.

Now wait a minute. This was maybe something altogether different. I mean, who wouldn't love Maurice's house? One of those high-ceilinged Garden District mansions. And who wouldn't want to transform it? Maurice hadn't done anything to it except turn the den into another law office after his parents died.

Maurice said, "I've decided we should be married by Christmas."

And this was November tenth. I felt panic rising rapidly.

"Maurice, you told me you've known her for less than two weeks."

"I know, but I'm absolutely sure. I haven't been as sure of anything since I knew I wanted to be a lawyer."

Which had been forever. Maurice, staring at me with those wide round eyes. Boyish. I think that's the word I've always used to describe him, even though he's about two years older than I am.

I fooled around lighting a cigarette for a minute before I said what I had to say: "I don't mind telling you I'm a little worried."

He smiled broadly at me. "Of course you are. You wouldn't be my friend if you weren't. I *expect* you to be worried. Until you meet her. Then you won't be worried anymore."

I didn't have an answer ready for that. I asked him what kind of work it was she did that she liked so much.

"She's a photographer," he said, "an excellent photographer. Of course, that's a hard way to make a living no matter how good you are, so she's been taking odd jobs when things get tight. She doesn't have to do that anymore."

"But that's exactly what I mean, Maurice." I decided I'd better tread gently, then I said, "I mean, maybe she's tired of all those odd jobs." I wanted to bite my tongue.

But he smiled at me with the greatest affection. "I understand what you're saying, that maybe she's using me. Don't worry, really. She's not tired of anything. She's only twenty-two years old."

Great. And Maurice was pushing forty.

A girl who liked to take pictures, who told Maurice he was sexy, and who wanted to move in and redo his house. Oh boy.

"Look, Maurice, I hope you don't mind me saying this, but it would make me feel a whole lot better if you'd stop talking about getting married for at least six months."

Another indulgent smile. "As soon as you meet her, you'll see we're made for each other. And you must meet her tonight, Neal. Get a date and let's go to dinner. Nita says that the only way we won't forget to eat is to make plans well in advance."

"I'll see if I can round up the princess," I said weakly. There was no talking to him; he was off the deep end.

"You'll love her, you really will. Nita." He said her name in two short, punctuated syllables. "Isn't that a great name? So crisp and pert and energetic. Just like she is." His grin was so wide I thought his face would split.

Isn't it funny how silly someone in love can seem? Unless, of course, it's you.

I left Maurice mooning around his office and went out into the reception area where Pinkie, Maurice's young, pert, energetic secretary, was sitting in front of a computer screen. Her short frothy blond hair curled behind a small, delicate ear. An earring like a beaten gold scythe swayed gently as her fingers flew over the keyboard making soft rapid plonks. I sat on the corner of the adjacent desk and waited for her to turn rose-shadowed sapphire blues on me. She rested her chin on her laced fingers and looked at me in her dreamy way, her lips slightly parted, asking to be kissed.

"What's it like working for a lawyer in love?" I asked.

Her long black lashes dipped once. "I like it," she said. "I give the orders now."

I really got a kick out of Pinkie. When she thought no one was watching her she was very childlike, jiggling her legs under the desk, chewing gum and blowing bubbles while she typed a letter, or eating candy, a long chocolate streak on her cheek, yawning with complete abandon. But in a situation like this, she was quite the sophisticate, very aware of herself—and her sexuality.

She smiled a slow conspirator's smile. "What *I* want to know about is detectives in love."

Pinkie had been after me for roughly the three years she'd worked for Maurice. It was the running joke between us, though she wasn't entirely joking and I admit to being flattered by the attention.

"What about them?" I asked. "What it's like to work for them?"

"No, that wasn't at all what I had in mind."

"Oh. Then let me tell you about detectives in love." I learned down closer to her, lowering my voice. "Detectives fall in love nearly every day. That's because they're such horny old buggers. They know women from all walks of life—lady cops, ladies of the night, high society ladies—that's not what they're particular about. What they're most particular about is that they're not seen with anyone too young or too innocent or too wholesome. They have reputations to protect."

And that was the running argument between us, the difference in our ages. Or, more specifically, the fact that I thought Pinkie was too young for me. She was just a kid. The same age as this Nita.

Her smile vanished while I was talking. "Of course," she said. "Their reputations as sex-crazed, gun-slinging adolescents who think the bigger a woman's mammary glands are, the more brains she has." She turned her slim squared shoulders away from me, to give her attention to the more cooperative computer.

Maybe she thought I was taking a crack at her figure, the type of build that some people might call boyish.

"You know I'm just kidding, Pinkie."

She kept her eyes on the screen. "Adolescent humor."

I sighed. "Let's face it, Pinkie, I'm too young for you. You need an older guy, someone you can match wits with. Someone into early senility maybe?" (All right, all right—it *was* despicable.)

I slid off her desk, ready to go, but not before the golden scythes sliced the air at the sides of her cheeks and I got a sharp bite of cold sapphire.

"You are," she said, "a despicable human being."

"That's good," I told her. "I hope you include that when you recommend me to your clients who are sleazy enough to need the services of a detective. In my business, 'despicable' translates as *effective*."

"A *low*life," she said with disgust.

3.

Diana

You might think what I said to Pinkie means I'm not particular about women. Not so.

Hell, I have a history of being particular about women. For instance, Diana DiCarlo. Thirty-two, five foot seven, dark brown hair that took a straight and elegant plunge before curling gently under her chin, a body that looked long and willowy under her fashionable clothes, but was substantial enough to give you something to hold on to. It's true—I always like something to hold on to. She said not to let the name fool you, that she was French—Parisian French—descended from the early French settlers, and she looked it, with that smooth fair skin and those chocolate-drop eyes.

Diana was the most imperious woman I'd ever known except maybe old Grandma Rafferty, who was just as haughty and demanding. Diana was also smart and independent. She had a glamorous job as assistant director of public relations for a swank French Quarter hotel.

Plenty of men lined up for a chance to take Diana out, and every once in a while she went with one of them. That was okay. It didn't kill me, and the less it seemed to kill me, the less interested she seemed to be in anyone else.

So the princess and I were having a pretty good time, mostly in between the sheets, but I figured one of us would get bored with the scenario sooner or later. I had no delusions about the permanence of our togetherness. We were from two different worlds, two different backgrounds, which I admit was one of the attractions. Not only that, I had decided I was set in my ways and liked living alone. Of course, I had assumed that was true of Maurice, too.

On the night of our dinner with Maurice and Nita, Diana had to go to a cocktail party thrown by some conventioneers staying at the hotel. I called Maurice and told him we'd be late, and lounged in front of the TV with a couple of Scotches before it was time to pick up Diana.

She was waiting for me in front of the hotel. I had warned her over the phone to be out there when she said she'd be so I wouldn't have to sit parked in the passenger zone like some damned chauffeur. Making people wait was one of the ways Diana controlled them, and I refused to put up with it.

The November air was cool and breezy. Diana had on a short fur cape over a black dress. I reached over and opened the car door. She slid into the seat next to me with the sound of silky materials rubbing against each other and the smell of Shalimar masking the odor of smoke-saturated upholstery. The cape slipped into the space between the seats when she leaned into me with a long deep kiss. The dress was strapless.

She broke the kiss off just short of hot house flowers sprouting full grown from the car seats. "Hello, darling."

One of her arms came from around my neck and her

hand began making its way down the front of my shirt. I held it against me, stopping it.

"Princess," I said, "we're on our way to meet the love of Maurice's life. Save it for later."

"Okay." She straightened herself in the seat and smoothed her dress down where it had ridden halfway up her thigh. "But not too much later."

I drove uptown to Franky and Johnny's, a bar and restaurant on Arabella Street, half a block from the river. It's actually in the basement of an old raised house, with a blond brick façade added on to the front of the lower half of the house that turns it into a business establishment. It looks like what it is—a neighborhood place, nothing fancy, plenty of ice-cold beer and fresh boiled seafood.

Diana stared at the neon Budweiser sign lighting up a picture window cut into the brick.

"We're going *here* to meet the love of Maurice's life?" she demanded.

"Their choice."

"But I don't want to go in there dressed like this." She pulled the cape close around her as if someone were going to try to rip it off. "Why didn't you tell me? I would have gone home and changed."

"Hey, you look great," I said enthusiastically.

"That is hardly the point."

"Well, it was too late for you to change. It doesn't matter anyway."

The way her mouth curled up on one side, I might as well have told her that money doesn't matter or that the American Dream is dead.

Just about that time a young guy wearing threadbare jeans and a Tulane T-shirt with the arms and neck cut out of it went through the front door.

"Do you want to leave your fur in the car and put my jacket on over your dress?" I asked her. The jacket was one of those lightweight all-weather deals, khaki.

She drew herself up, let the fur fall so it appeared to be casually slung over one shoulder, and said in her most imperious voice, "No thank you."

We walked into the front room of Franky and Johnny's, which has a long bar against the left wall and a jukebox on the opposite side. The light from the jukebox bathed the room in purple, and a lavender sheen radiated from Diana's bare shoulder. Whenever the front door opens the beer swillers at the bar usually turn around to see who's coming in, and immediately lose interest. But they leered appreciatively at Diana, and as we went toward the back, one guy shivered with lust and called out, "What's hap'nin', mama!" Diana flashed him an evil look. A couple of steps behind her, I gave the thumbs-up sign to the guy. Diana's pointed heels on the old vinyl floor snapped like reprimands.

The back room was the restaurant. From the luridly romantic light of the bar we emerged wincing into a bright fluorescent wash that is the trademark of a New Orleans seafood joint. Diana strode with certainty to a table for four in the rear. The man who jumped up from the table looked vaguely like my friend Maurice, but this man had the sleeves of a blue Oxford cloth shirt rolled up so he could eat the mound of crawfish in front of him, and he had on a pair of jeans. I stepped closer, squinting.

"Maurice?"

"Diana, Neal, this is Nita Greene." The hand he gestured with dripped crawfish juice.

I did a double-take, to Nita, to Maurice, then back to Nita. She was Maurice's clone. I mean it. Her hair was longer than Maurice's, but it was the same color brown, parted on the right, bangs swept to the side above glasses. Hers were tortoiseshell. She had on an Oxford cloth shirt, too, white, button-down. If he was boyish, then she was girlish, both of them with their round faces and their brown eyes looking big and innocent behind lenses.

Diana and I sat down and I ordered another pitcher of beer and more crawfish, some of the first of the season. I was ready to dig in after a six-month-long abstinence. The princess, however, wouldn't eat crawfish. She declined to eat anything at all that night, preferring to let me know through food deprivation that she was not happy. She ordered a Dubonnet on the rocks.

As soon as the waitress left the table, Nita said, "Neal, doesn't Maurice look great?"

"Yeah, I was gonna say . . . yeah, you look great, Maurice."

Maurice nudged her with an elbow. She angled her body a bit more in his direction.

"I told him he was too sexy to go around looking like a high plains undertaker all the time," Nita said.

They both blushed and we all laughed. Diana dug her nails into my thigh. Then she pinched me when Nita picked up a big red mudbug and sucked its head.

Let me explain that no true New Orleanian eats the tail of a crawfish without first sucking the juices from its head. There's no way to describe it delicately, I suppose. It's not a delicate act. Which is why the princess wouldn't eat crawfish.

Nita asked Diana about her job at the hotel while she peeled a rung of shell from the crawfish tail and popped it out. As soon as Diana answered one question, Nita asked another. She was fascinated by public relations work. A couple more questions down the line and I detected a note of boredom creeping into Diana's voice.

"Why are you so interested in public relations?" Diana asked finally. "I thought you were a photographer. Are you interested in doing photography for a public relations firm?"

"I take photographs," Nita said, "but that's not how I make money."

"She could if she wanted to," Maurice interjected.

Diana looked at him for a moment, but her eyes snapped back to Nita. "Then why don't you?" she asked.

"I'm not sure I want to. Not yet. I'd rather take odd

jobs and have fun with photography. I guess I'm afraid that if I get too serious about it, it won't be fun anymore."

"What kind of odd jobs are you talking about?" Diana wanted to know.

"Clerical jobs, sales jobs, whatever I can get."

"But nothing to do with photography," Diana said.

"Well, no. I take the pictures I want to·take."

"So." Diana sat back. "You're an *artiste*, not just some workaday drudge. Actually, that sounds fairly serious."

When Diana said something like that, it was hard to know how to take it. Was *she* being serious, or was she goading Nita? Her tone betrayed nothing. I certainly didn't know how to take it. I looked at Nita, stole a sidelong glance at Maurice . . .

Nita knew how to take it—undaunted. "I don't think of myself as an artist. I don't want to take myself that seriously."

"Then," Diana said, "why not make money at photography, do portraits or some industrial photography or morgue photography—whatever you can get."

Maurice spoke up, a little too loudly. "I believe, Diana, that Nita is trying to tell you that she'd like to nurture her art for a while. There's nothing wrong with that."

This was making me awfully nervous. I have nerves of steel when it comes to entering dark places at night or finding the bodies of murder victims, but these social situations . . .

Nita, however, seemed determined to make Diana understand her point of view. She leaned toward her. "Look, I don't want to get bored taking pictures. I'd rather be bored answering somebody's telephone or being a file clerk. I want to feel alive when I'm behind the camera. I want to be intensely interested in my subject. But I don't want to be like those ambitious self-important artists either, who think their art is the most serious, most important thing in the world, and if they don't get into the right gallery, and if they don't get enough recognition, they want to die. If I try to make money doing what I want to do, then I have to deal with all that. I don't want to always be seeking someone else's approval."

Diana tilted her chin back and stroked it with an index finger. "All that sounds pretty good," she said to the acoustical tiles of Franky and Johnny's ceiling, "but are you sure you're not just afraid of rejection? Or failure?" Now she leveled her gaze at Nita. "Or could it be that you're afraid to succeed? Then you wouldn't be able to work so leisurely anymore. Are you afraid of hard work, or are you afraid of competition?"

Maurice, I could see, was hot. He started to speak, but Nita put her hand on his, and said to Diana, "Maybe I am afraid of rejection. Maybe I'm afraid of competition, too. I don't know. It's easier for me not to worry about those things right now. I'm not afraid of hard work, but I'll be honest with you, I'd rather work leisurely right now, and think about Maurice." She smiled at him and closed her hand around his. "He's what's important to me right now and I like to concentrate on one thing at a time. But it just so happens that I'm also working on some portraits. No one's paying me and I can do them whenever I want to, and whenever the women are available, and I could get pretty excited about it. Eventually, I'll work it into an entire series of portraits."

"What women?" Diana asked.

Nita wouldn't tell her who they were, but she went on about them, using words like grotesque and vulnerable, and phrases like slice of life, though she did say that all the women she'd taken pictures of so far were on the West Bank. Diana didn't sneer when Nita mentioned the West Bank, and after a while I relaxed and started to lose interest.

But then Diana said, "All right, Nita, I'll make you an offer, call it a challenge. At the hotel there's a small gallery. It's a space leading out to the courtyard where we showcase a single artist's work."

Nita nodded. "I've seen it. Someone I know had a show there. It's very nice."

"I've had a cancellation for January. Get fifteen or twenty portraits ready and I'll give you a one-woman show. We do a very elegant presentation folio and on opening night provide cocktails and hors d'oeuvres. In a month hundreds of people will see your photographs. We also have a good sales record, and we take a fraction of the percentage an art gallery takes. Just enough to cover costs. All you have to do is get the portraits done. We'll do the rest. What do you say?"

Challenge my foot. It was an outright dare. And Maurice didn't like it.

"I don't think so," he said. "We have plans. We'll be tied up for most of January."

That's right—he wanted to get married at Christmas, take a long honeymoon trip, I supposed. I was beginning to like Diana's challenge more and more.

Poor Nita, though. All this time, throughout Diana's grilling and her explanations, she had seemed very self-assured, especially for someone so young. Now she looked at Maurice, emotion obviously pulling on her. He'd given her an out, but she wasn't taking it. Part of her, at least, wanted to accept Diana's offer. There was a wicked smile curving Diana's mouth.

Nita looked at the red-checked cloth. "I don't know," she said quietly. "No one's ever offered me a show before. I'll have to think about it."

Diana said, "I'll need an answer within the week. You'll have to figure out if you have the time to do it. And the self-confidence," she added. With that she got up and went to the ladies room.

None of us said anything right away. Then Nita was saying to Maurice, "I think I want to do it."

"But we're supposed to get married at Christmas."

I was on the edge of my chair, thinking I ought to excuse myself, but I waited too long.

"We haven't made any plans yet," Nita said. "Couldn't

we postpone it for a month? How about Valentine's Day?" she asked, trying to entice him. Then quietly again, almost shyly, "It's a good opportunity for me."

"She's not doing it for you," Maurice told her. He never was one to beat around the bush. "She's doing it to prove her point, or at least she's hoping to prove it," he revised. "She's trying to make you do something you've already decided you don't want to do."

By this time I was feeling quite sorry for Nita. She couldn't look at Maurice. She went back to examining red checks. "But she's right. I'm afraid of competition. I'm afraid of being rejected. I'm afraid I'll never be able to take a photograph that's good enough to sell. Even if she's not doing it for me, she's giving me the opportunity to get over all that."

Maurice put his hand on the back of Nita's neck. "You'll get over it when you're ready to get over it," he said as lightly as Maurice is capable of saying anything.

"You were never afraid," Nita said to him. And then by some kind of tacit agreement, they dropped it, Maurice's hand falling off her neck.

The next thing I knew I was babbling away, trying to keep up my end of the chitchat, talking about playing pool and Murphy Zeringue and the boys over at Grady's.

Well, that did it. It turned out that Nita loved to play pool, and the next thing I knew Maurice was suggesting that we go over to Grady's Irish Channel Bar so Nita and I could play.

I want you to realize how remarkable this was: All the years I'd known Maurice, and all the times I'd asked him to go over to Grady's with me, he'd never gone, and now here he was suggesting we go over there—all because Nita liked to play pool.

I suggested, however, that we go to Robert's over on Calhoun and Claiborne instead, that it was closer. That's doubtful, and it's true that the best of the local hustlers, like Murphy, are at Grady's, but I don't like to take women there. Especially a woman like Diana. Especially dressed like she was. If we went there, Murphy's pointed ratlike face might have to be surgically removed from her cleavage before the night was over.

"I can't believe you agreed to play pool with her." She shot it at me as soon as we were alone in the car.

"Hang in there, princess." I put the car in gear and slid from under a crepe myrtle tree. "We won't be long. I'll let her think she has a fighting chance before I wipe her out." (I hate like hell admitting I said that.)

"Sure. And then we'll have to sit around and have more discussion about how sad and funny and grotesque and fascinating people are."

"She said all that?"

"Neal." Two syllables that carried a threat.

"She was just trying to tell you something about herself and her photographs."

"Right. I'll bet her favorite photographer is Diane Arbus and that she reads Flannery O'Connor for inspiration."

"Who? Give her a break, princess. She was trying to impress Maurice's friends."

"God! All that lovey-dovey stuff—it's absolutely nauseating!"

"Is that so?" I asked, going for poignancy.

"I mean in a public place. Making eyes at each other, constantly touching each other . . ." She settled back in the seat, crossing her legs. "Do you think she'll accept my offer?"

"*Dare*," I amended.

"It's a perfectly legitimate offer," she said testily.

"So it is. Quite generous, considering you've never seen any of her pictures. What if she's no good? Aren't you taking a chance?"

"I don't think so," she said confidently, but I had no idea if she meant she thought Nita would turn out to be a good photographer or if she thought Nita wouldn't accept her offer at all.

Actually, my bet was on the latter. "Don't underestimate her, princess. I think she's going to do it, and you better hope she's good or you've just stuck your pretty little neck out way too far. She's got what counts—an awful lot of youthful exuberance."

"Well," Diana said, "her youthful exuberance bores me out of my mind. So does watching you play pool," she added.

"But you've never watched me play pool!"

"That hardly matters."

Her hauteur always brought out the tease in me. "Let me get this straight. You're bored if we're not dressed to the teeth and dining in some elegant restaurant, or undressed and in bed. Is that right?"

But as soon as I said it, I realized it was essentially true. That's the way it had been for the nearly two months we'd been seeing each other.

She let half a block of silence pass before she said, "Yes, that's right. I suppose it does sound a little selfish," she admitted.

"And maybe a little boring?"

She didn't answer that. I parked in the closed gas station next door to Robert's. Maurice's car was nowhere in sight. I didn't want to fight, and I certainly didn't give a damn about playing pool with Nita. I left the keys in the ignition, fully intending to tell Diana that as soon as Maurice and Nita arrived, I'd take her home, that I'd much rather be in bed with her than leaning over a pool table. I put my hand on her neck, underneath her hair, and pulled her toward me.

She resisted, huddling in her fur as if she were cold. Her voice was icy. "Would you please be kind enough to call me a taxi? I'd like to go home now."

Instead of telling her I'd be happy to take her myself, I said, mostly kidding but not totally, "You know what, princess? You're being a royal pain in the ass."

She popped me in the face with the flat of her hand. I think she was as surprised as I was. We just stared at each other for a few seconds, then I got out of the car and went into Robert's, heading straight for the phone hanging on the wall at the end of the bar. I could feel her standing behind me before I finished dialing the number of United Cab. I gave the dispatcher Robert's address, turned around, took Diana by the arm and headed out the front door to Claiborne Avenue.

I smoked a cigarette and wouldn't look at her. When the cab pulled up, I opened the back door and stood there.

She didn't get in immediately. I knew she wanted the last word, but I was surprised when she said, in the best Mae West tradition, "Why don't you come on over when you're finished?"

I waited until she pulled her slim, elegant legs inside the taxi, handed the driver ten bucks, and closed the door.

She must have considered the fight a draw.

I could say that my concentration wasn't good or that the scene with Diana had unnerved me, but the truth is Nita was *that* good a pool player. The first game, I suggested eight ball because that's what most women like to play. She merely nodded and set the cue ball up to break. The strength of her break was impressive. She sunk one ball after the other. She won before I had a chance to play. She suggested nine ball, and won fair and square.

I decided I was going to take her to Grady's one night and make a bundle off Murphy and the boys. I wouldn't pretend she wasn't really good or act as if I were trying to indulge her. I would tell them the truth right from the beginning. I knew it wouldn't matter; they wouldn't believe me anyway.

4
The Emerald Lizard

So that's how I came to be propped up in bed with a Scotch, expecting a call from Diana. Instead, it was Jackie Silva who called.

When Jackie said she might as well be in China if she was in Westwego, in one way she was right: to a lot of people in New Orleans the West Bank is on the other side of the world. It would be considered a fate worse than death to have to live there. If threatened with death, however, they might consent to live in Algiers, which is part of New Orleans. They would tolerate it because in some sections Algiers still looks like New Orleans, with raised, high-ceilinged homes, camelbacks, doubles, and structures with a lot of architectural gingerbread. Otherwise, these people think the rest of the West Bank has no character. It's nothing but suburbs, shopping centers, and convenience stores.

But to the people from the West Bank, the West Bank is the Best Bank. To them New Orleans is too crowded, too dirty, too expensive, and too scary.

Algiers aside, the rest of the West Bank is part of Jefferson Parish and, with two exceptions, is patrolled by the Jefferson Parish Sheriff's Office. Those two exceptions are Gretna and Westwego. In both cases, the people from those towns got together and incorporated, electing their own mayors and city councils, forming their own police departments, and sending their own representatives to the legislature. In Gretna this action seems understandable. Gretna covers a large area and a lot of people live there. In Westwego, it's something else. I can't give you an exact explanation, but maybe I can give you a feeling for the way it is. I have a friend who was born on the West Bank and lives in Marrero. He thinks the people from Algiers are snobbish because they're part of the Big Town, but he grew up being told not to associate with anyone from Westwego. I guess the people from Westwego always felt they were different, separate from everyone else across the river, and decided to make their separation official.

I'm a good New Orleans boy, so I'll admit to a certain prejudice against the West Bank. You know, sort of an "Our team is the best team" attitude. But I grew up in the Irish Channel, and a lot of people on the other side of Magazine Street were told not to associate with anyone from the Channel. I know the West Bank is different from the East Bank, but I also know that no matter which side of the river we plant ourselves on, our roots grow deep. In the end we're all from the same hot bayou country. Also, I like the names of the towns across the river—Algiers, Gretna, Marrero, Avondale, and farther down, Crown Point, Barataria, and Lafitte.

Okay, so Westwego doesn't sound so picturesque. Nevertheless, I was on my way to Westwego.

The afternoon after I talked to Jackie, I drove out to Jefferson Parish and took the Huey Long bridge across the Mississippi. I ended up at the traffic circle in Bridge City, which I followed around until I got to the road that shot off to Westwego.

I was completely out of my normal territory and used a map to figure out that Highway 18 eventually became Sala Avenue and then 4th Street where the lounge was located. According to the map I was on the Old Spanish Trail. This gave me a sense of adventure. Then I was on River Road, which runs right up against the levee that does its best to keep the mighty Mississippi in check. I went past a part of Avondale Shipyards. The hulls of ships and tugboats looked surreal, their keels seeming to cut deep into the earth from a distance. I was so busy taking in the scenery that I missed my turn and had to go back.

The Emerald Lizard was a plain, one-story, weather-beaten frame building with a couple of incongruities. One was its front door, a piece of black glass, with *The Emerald Lizard* written on it in a bright flowing green. The other was the sign, an emerald green lizard studded with small lightbulbs. It looked, too, as if lightbulbs would flash on and off at night so you could see the throat of the lizard puff up. I wasn't sure I considered this inviting, but, what the heck, the black door was open even though the lounge was closed, so I went on in.

Inside was almost as black as the door, even on this sunny, though somewhat hazy, afternoon. My eyes adjusted to the darkness enough for me to feel as if I'd entered a womb carpeted in green and black. It was on the floor and the walls, a green mottled with black, bright enough to seem lush, dark enough to be romantic. Close and warm and stifling.

That was all I noticed before Jackie came from behind the bar, where she'd been standing with a man. She came toward me, across the dance floor, walking that slow, sensuous, provocative walk, smiling that intimate, con-spiratorial smile, and twenty-two years melted away like a sweet meringue on the tongue.

The changes in Jackie seemed mostly a matter of style. She no longer tortured her hair into an ornamental shrub the way girls used to. Instead it was curly now, soft curls rolling and tumbling from her crown until they fell to her shoulders and floated gently there. It was blacker now than it used to be, so black that the smooth curve of a curl here and there glinted blue from somewhere deep inside like a kaleidoscope of blue stones that moved and changed as she moved. Her lips were a rich cherry red instead of those iridescent pinks and lavenders, and she didn't wear nearly as much eye makeup as she once did. Her eyes were shadowed with a hint of green to go with the green in the sweater she was wearing, the emerald green of the Lizard.

But as she came closer I could see there was a hardness to her face, a set to her mouth and a puffiness around her eyes. Either she hadn't been sleeping too well or she'd been drinking too much or both. The puffiness, though, couldn't disguise those slanted, seductive eyes. And her crooked smile still ended in two crescent-shaped lines, but the lines cut a little deeper now. So much the better—I'd always liked them.

Jackie took both my hands and we kissed lightly on the mouth. She stared at the scar on my face that ran from my left eyelid down to the lower tip of my ear, an arc like the marking on a tabby cat. It caused my eyelid to droop a little, and on the whole gave me a rather sinister look that might come in handy if I ever needed to scare the pants off anybody. It still scared the pants off me to think about how I got it. Jackie released one of my hands, and I thought for a moment she was going to trace the scar with a fingertip, something some women seem to like to do. I involuntarily braced myself so I wouldn't flinch away, but she didn't do it.

"Knife?" she asked. I nodded, not anxious to go into the gory details of late one night in a dark alleyway. She followed up with, "Was it a woman?"

Jackie, it seemed, had not lost her ability to kick aside preliminaries and get into the more penetrating questions.

"Is that what you'd go for," I asked her, "the eyes?"

"Hell no," she said, "not unless I was ugly."

I smiled. "Why don't you tell me about Bubba Brevna," I suggested.

Still grasping my hand, she led me to the dance floor, a light oak parquetry, one end of which was covered over with a crude numbered board.

Her hand flew out toward the board, boomeranged back and landed on her hip. "He's running chicken drop contests on my dance floor."

She told me that one day when she wasn't there, two of Brevna's hoods, the Impastato twins, had arrived at the lounge, paint cans in hand, and told the bartender they had permission to paint the board.

"If they had permission, it was from Brevna, not me," she said indignantly. She said the paint was barely dry when they showed up that evening, built a wall of beer cases around the board, took bets on the numbers, and threw a chicken out on them.

"Have you ever felt sorry for a chicken," she asked me, "everybody yelling at it to crap on their number?" Her voice had gotten so hoarse that some of her words were soundless. She wiped under each eye with a finger. I'd never thought that Jackie would be so emotional, not, at any rate, about a chicken. She'd been pretty tough when we were kids. But that's not what she was upset about.

"I mean," she said, "does this look like that kind of place?"

Now that my eyes were fully adjusted to the dimness, I looked around some more. Tall furry black chairs surrounded gleaming black tables. Across from where we were standing was another level, raised a step off the dance floor and separated from it by a low iron railing. There was more tables and furry chairs, and also black upholstered booths with green carpet on the wall behind them. All in all, a very intimate setting. A little too intimate for me. Even though the place was empty, I was beginning to feel uncomfortable. Above us the ceiling was draped, tentlike, gold spangles on white. A disco ball hung from the central point of the tent.

Jackie called out to the guy behind the bar, "Hit the light, Jeffrey."

The ball began to revolve slowly, colored lights sending out rays reflected off its mirrored pieces. I thought this sort of lounge decor had gone out in the early seventies. Of course, this was New Orleans, the West Bank yet, everything so slow and lazy that things caught on several years after leaving the rest of the country.

The decor was dazzling, claustrophobic. I imagined the lounge full of people. I could see couples overcome on the dance floor, twosomes suffocating from all the fabric on the booths and walls, the flaming tent falling on the helpless, bedazzled patrons.

I looked back at Jackie. "Not the sort of place for a chicken," I told her.

A tear edged its way over one of her bottom eyelids. She wiped it away. Her hoarse voice cracked with the effort of staying dry-eyed. "The Impastatos say they're running the chicken drop contests to help me pay off my debt."

As I said, the Jackie I remembered had been tough, self-confident, aggressive, and sometimes abrasive, but there had been a vulnerability about her, too. Somehow that vulnerability came through mostly in her voice. She was older and it was deeper, which is why I hadn't recognized her right away on the phone, but it was still sexy as hell, even when she was talking about a chicken drop contest. The voice was somewhat of a contradiction, sex and toughness and vulnerability all at once. It wasn't a fragile voice, but it told you she was fragile.

I put my arm around her shoulders. She leaned into me easily, still fighting tears, and put her arm around my waist.

"Thanks for coming," she said, her voice not much louder than a sigh. "I feel better now that you're here."

The guy behind the bar hadn't been doing much besides throwing a couple of light switches and watching us. His name was Jeffrey Bonage. He was probably in his late twenties and he stood behind the black-and-gold marbleized Formica bar with his hands thrust deep into his pockets. He was skinny, too skinny, his shoulders rounded and his chest caved in, his neck a little too long. His face was thin, but nice looking, his eyes big and watchful. His not quite blond, but not quite brown hair was clipped short, and I could see the back of his head with its crimped waves reflected in the smoky gold-veined squares of mirror behind the bar. His movements were crimped too, jerky. When Jackie introduced us, he moved an elbow away from its close hug against his body to acknowledge me.

Jackie asked me what I wanted. I said I'd have a beer and she told Jeffrey to bring us a couple of Dixie Longnecks. We went to sit in a booth toward the front of the lounge. Jeffrey accommodated us by turning on a small spotlight above the booth.

"I'm not a cop anymore, Jackie."

"I know. I've kept in touch with Reenie off and on through the years."

I hadn't known that. I nodded. "So how much do you owe Brevna?" I asked her.

"I borrowed ten thousand dollars from him. I thought I'd be able to pay him back in a year or two except I didn't count on the oil industry going bust. Most of the people who live in Westwego are tied to oil in some way or another. The ones who can are getting out. People are going bankrupt, losing their houses. They're probably drinking more, but it's cheaper to drink at home."

Jeffrey put a cardboard coaster, a Dixie, a napkin, and a glass down in front of each of us. He poured Jackie's beer and stood a couple of steps away from the booth, his hands jammed in his pockets. Maybe he was awaiting further instructions, or an invitation to sit down. Jackie paid him no attention and didn't stop talking.

"I got behind on my payments," she said, "and now I

owe him more than I borrowed. I'm paying fifty percent interest."

If you're wondering why I didn't choke on the mouthful of beer I'd just taken, it's because interest rates like that are not unusual for privately financed high-risk businesses like barrooms. If you want to open a neighborhood bar anywhere in New Orleans and don't have the capital, you wouldn't go to a savings and loan or a bank unless you didn't know any better. I'd heard of amusement company operators and liquor and cigarette wholesalers forming silent partnerships with lounge owners or lending money outright. Part of the deal was they put their vending machines and games in the place to help pay off the debt. Brevna apparently put in chicken drop contests.

Jeffrey slunk off in the direction of the bar and I asked, "What kind of business is Brevna in?"

"He says he's a fisherman, but he thinks he's the Carlos Marcello of the West Bank," Jackie said sarcastically.

Marcello had been the reputed Mafia boss of New Orleans at one time. He had survived family wars, a 1938 marijuana conviction, and deportation only to be imprisoned on a federal racketeering conviction at the age of seventy. He was currently making a fuss from prison, demanding his social security benefits.

"Marcello always gives his occupation as tomato salesman," I said.

"Yeah, he probably has a few trucks parked around town selling tomatoes off their rear ends. Bubba has an interest in some fishing boats out of Lafitte."

"I don't know, Jackie. There's too much in a name. The idea of a Mafioso type named Bubba is ridiculous."

"This is the West Bank, Neal. Bubba has a gang of small-time hoods who burn cars for insurance money. They pimp, they gamble"—she pointed toward the numbered board—"they specialize in bargain-basement intimidation. They do anything their walnut brains can understand well enough to vilify." The words rolled off her tongue.

Jeffrey returned and put a black suede cigarette case studded with rhinestones on the table.

"Thanks, honey," Jackie said and treated him to one of her lopsided smiles.

"Does Brevna do this kind of high-risk financing as a business?" I asked her.

She flipped a hand and said hotly, "I don't know. I don't know what the hell he does. Lately he's been trying to figure out ways to help me make more money. He's got Godzilla running whores out of here now, and of course the inventive Impastatos can always find something new and exciting to do, like two-dollar limit poker games in my office while they stuff the chicken for the next contest."

"Calm down, Jackie." She was angry and I could see she was set to rave on. "Who is Godzilla?"

"The nation's first brain transplant," she sneered. "He makes the Impastatos look like Einstein. He makes my bouncer look like Peter Pan. Next to him, Helen Keller was talkative."

"But who is he?" I raised my voice, though I wasn't anywhere near yelling. Suddenly Jeffrey appeared somewhere in my peripheral vision.

"He's the head henchman."

"Does he have a name?" I asked. Jeffrey was wiping off the already gleaming black tables nearest us. I slid further into the booth and sat against the carpeted wall so I could watch him.

"Rodney Nutley, but the girls call him Godzilla. It suits him better."

These people sounded like sleazeballs from a Mel Brooks movie about the Mafia. I retreated back to reality. Jeffrey retreated back to the bar.

"Why did you go to Brevna for the money?"

"Bubba was the only person I knew who had enough money"—she stopped to laugh bitterly—"except my father. Hell, maybe I should have asked him. I wanted to divorce Larry. We were already separated. He might have given me *twenty* thou."

"How do you know Bub—Brevna?"

"Larry knew him, probably from the barroom over in Marrero that the Impastatos own. He got Larry to invest in a fishing boat, too. Larry used to make good money before the accident."

Then she told me a sad story. Larry Silva had been doing some deep-sea diving out in the Gulf of Mexico, oil pipeline work, and something went wrong. A bubble of air forced its way through his lungs into his bloodstream. Jackie referred to it as a bubble on the brain because, she said, that's where it lodged. At any moment it could move and cause a brain hemorrage or, more likely, travel to his heart and kill him. It had been nearly four months since the accident. Jackie dropped the divorce proceedings, and Larry moved back in with her, but she'd kicked him out again a couple of weeks ago.

"I told him I'd think about letting him move back in after he'd been to court and was rich." The left side of her mouth curved up. "I know that sounds terrible, but you have no idea how awful it is to live with someone who thinks he's going to croak any minute. He's either scared, depressed, getting reborn, or gambling like there's no tomorrow. One way or another, death is always on his mind, which I suppose is understandable, but he also talks about it constantly. I can't stand it."

No, Jackie was much too alive, but nevertheless I felt sorry for Larry Silva.

She leaned across the table toward me. "Look, Neal, Bubba knows I'm going to have the money to pay him every cent I owe him, plus the interest, once Larry goes to court. He's just harassing me."

I asked her why.

"Because I shot him off the saddle, that's why."

Jackie took the last sip of her beer, and a cigarette out of the suede case. Before I could get my lighter out,

Jeffrey had a flame to the end of her Kool and had put a whiskey on the rocks down in front of her.

"You're a sweetheart, Jeffrey."

Jeffrey ate that up, then he turned to me and asked if I'd like anything else. He didn't seem at all happy to hear I'd have another beer, but he went off to fetch it.

"Jackie," I said, "Jeffrey is hovering."

"He's psychic. He knows what I want before I do."

"I mean he's acting like a jealous lover."

"He is—he's crazy in love with me," she told me as if it was the most reasonable thing in the world.

"Oh. And Brevna?"

"Bubba thinks he is. What Bubba is really in love with is power. He thinks he should have everything he wants because that makes him more powerful. And he thinks he wants me. I made the mistake of seeing him while Larry and I were separated the first time. He took it pretty well when I told him I was taking Larry back, but when I booted Larry out again, he thought I should take *him* in. I told him trading Larry Silva for him was like trading in herpes for AIDS."

Unfortunately, I'd just drained off the last of my beer and was trying to swallow it. I choked and coughed and wiped off my chin with the napkin from under my glass.

"Would that," I started and had to cough again, "have anything to do with Bubba's threat to have your tongue cut out?"

"I'm afraid so."

She wanted me to go talk to Brevna because he refused to talk to her, and there was no way she could come up with five thousand dollars by Friday, which was tomorrow.

"Look, Jackie, I don't want to get in the middle of some lovers' quarrel."

"Lovers' quarrel! The man is threatening me!"

"Do you really think he's serious about this contract?"

She told me she thought Brevna was perfectly serious, and repeated what she'd said over the phone, that Brevna was essentially a stupid man, stupid about everything except how to hurt people, which he liked to do.

"I'm afraid of Bubba, Neal. I'm even more afraid of that goon of his. There are all kinds of rumors around about him—that he killed a young girl a long time ago and didn't even know it, or he left her for dead or something. I don't know—I want him out of here. Please go talk to Bubba, Neal. Please, for old time's sake."

I wished she hadn't said that.

"You didn't have to say that, Jackie."

But that's exactly why I was going to go talk to Brevna, for old time's sake, and sometime later I remembered that, and it made me wish that all those years ago, things had ended up a bit differently. If they had, I don't think Jackie would have had the nerve to keep in touch.

She gave me Brevna's address, a trailer park in Marrero.

"Brevna lives in a trailer park?" I was astounded. There is probably nothing more depressing than a trailer park on the West Bank unless it's a trailer park in New Orleans East. "I thought you said he had money."

Jackie said, "The thing about Bubba is that he lives as well as he knows how to live. It's a very nice trailer, the best one in the lot. He likes living over there. He's king of the trailer park."

5

King of the Trailer Park

Roughly speaking, I drove east on 4th Street after I left The Emerald Lizard. I say "roughly" because in New Orleans we don't give the standard north, south, east, west directions. We say lake, river, uptown, downtown. That's because New Orleans wasn't laid out on a grid; it was built into a crescent of the river, and most of the streets run northeast, or south-southwest and so on. But I was on the West Bank, and there was no Lake Pontchartrain to the north. To the north was the river, to the south Lafitte. According to the map, I was traveling roughly east. Like Jackie said—China.

I turned on Ames Boulevard away from the river to get to West Bank Expressway, a huge thoroughfare divided by a wide median. It slices across the West Bank on about the same curve as the river, and it's bordered by shopping centers, car dealerships, fast food places, ad infinitum. Jackie told me the trailer park was located off the Expressway, not too far past Barataria Boulevard. A couple of blocks after Barataria, I headed back toward the river.

Once you're off West Bank Expressway, there's a feeling of space, as long as you're not in a planned subdivision. There'll be a stand of tall lacy cypress trees or dense overgrown woods or several lots of tall grass waving gently in the wind. Here it was, November, and the foliage was still a dark, lush green fringed with the lighter green of new growth that seemed to take no heed of the approaching winter. The cypress trees hadn't even started turning the reddish-brown they become before they bare themselves.

The Marrero Trailer Court was like some blight in the woods, an enclave of irregular shapes that kill off anything too close to it. The field of tall grass on one side of the court was edged with bent brown stalks. On the other side were a few scraggly trees missing most of their leaves, though the leaves that remained were still green. The Marrero Trailer Court sign itself looked like the victim of some pestilence or pesticide, the white behind the letters now a dull dead gray with a pox of rust, its galvanized pole pitted by some powerful corrosive, maybe nothing more than the swollen swampy air of Louisiana marshland.

The car wheels left asphalt and crunched on a bed of oyster shells, ground cover for most of the front part of the trailer court. I pulled over into a space reserved for cars. A little kid, couldn't have been more than two, stood beyond the parking space, his bare feet on the shells, wearing nothing but a dirty plastic diaper and a short-sleeved T-shirt. His nose was running. So were a couple of sores on his dirt-streaked legs. I got out of the car and smiled at him. I might as well have growled. He took off across the shells, the bottoms of his feet striking hard against their sharp jagged edges.

The trailers, twenty-two of them, were set close to each other, drawn up around an elongated oval clearing. It reminded me of a wagon train, the wagons huddled together for protection. At their center was a rusting swing set atop a mound of dirt, a few benches and chairs around a slab of concrete, the courtyard. The courtyard foliage, a few withered bushes and some droopy flowers in pots, served to accentuate the fact that nothing seemed to be able to grow there. The kid disappeared into an old bullet-shaped aluminum trailer, its door banging shut behind him. He was the only sign of life around.

Toward the back was a new-looking trailer that was at least twice as wide as any of the others. It seemed to be set off to itself, but that was only because of its size. A shelled driveway skirted the right side of the circle of trailers. I walked over to it. It went from the parking area to a clearing large enough for a couple of cars at the rear end of the big trailer. Pulled up into the clearing was a long green aluminum flatboat with an outboard motor, and next to it a dirty white Lincoln Town Car with a trailer hitch.

My shoes scrunched on the shells as I made my way down the driveway. I'd gone this way to be less obtrusive in case there was anyone home besides a snot-nosed two year old. His mother was. She eyeballed me from a crack in the door of the silver bullet. I smiled at her and she closed the door.

It was silly to be so circumspect, but it's a habit I have whenever I'm on foreign turf, and I was certainly a stranger in a strange land. I was out of place, wearing a medium-gray flannel suit with a light-gray pinstripe. I was high profile dressed like that here, but low key, conservative, and credible in the courtroom. The lawyers I do work for like it. So do the judges. It was my power suit, and my going-to-court suit, though I'd gone to court that morning only to hear that the trial was continued until the next Monday. But no matter how I was dressed, I was, to say the least, on a dubious mission. If this Bubba Brevna really went around putting out contracts on people and committing arson, why wasn't I en route to the Jefferson Parish Organized Crime Unit instead of getting ready to knock on Brevna's trailer door? But there you have it: a man named Bubba who lived in a trailer. Imagine the field day the OCU would have with that.

I banged on the door, making quite a racket and getting no response. He must have been in there if the car and the boat were parked outside. I'd given up and was toying with the idea of breaking and entering, frankly afraid of what I might find, when he opened the door and stood looking down at me, his eyes a wet, watered-down blue in a broad, ill-tempered, blunt-featured face. His mouth curved down and was flanked by two folds of skin that ran from the sides of his nose to his jawline. He had on a pair of tan slacks, an undershirt, and a brown towel around his neck. There were leftover tufts of shaving foam on his chin and on the lobe of one ear.

I apologized for interrupting his *toilette*, introduced myself, and told him I was here to talk about Ms. Jackie Silva's debt.

He didn't quite know what to make of me, a guy with beefy shoulders, in a gray pin-striped suit, a cigarette butt sticking out of his mouth, and a ragged scar on his face, who used words like *toilette*. But he couldn't resist talking about Jackie Silva's debt. He invited me in by standing aside.

I could see why Bubba needed an extra-wide trailer; he was an extra-wide man, his frame square-looking because he wasn't very tall, maybe five eight. I bet he had a good thirty-five pounds on me, though, in spite of my being four inches taller. His gut hung a bit over his Sansabelt slacks, but, actually, he carried his weight fairly well. Once he had a jacket on, I imagined he would be quite presentable, a real presence with his bulk, his bald head, except for a graying fringe, and his pugnacious expression.

Bubba eyed me warily and didn't ask me to sit on the tweedy high-backed sofa with maple trim or matching recliner in the living area. The maple coffee table was stacked with power boating magazines. On the walls were plaques glorifying dirty old men. On top of a portable bar were Mardi Gras glasses and swizzle sticks shaped into naked ladies. Knickknacks promoting sex and party-ing gave evidence to Bubba's lifestyle. A counter with two rattan stools divided the living room from a kitchen that appeared to have every convenience.

"Nice trailer," I said. I hate trailers. The worst thing I can think of is having shelter that could just roll away on you.

Bubba grunted and got a point for having no other reaction to hypocritical flattery. All he did was watch me. A quiet sort of guy, this Bubba, to be such a party animal. Maybe that explained his rather bizarre tongue removal contract.

I gestured toward the sofa. He repeated the gesture and I sat. Then Bubba left me. I heard water running and a toilet flush. That's another thing about trailers—the problem of waste removal.

He came back wearing a light blue shiny shirt, the same tan slacks.

"Mobile home," he said.

"What's that?"

"It's a mobile home, not a trailer. My flatboat's on a trailer. I hook the trailer to the back of my mobile home and truck the whole rig down to Lafitte, you know, if I want to do some extended fishing. 'Course there's no reason to go to the trouble. I can drive down to Lafitte in no time."

Boy, put a shirt on this Bubba and he talks up a storm. I bet he was one of those people who is practically defenseless naked. I made a mental note that if I ever had any trouble with Bubba to just strip him down.

"You got money for me?" he asked.

"I said I was here to *talk* about Ms. Silva's debt. No, I don't have any money."

"What's this *Ms*. Silva shit? You her lawyer? Her banker, maybe?" He laughed with his mouth closed, the sound of a bass string twanging. "I don't like the way you talk." Not being very humorous now. "Who the hell are you?"

A moody guy, mean looking with his mouth clamped into an upside down smile and his jowls hanging low like a bulldog's.

"Ms. Silva said you refused to talk to her."

"You can't talk to that woman! She won't shut up long enough for you to talk to her. I want her to pay up and shut up. You tell her that. While you're at it, tell her not to send any more of her fancy trained dicks around."

This was not, you understand, a reference to my profession since he didn't know it, though it may have been to my suit. I stood up and locked into Brevna with an impersonal, hard-ass cop's stare.

"You threatened Ms. Silva," I said in a menacing monotone.

I could almost see him think: If he was a cop he would have identified himself; he's got ten or twelve years on me, longer reach and agility. I saw him decide to lighten up.

His upside down smile righted itself. He walked over to the counter, the floor of his house on wheels shaking under his weight, and sat heavily on a rattan stool. The rattan creaked. He sat with his side to me, his arm stretched over the counter. I moved so his body wouldn't block my view of his hands.

"Hey," he said, "I'm a business man. I kept my part of the deal. I'm asking her to keep hers." Like it was all on the up-and-up.

"Legitimate businessmen don't threaten to have people's tongues cut out."

The expression on his face changed suddenly, as if I'd snapped on the light; as if all of a sudden he understood the purpose of my visit and he found it funny. With his mouth open his laugh had a raspy scraping sound.

"She believed that?" he shrieked in wonderment. "She took that seriously?" He was getting pretty raucous now.

Too much more hilarity and he might raise his rolling rooftop.

"Not only that," I said over his laughter, and he quieted down enough to hear me, "she doesn't owe you five thousand dollars. Not quite. Not according to the schedule you worked out."

Bubba shrugged. "I was talking in round figures. Look, all I was asking for was a show of faith. A little something to let me know her intentions, you know?"

He got up and went to the refrigerator.

"That's not the way she understood it."

He was peering into the refrigerator, speaking deep into its interior. "I don't believe she took that seriously." Laughing still. The door was blocking my view of everything except Bubba's rump. I hoped he didn't keep a piece on ice.

He straightened up, something long and brown in his hand. He farted and threw a rasher of bacon on the counter next to the stove.

"You know why I told her all that shit? 'Cause I got tired of listening to her. Look." He leaned against the refrigerator, a finger casually hooked into the side of his waistband. "I can't help it if she don't understand what I told her. She don't listen long enough to understand much. Her and me, we had a relationship for a while. It's all over now. It's *been* over, but she seems to think this debt has something to do with all that, like maybe she don't owe me nothin' because we had a thing once. She talks about what she owes me and she starts talking about sex. I don't see what the one has to do with the other."

"Neither do I, but it seems to me you're the one brought it up this time."

"What the fuck do you want?" he demanded. Apparently I wasn't being sociable enough for him.

"I want to leave here assured that you won't threaten Jackie anymore. There's no way she can come up with anywhere near five thousand dollars by tomorrow, but since you say all you're looking for is a show of faith, I'll tell her you're willing to take five hundred next Friday. She plans to pay off the debt, the whole thing, as soon as her husband goes to court and settles his diving accident."

"Yeah? Lemme tell you who's gonna get most of Larry Silva's money—his lawyer, his bookie, and that bogus church he belongs to. He isn't even going to get much out of workman's comp. He's over the hill, working on borrowed time. Divers don't age well, and Larry Silva is forty-five going on sixty. He's dead broke, in debt to his ears and you think he's going to pay off his wife's debt when she won't even fuck him?"

Seemed like Bubba was determined to tell me as much about Jackie Silva's sex life as he could. He opened the refrigerator door and got out half a dozen eggs, three in each hand, and put them next to the bacon.

"I thought Larry made an investment in a fishing boat. Isn't that making any money for him?" I asked.

Bubba, getting out a box of grits, a loaf of bread and some pots and pans, explained things to me with a certain amount of condescension. "You make an investment in a fishing boat, you got to maintain your investment. It costs to keep a vessel like that going. You don't maintain it, you don't get paid forever."

"Thanks for the economics lesson."

"Sure." Instructing me in the ways of big-business fishing put him in a better mood toward me.

"While we're on the subject, I'll tell Jackie you agree to five hundred next Friday. After that we renegotiate."

Bubba was positively jovial. "No problem. You tell her. You tell *Ms*. Silva not to worry, she's got nothing to worry about at all."

"She's worried about that goon Godzilla. Get him and the whores out of the lounge."

Bubba's good mood disappeared like the sun blotted out by a rain cloud. His face became dark and threatening. "You said you came here to talk about money. We talked about it. Now get out."

"We're not finished. Godzilla goes. Consider it part of the renegotiation."

He stood with his fists balled up at the sides of his thighs. "Don't call him that."

"Okay. Nutley goes and takes the girls with him. And call off the Impastato twins. No more chicken drop contests at The Emerald Lizard."

He stared at me stupidly for a few seconds before his face fractured into a grin that exposed a lot of predatory teeth of a fuzzy dull white, the color of a dirty porcelain sink.

"Chicken drop contests at The Emerald Lizard!" He pitched his voice high, like the scream of some swamp bird. He hit himself on the thigh, then pounded the counter with the bottom of his fist. The eggs shook and a toaster hopped toward the sink and got ready to take a dive. "God," getting himself under control, "those Impastatos have got some imagination!"

"Call 'em off," I repeated.

"Yeah, okay." He turned his back to me, put a fire under the frying pan, picked up an egg in each hand and cracked them into a bowl before picking up two more. "Chicken drop contests," he crooned in a high voice, his falsetto cracking like the eggs with laughter, "at The Emerald Lizard." Oblivious to my presence, unafraid with his back to me, the king of the trailer park got down to preparing his moveable feast.

6

Too Many Lovers

I resisted an urge to brush myself off before I got in my car. The trailer wasn't dirty; Bubba himself was. Dirty, petty mind. There was no way I could help wondering what in the world Jackie was doing to ever get herself involved with someone like him.

Bubba put on a good act, but all he'd really done was boast about how virile he was which meant he probably wasn't, though you wouldn't catch me asking Jackie about that. Otherwise, he'd been doing some form of appeasement, the way he'd said, "Yeah, okay," and turned his back on me when I insisted he call off the Impastatos. I translated that as, "Yeah, okay, just get outta here." He was the big fish in his pond, the bully on the block. There was no reason in the world to trust anything he said. Jackie would have to decide for herself whether she was in any danger from him.

"Why don't you call the cops, press charges against the Impastatos for defacing your property, tell the Organized

Crime Unit everything you know about Bubba's activities," I suggested when I got back to The Emerald Lizard.

It was about four-thirty in the afternoon and there were a few patrons in the Lizard, up on the higher intimate level above the dance floor. A spot lit up the numbered board.

We were sitting at the bar alone. Jeffrey had just given me a Scotch and water and Jackie a bourbon on the rocks.

"I already went and talked to a Westwego cop I know, Aubrey Wohl. But he's a wimp. He thinks chicken drops are an all-right way to make some money."

"Is this Aubrey aware of Bubba's criminal activities?"

"He may be, but he can't prove it. Some guy's ex-wife claimed her husband put Bubba up to burning down her restaurant, and pimps don't usually get run in, the prostitutes do. Anyway, Godzilla would take that fall. I don't really know what Bubba does. I just hear things."

Jeffrey, as usual, lurked close enough to hear our conversation.

"Tell him about the Lizard getting broken into," he said to Jackie, and added, "twice," for my benefit.

"That's true," Jackie said, "but who can say that was Bubba. Mostly what they took was booze."

"But that was since your falling out with Brevna?" I thought that was a delicate way to put it. Jackie nodded.

"I'll never get rid of Bubba," she said. "If he can't possess you, then he wants revenge on you."

She began to get maudlin, crying into her drink that she'd never get out of debt to Bubba. I reminded her about Larry's court case, wondering if I should repeat what Bubba had told me, but before I could finish, she started berating Larry, calling him stupid.

"If they award him anything at all," she spit, "he'll give half of it back and the other half to his hokey church, the Universal Church of Love and Light, or whatever they're calling it these days. Every time one of their leaders absconds with the treasury, they hire a new minister and change the church's name. Whatever they do is fine with Larry, he keeps contributing. The man doesn't have a brain in his head about money."

Her anger was hard to take because even if it wasn't directed at you, you felt as if it were. But that was better than when she stopped being angry and became sullen and hopeless. No matter what I said, she said she was doomed, by Bubba Brevna.

Maybe it was the booze. Jackie lifted the glass to her mouth and the last of the bourbon slithered around the rocks and down her throat.

I tried one more time to get her to at least go talk to the OCU. She gazed at me out of already glazed eyes—it wasn't even the righteous cocktail hour by my watch—and smiled playfully, but when she spoke, her voice was as chilled down as the next bourbon Jeffrey put in front of her. "Once a cop, always a cop, huh, Neal?"

That would do as a cue, I decided, not wanting to bother finishing off the Scotch before I left.

At that moment, however, two men came in through the front door. They were arguing. I thought one of them was Larry Silva. My eyes went automatically to the backs of his hands. The tattoos were there, one a bird in flight, the other a large **X** filled with smaller **x**'s.

The other man was tall, extremely tall I thought until he got closer. He looked tall because he was walking next to Larry, who was short, about five-six, and also because he was extremely thin and accentuated his thinness by wearing very tight jeans and a cowboy shirt with a vest over it that didn't quite reach his waist. He wore brown lizard cowboy boots. I wouldn't say cowboys are prevalent on the West Bank, but there are a few of them around and Western wear is trendy. This cowboy, though, talked like a Texan.

Wouldn't you know it—they were arguing about Jackie.

"She don't want you around," the cowboy drawled to Larry. He may also have slurred. Afternoon teas could have been more of a custom on the West Bank than I realized.

Larry handled the cowboy's belligerence with humor. "Sure she does. The more men the merrier, right, Jackie?" he called.

Bubba was right about Larry, he wasn't aging well. He wore a beard streaked with gray that covered most of his face, but he couldn't cover up all the wrinkles, especially around his eyes. His posture wasn't good either. And he, too, was too thin, not like the cowboy who was wiry and energetic, but more like Jeffrey, a sick look, bad diet or something. Lovesick was a definite possibility.

"Jackie, honey, tell him to just run along now like a good little dogie."

I'm not kidding—the cowboy said that. If we'd been in Burbank, California, I wouldn't have thought a thing of it.

Jackie ignored him. She and I had turned around on our stools and now she put a hand on my thigh, which got the cowboy to notice me right away.

"Larry, look who's here. You remember Neal Rafferty, don't you?"

Larry did, I stood up, we shook hands and were cordial. I was remembering Jackie's parents' reaction to her marrying him, her father so angry, her mother so heartbroken. He didn't seem like such a bad guy. Of course, maybe I was feeling sorry for him, not to mention that after I spent part of an afternoon with the likes of Bubba Brevna, anyone would look like a sterling piece of humanity.

What happened next is a little hazy in my mind, I guess because it happened so fast. The cowboy tried to go around Larry to get to Jackie, who was still sitting on the bar stool. Larry moved, taking a step backwards as he reacted with gratifying jocularity to something I'd just said. It didn't seem to me that he was deliberately trying to block the cowboy's path to Jackie, but the cowboy thought he was and turned mean, shoving Larry while he spewed and drawled at him to look where he was going. He almost knocked Larry down, and Larry was entirely too feeble to fight back. So I grabbed the cowboy at the shoulder by his vest and told him to back off. He was quick, and in the dim light of the lounge I almost didn't see his right hooking around toward my head. I moved so that he connected, but not very solidly, on my chin. I immediately delivered an uppercut to his ribs followed by a good punch in the eye as he came forward, and the cowboy went down.

He stayed down, flat on his back, out. Yelling came from the level above the dance floor, two women standing in the intimate darkness cheering my KO. One of them was wearing a leather halter cut to the solar plexus and a below-the-belt (though not by much) skirt. The other one had on red crushed velvet. They had come down to the railing to see the action. Their dates stayed where they were, two faceless men shadowed the way they are on those news shows when someone wants to give an exposé without being recognized. There was someone else, too, standing against the wall at the side of the bar where a small hallway led to Jackie's office. He was a regular dinosaur of a man, close to seven feet tall, and about twice as wide as Bubba Brevna. His head would be up in the tenting if he walked out on the dance floor. His face was a wedge of bone with a black beard. His hair hung in strings past his shoulders. His eyes were onyx slits under a brow like the blunt edge of an ax. He stood with his arms folded over a white T-shirt, and below that he wore jeans and black motorcycle boots. I hadn't been aware of him coming in, in fact, I was sure the door to the lounge hadn't opened, which meant he'd come in through the office. He took one step out from the wall, turned his face toward the girls, and they stopped cheering and went back to their dates.

"Well, that'll show Clem Winkler a thing or two," Jackie said, her eyes no longer glazed, some life back in her rich voice. "Another drink for our champion."

"You bet!" Jeffrey's attitude toward me had turned enthusiastic.

"Thanks, but I've got to be going," I said. "I've got an early dinner date." Jeffrey liked me even better.

Larry was the only one who was distressed. He was bent down over Winkler, pulling back one of his eyelids. Winkler began to snore. No one at all seemed to notice Godzilla up against the wall, whose eyes followed Jackie when she got up and limped behind the bar. The look on his face was malevolent, but there was nothing he could do about it, that's how he was put together. Hell, the way his eyes were glued on Jackie, for all I knew he was in love with her, too.

Larry stood up. "I hate all this violence, Jackie. Every time I'm here a fight breaks out or a woman throws her drink in some guy's face and he slaps her, or something. Why do you let guys like this Winkler in here? He comes in looking for a fight."

"No, he doesn't," Jackie snapped. "It's your timing that's bad."

Larry spoke to me, a small smile peeking out of his beard. "No matter what," he said, "it's always my fault."

Before anything else happened, I wanted to leave. I gave Larry a light biff on the upper arm and told him I was glad to see him.

The black glass door opened again and this time two young guys, not over twenty, came into the lounge. They had to be the Impastato twins. They were both small, they both had mustaches and dark brown limp hair they brushed straight back, except that the front hank of hair on each of them didn't want to stay put and fell forward onto their foreheads with the same twist. The only difference between them was that one was very sullen looking and the other smiled a lot. The smiley one was carrying a box with holes in it. From inside the box came some cackling sounds.

He held up the box. "We got a new chicken, Miss Jackie, going to make lots of money for you tonight."

"Ugh," Jackie said. "Put him in the back, will you? And then will you Imps come get Clem and put him on the sofa in the office?"

"Sure, Miss Jackie. Mr. Clem, he never made it home last night or what?" Even the sullen twin grinned now, good-natured boys, polite, resourceful. I was confused. They were acting like they worked for Jackie. So was she.

The Impastatos walked right past Godzilla without giving him a nod. As for the monster, he was still watching Jackie's every move.

As the twins carried Winkler into the office, Jackie walked outside with me.

"For a giant," I said as the door closed behind us, "that Godzilla makes his appearances with very little fanfare."

"Creepy, isn't it? It's always like that. You don't even notice it, then all of a sudden he's there. I really don't like him being around."

"I don't know. The way he was looking at you, I bet he would have moved Winkler for you if you'd just asked."

"I don't say anything to him. I just smile at him every now and then so he'll think I'm friendly."

"Well, that explains it. The giant has fallen for your lopsided smile, Jackie."

We were standing next to my car. I reached into my pocket for the keys. Jackie stepped closer, her head tilted up at me, trying to put me under her smile's spell.

"Why don't you stick around, Neal? Let's get to know each other again."

"Oh, I don't think so, Jackie." I looked up at the darkening sky. "It would make me feel like part of a side show"—I gestured at an invisible marquee—" 'The Suitors of Jackie Silva.' "

"Married women don't have suitors."

"Not usually," I agreed, "but there's nothing usual about your life as far as I can see."

"It's a life, all right." She gave me an intense look, then she reached out and touched my scar. I tried not to, but I flinched and she withdrew her hand. "Looks like we've both done some pretty hard living," she said.

"Somehow I think you're going to make all of it work for you, even Bubba Brevna," I told her.

"Maybe." She stood on her toes and gave me a peck on the cheek. I think I patted her on the shoulder.

I watched for a moment as she limped back into The Emerald Lizard. The limp didn't do to me what it once did. I unlocked the car and got inside.

Just as I was getting ready to start it up, I saw something moving on the other side. Through the window I could see Godzilla's torso. He was so tall I couldn't see his head or shoulders. His arms were still folded over the white T-shirt. He stepped up and butted the car with his enormous gut. The car shook violently.

A couple of months before, I'd finally retired my old car, which was so beat-up that when it died it was pronounced generic. I'd bought a brand new Thunderbird, the first new car I'd ever owned. I was in hock up to my eyeballs, but I didn't care—the car was beautiful, a smokey gray with a razor-thin maroon racing stripe, the windows tinted a gray almost as deep as the color of the car. I was extremely fond of it. I didn't like Godzilla abusing it. He reared back and rammed it again.

"Hey!" I yelled. "Cut it out!"

He paid no attention to me, and slammed into the car once more, so hard that I was actually afraid he might turn it over. I turned the key and laid rubber backing up. Godzilla moved in front of me, almost daring me to try to run him down, his arms still folded, the expression on his face exactly the same as it had been inside, malevolent. I wondered if Brevna had called him and told him to let me know my visit hadn't been welcomed, or if Godzilla had taken it upon himself to let me know he didn't want me fooling around with Jackie. Either way, I was all for getting out of there, out of Westwego.

7

The Mean and
the Hungry

It had been a complete waste of an afternoon. I got off
the Mississippi River Bridge in New Orleans where it is
too crowded, too dirty, too expensive, and too scary,
glad to be back. To be honest, I couldn't imagine why
anyone would want to live in a place like Westwego. I
realized, though, that it suited Jackie perfectly. Just as
Bubba was a big fish in the pond, so was she. She seemed
to have the market on men pretty well cornered. I'd
almost asked her why she didn't sell The Emerald Lizard
and move back to New Orleans, but I knew why. She
had a place where she could hold court with her lounge
lizards, do her flirting, and if she didn't like the way
someone flirted back, she could have her bouncer toss
them out. Or Godzilla. Somehow I felt sure he would be
glad to accommodate her. If only she would ask.
　The more I thought about it, the more I saw Jackie
and Bubba being a lot alike. Both of them were selfish
and ruthless in their own ways. It was no wonder they

were adversaries, probably good adversaries. They'd keep each other's life from getting too boring. When I'd said that about Jackie making everything work for her, I'd said it for something to say, but I believed it was true. I bet I could look her up in a couple of months and find out that she and Brevna had worked out a peaceable solution with, of course, a show of forces now and then to keep things interesting. Godzilla would be the new bouncer, the Impastatos would have cowboys, bikers, and johns gambling on their newest craze, maybe bear wrestling contests, and Jackie's clientele and list of suitors would have substantially enlarged.

All those people were in their own little world, a world so different from mine that I'd never completely understand it without being born into it or moving myself into it the way Jackie had done. It was a world as hard to crack as uptown New Orleans was, a closed society, open only to those who grew up there or were accepted by tacit agreement. It was that way in the Channel and it was that way in the Garden District. So it was in Westwego. The same laid-back, hot bayou country where people carved their niches the way you carve a school desk or a tree with your initials. You stake out your territory, you know everyone in it, and you stay there. Everyone has always agreed that it's too hot to move around too much.

So I didn't understand why Jackie had bothered to call me. She had the situation under control. Was it part of the game she was playing with Brevna, or had she gotten nostalgic after too many bourbons one night and decided to look up an old friend? And lover. Her first, in fact.

Whatever it was, the more I thought about it, the angrier I got. She hadn't thought a thing about using me or adding me to her list of ass-kissers.

I'd lied. I didn't have an early dinner date or any date at all. I still hadn't talked to Diana. I resisted the urge to take time to stop at the Euclid and have a quick drink while I used the phone. The Euclid was the apartment building where I lived. It was on St. Charles Avenue just a couple of blocks farther, but instead I stopped at a pay phone and checked with my answering service. There were no messages from Diana. Unless she'd had some event to attend, she'd be getting home from work about now. Or she might have a date. I decided to take my chances and go over to her apartment.

I'd begun to know Diana's ways pretty well. I had a hunch that since I hadn't gone to her place last night after playing pool, she wouldn't be inclined to be very kind to me. If I called her she would almost certainly tell me not to come over. If I arrived and she already had a date there, she would use the situation to be as beautifully and desirably cruel as possible. Thinking about how mean she could be made me feel mean toward her.

Diana lived on the top floor of a 1930s duplex on Baronne Street where it ends at Dufossat. It was a nice old building, not fancy on the outside, but stately. It was on a corner, and the entrance to the upper and lower floors were each on different sides of the building, the upper on Baronne, the lower on Dufossat, so that from either side the house looked like a single dwelling. The place was big, three bedrooms and a sun room upstairs that made you feel as if you were in a tree house because of a giant oak right outside. The duplex was owned by Diana's daddy. It was also not too far from the family home on Calhoun Street which Diana had pointed out to me once—a large shuttered house they call a raised cottage around here, with a wide veranda and opulent side yards full of magnolia trees and camellia bushes.

Diana was from a wealthy and social uptown family and the way she talked she got along with them well enough, but she was rejecting her place in society. Her parents wanted her to marry some lawyer named Wiley St. Cyr, who was from another prominent family and also a member of the Boston Club, the Krewe of Comus (the oldest carnival organization), and the Lawn Tennis Club, all of which meant he was as blue-blooded a New Orleanian as you can be. He also happened to be madly in love with her. She refused to marry him so he hung around with her parents when he couldn't be with her, poor lovesick pup. Wiley St. Cyr seemed to be the one area of conflict Diana had with her parents.

Diana worked in the French Quarter but lived uptown because Daddy thought it was safe, and she agreed. She dated mostly out-of-town men she met at the hotel, I gathered, and talked about the uptown men with distaste, saying they all were either ultra-conservative, like Wylie, or closet gays. I was an exception, but of course I wasn't one of the group she was talking about—I was from the wrong side of the tracks, born too far away from St. Charles Avenue. I didn't regularly attend carnival balls, museum and art fetes, charity dinners, or most of the multitude of soirees that happened constantly in private homes. But I attended some of them now and then, and I was presentable enough. Diana attended some of them now and then, too, but not with me. When we were together we mostly stuck to restaurants, hotel lounges, and her apartment.

When I rang her doorbell, I was still feeling mean. She buzzed me in at the downstairs door. I pushed the door open and walked into a small foyer with a marble-top antique table, a gilt-edged mirror, and a black iron umbrella stand. The wide palatial stairs were carpeted in a deep red, the mahogany banister stained to a satiny reddish-brown glow by many years' worth of palm oil.

Diana waited in the upstairs doorway. I took my time, feeling each spongy carpeted stair as I went. She tapped one foot. I reached the landing and put out the cigarette I was smoking in a Chinese vase on another antique table. She stood in the doorway looking at me contemptuously and blocking my way in, and it made me feel meaner. She was dressed in another one of her elegant little black numbers, silver collar around her throat. She was dressed to kill, but the only car parked outside was mine.

"Just finishing your game?" she asked with the kind of condescension that rolled over you like Sisyphus letting go of the rock while you were at the bottom of the hill.

"You should have stuck around, princess. It was over real fast."

"Is that so?" There was a wicked curve to her mouth and a cutting edge to her voice. "You do lots of things real fast, don't you?"

I grabbed her upper arm so it hurt and pushed her backwards into the living room, closing the door behind me with my foot. She tried to twist her arm away from me, but that only hurt her more. As soon as she opened her mouth to protest, I clamped mine over it and pulled the zipper down on her dress. Her free arm reached back to stop me, but I'd been too quick. She stood there as tense and unyielding as she could be. I finally let up, but still held her arm.

"I have a date," she informed me, breathing hard with anger.

"Where," I said and let my eyes take in the empty living room for a couple of seconds. The moment she started to answer I put my mouth over hers again.

My grip on her arm must have gotten stronger because she started pulling her shoulder up and making little hurting sounds in her throat. When I released her we both could see the beginnings of a bruise where my thumb had pushed against bone.

I fastened her mouth this time with a stare that dared her to complain. She didn't. But she was furious, her body rigid with barely controlled anger. I pushed one shoulder of her dress down. Underneath she was wearing a filmy black slip held up with a skinny round strap. I pulled that down, too.

She slapped me hard in the face. Without thinking, I slapped her back. She was shocked for a second, but just a second. She belted me again, harder. It wasn't a reflex this time. I hit her deliberately, but not nearly as hard as she was hitting me. She lifted her hand to strike again, but I caught it.

"We could do this all night," I said.

She smiled, almost as if she couldn't help it. I relaxed my grip on her arm and she attacked, her fingernails catching me at my jawline and raking my neck.

It was my turn to be shocked. Not for too long, though, because she was getting ready to start again. I could see it in her eyes. I grabbed her, pinning her arms. She started to kick. I smacked her on the behind.

Now she fought, viciously and strongly for a woman of her size and build, for any woman. We fought all the way down the hallway and into her bedroom. She got me again with those fingernails, on the cheek. I shoved her backwards onto the bed.

She landed stretched out full length, sideways across the bed, propped on her elbows. She stayed where she was and gazed at me coolly, clearly enjoying the hell out of herself.

"Get undressed," I told her.

"Make me," she said insolently and with about the most inviting look I've ever seen on a woman's face.

I did. Everything else I did, she took, and it was clear she could take more. We were going at it pretty good when the doorbell rang.

Diana's date. We both had forgotten all about him.

She jumped up, grabbing a robe hanging over the back of a chair. "I'll tell him I'm sick," she said and flew toward the front door.

Sick? She was radiant, her eyes shining, her cheeks flushed, her hair tousled, her bare body underneath that loosely wrapped robe all soft and rosy. This guy wasn't going to know what to think. I supposed it was possible he would think she was flushed with fever, her eyes rheumy. It sure as hell wouldn't have fooled me.

I wondered if her date was one of those ultra-conservative uptowners. It suddenly occurred to me that when she used that term, it had nothing to do with politics.

Sounds of voices, the door closing solidly, and Diana was running back along the hallway.

Afterwards I took the princess out to dinner at a fancy restaurant.

8

Of Home and Cheap Hoods

After a particularly frustrating Monday—spent cooling my heels in a corridor outside a courtroom until almost two o'clock while waiting to be called for a personal injury case, and then nearly missing my appointment with a man whose case I decided not to take after all because he needed a sex therapist, not a detective—I was looking forward to taking a long shower and having a long drink and dinner at home, alone. It wasn't that I was tired of Diana . . . well, yes, it was. We'd spent the entire weekend together, something we'd never done before, never leaving her house except to eat. I suppose it was a sign of something to do with age, but I needed a break.

The first thing I did after pulling into my slot in the Euclid's garage was go across the street to a grocery store where I bought a couple of New York strips, a large Idaho, a head of Boston lettuce, some brussels sprouts, and a bottle of Glenfiddich. I'd had it with béarnaises, bouillabaisses, bisques, blackened redfish, and French wine. Then I walked along St. Charles Avenue to the front doors of the Euclid, stopped at the mailbox, threw the mail in the grocery bag, and rode the elevator up to the sixth floor.

One of the reasons I'd moved into the Euclid was because it was a building that could have been anywhere, in any town. It was a boxy ten-story building with a bland, light brick façade and an impersonal lobby. My apartment had wall-to-wall carpeting of nondescript beige, a bathroom right off the bedroom, and nine-foot ceilings which meant you could actually keep the place cool in the summer and warm in the winter.

My apartment was completely unlike the camelback double where I'd grown up, with one room lined up after another, but the doors staggered so you couldn't shoot a shotgun straight through the place, which would have made it a shotgun double. In the back, before you got to the kitchen, there was a steep narrow stairway that led to two small bedrooms, mine and my sister's, no bath. Downstairs the bathroom was tacked on behind the kitchen. It hadn't existed before the 1940s. If you were in the bathroom at the same time as your neighbor on the other side of the double, both of you turned the water on in the bathtub whether you were taking a bath or not. As for the rest of the place, the walls were so thick that someone could have been killed on the other side and you wouldn't have known it.

The summers were better than the winters because every room had a ceiling fan hanging from a pipe dropped low enough off the fourteen-foot ceilings that you could feel it. The house was so drafty and full of humidity that the old flowered wallpaper peeled away from the walls, always up high where it was hard to reach, releasing ancient smells of must and mold. A whiff of that smell anywhere is strong enough to call up a string of memories, some of them as comfortable as your granny's rocker in front of the fireplace, and some of them that just make your nose twitch with impatience to be rid of them.

Coming from that, the Euclid was modern to me. There were no plaster ceiling medallions to crack and fall, or mantel pieces to get cluttered with old photographs and bric-a-brac, or fancy moldings to decorate the tops of the walls and catch dust balls; no memories to coat your tongue and pinch your nostrils; no resemblance to the past.

But it was still a swell address on St. Charles Avenue for an ex-cop turned private detective ready to make a living off conservative uptown lawyers and the intrigues of the uppercrust.

The Euclid had gone through a few changes in the five years I'd lived there. Sometime toward the end of the first year, a number of sophisticated call girls had moved in and dressed up the place. Because they were there a lot of the new tenants were pretty seedy, and eventually the call girls moved out to find classier digs. For a while things were bleak, broken elevators, a trashed-out lobby, very little general maintenance, until new management took over about a year ago and the place got fixed up. I was happy at the Euclid. I thought I could live there forever, although lately I'd noticed a little seediness creeping back in, small things left unrepaired, garage graffiti no one bothered to remove.

I unpacked the groceries, poured a drink, and started going through the mail. And there it was, another of life's unpleasant interruptions, an eviction notice. They wanted us out, everybody in the building, by the first of the year. The Euclid was being turned into a hotel. Well, that explained the creeping seediness.

Hard as I tried not to let this piece of news change the mood of the evening, I kept thinking about where I would move. During the time that the Euclid's decor was postmodern derelict, I'd thought about moving out of uptown New Orleans altogether, maybe to the Bayou St. John area or downtown to what had been a part of the warehouse district and now was being turned into swank apartment buildings and condos. I could think about that again. But I didn't have to right now. Because the oil industry was practically paralyzed, people were moving out of the city, so there were plenty of places to rent, and the prices of apartments were falling every day. In fact, that was undoubtedly the reason the Euclid was being turned into a hotel and not a condo. Tourism was the only industry left to save the city.

So the only problem I was going to have was deciding where to go. In the words of that famous Southern temptress, I'd think about it tomorrow. I took my drink into the bedroom, turned on the shower so the bathroom could get steamy, and started getting undressed. One foot was wet when the phone started ringing.

I almost let it fly, but it wouldn't have mattered. She would have kept calling. She wanted to chew somebody out. Anybody. Everybody.

Leaving the shower running, I crossed the bedroom to the telephone. For this conversation hellos weren't considered necessary. She lit in before I could get one out.

"I thought you could handle a cheap hood like Bubba Brevna." Her husky voice purred like a large hungry cat about to turn mean. I thought about telling her I was fine, thank you, but she didn't have time for that either. "I should have known better than to send some spruced-up, suited-up, blue-blood ass-kisser to try to talk sense to a shark."

"Isn't this a twist," I said. "In my neighborhood I'm usually the tough guy."

"This is a different world over here—"

"You keep telling me that," I interrupted, not pleasantly either. "A cheap hood is a cheap hood, even in China."

"What the hell did you say to him?"

"You know damn well what I said to him. You want to tell me what the hell this is all about?"

There was a pause, then I realized she was crying. "He torched the Lizard, Neal, burned it to the ground."

With the phone under my chin, I unleashed the expletives that count. She had me so damn mad they were right on the tip of my tongue anyway.

"When did it happen?" I asked her.

"Last night—early this morning. We closed up about two."

"You and Jeffrey?"

"Yes."

"What about the Impastatos and that ape?"

"Oh no. The Imps, they left about midnight—God, before that. All the girls were out working by eleven."

The nicknames sounded almost affectionate. I heard ice clink in a glass and she got mean again, that purr of hers drowning in venom. "But they could have come back. Any of them. One of them did 'cause you can bet Brevna wouldn't get his fat hands dirty. That fat pig was either in his chintzy trailer having a party or out on his smelly fishing boat having a party. You can bet on it."

"You told the cops you think it's Brevna?" The cops would have been the Jefferson Parish Arson Unit.

"Sure I told 'em." Then she said, with such irritation—as if I were a total idiot—that I wanted to throttle her just then, "Remember, I *told* you how he torches things for insurance money. He *knows* he'll get his money back from me now." At that moment Bubba Brevna's contract seemed like a flash of inspiration.

"Did you tell the cops I went to talk to him?" I spit it at her, letting my irritation show, too.

She paused and I heard the clunk of ice hitting bottom, as if she'd just run out of gas. "No," she said, tamed a little. "That was the right thing to do, wasn't it?"

If she hadn't, Brevna would. The cops could make of that what they wanted. I asked her if anyone was in the lounge when she and Jeffrey closed up.

"No, Sundays are slow. Jeffrey and I sat around and

had a couple of drinks while I waited for Clem to get finished with his barhopping over at the Gemini."

The Gemini was the Impastatos' bar in Marrero. "What was he doing there?" I asked.

"How the hell should I know? You don't think it pisses me off that he's out patronizing the Imps' bar while they're over at the Lizard crapping up the place?" She started to cry again.

"Who runs the bar when the Impastatos aren't there?"

"A woman named Mave Scoggins." Suddenly Jackie laughed, a short low burst like a big engine trying to turn over. "She comes on like Miss Kitty out of 'Gunsmoke,' boobs as big as Sylvester Stallone's balls. Maybe that's what the cowboy goes for."

"Did he stay with you last night?"

"We had it out last night. I'm finished with him." She sniffled a bit and said in a small breathy helpless voice, "What am I going to do, Neal?"

It was a mystery to me how she did it, but after being supremely aggravated with her, I suddenly felt sorry for her and wanted to help. "It's time to go to the organized crime people, Jackie."

"I've been talking to cops all day," she complained, then she slipped smoothly into an invitational purr. "Why don't you come over. We'll talk some more."

Right. I'd had a similar invitation just a few days before, and it wasn't to talk either.

"Once a cop always a cop, remember? I'll come 'round in the morning and take you to the OCU."

"Why don't you just come over now," she said, hurt, but a second later, recovered. "You think they can get him, Neal?"

"That's what they do."

There was no purr left now, nothing but a scratchy hiss. "That fat pig's gonna know what it feels like to burn."

9

The Last Lick

Nope. The game wasn't over. Brevna might have torched her lounge, but Jackie swore she'd have the last lick. She called me back a couple of hours later to tell me so. She was drunk and raving, going on about how she could tell those organized crime people some stuff about Bubba Brevna. She kept bringing up another of Brevna's torch jobs, the restaurant she'd mentioned the other day, the one owned by the ex-cop of a friend of Brevna's. It was difficult to understand her, partly because she was so drunk, but also because she became so hostile. If I tried to interrupt her to get something straight, she attacked me as if I were taking Brevna's side against her. This went on endlessly.

"What restaurant is it you say he torched, Jackie?" This was the third time I'd asked.

"You think I'm just saying that? You think he didn't do it?" Whatever she said next was muffled, as if she were reaching for something and not speaking directly into the mouthpiece, but I'd have sworn she used the word hire. I told her I couldn't hear her and she yelled into the phone, "I said, if that's what you think, then you're an idiot. 'Cause I can give the cops the person that torched it. I *know* who did it. I'll get the fat pig."

"Who did it, Jackie?"

"*Who*? I just told you *who*. That pig Brevna. And that's not all he did. He took money to fix cases, but he never fixed any cases." One of her wild raucous laughs before she said, in a baby voice, "He put the ten G's in Jackie's place."

And that's all it took to start some serious water flowing out of those cat eyes.

"Who torched the restaurant?" They say persistence pays.

It got me a deep stupefied laugh. "He did it to get money for his new shrimp boat. Nothin' but a goddamn fool."

And that was all I could take. I told her to try to get some sleep. Mostly I was hoping she'd let me get some. I hadn't had much over the weekend.

But I didn't hear from her again that night. She left me in peace to eat what I don't mind telling you was a sumptuous steak dinner and to give some thought to a couple of things that were bothering me.

One was why Clem Winkler hung out at the Gemini when his girlfriend owned The Emerald Lizard. The other was why the Impastato boys hung out at The Emerald Lizard if they owned the Gemini.

Well, if I wasn't bothered enough to go try to talk to Jackie in her drunken fit that night, then neither of those things was bothering me enough to do anything about them then or—I thought at the time—ever. My intention was to take Jackie to the Jefferson Parish Organized Crime Unit where she would tell her story and whatever she remembered telling me while she was drunk. The OCU, which is a research team and not an investigative unit, would do their research and decide if the Feds should be called in. Meanwhile, exit Neal Rafferty from The Emerald Lizard affair and Jackie Silva's life. I'd had it with her hostility, her come-ons, and her reckless angry talk. For old time's sake just wasn't enough.

The next morning I didn't bother going down to the office. I drank coffee while from my living room window I watched the streetcars going up and down St. Charles Avenue. That was another thing about my apartment at the Euclid, the great view of St. Charles and of the old Victorian house that had been converted into a dress shop across from me. I liked watching those sleek glossy ladies entering and leaving it. I should have gone to the office because sitting there made me think I liked living at the Euclid too much, that I didn't want to leave. I consoled myself, however, with the thought that I would no longer have to throw a shindig on Mardi Gras Day. It wasn't my friends who came, not for more than an hour anyway. Hell, Maurice only fielded answers from witnesses in courtrooms, not Mardi Gras beads, and not much penetrated the consciousness of the gang at Grady's other than the clicking of hard balls on the baize. No, it was the old man's friends who came mostly.

At nine-fifteen I put my coffee cup in the kitchen sink, went down to the garage, and headed the T-bird across St. Charles to Melpomene and the bridge entrance. I wasn't wearing my courtroom suit, but a dark blue sports coat slightly shiny with age, no tie. I even left undone the third button down the shirt. However, if I'd really wanted to achieve that Jefferson Parish look, I'd have worn at least one gold chain. But I didn't own any gold chains, so a few chest hairs would have to do.

Before I went to Jackie's house, I wanted to see what was left of The Emerald Lizard. I drove slowly along 4th Street expecting to see men from the arson unit still sifting through the rubble, but no one was there. Fourth Street itself seemed awfully quiet for a weekday, though the cars that came by slowed down to look at the charred ruins.

Jackie hadn't exaggerated when she said the place was burned to the ground. Only a couple of timbers were left standing. All the lush green of the Lizard had been turned black, aged overnight into ruins by the fire. I got out of the car for a closer look. A few emerald patches showed here and there, as if to highlight the contrast between what had been and what was now.

I didn't like looking at the ruins of Jackie's dream, the collapse of her way of life.

The Emerald Lizard was where Jackie had really lived, though her house was located within a grid of lettered avenues and numbered streets that ran between 4th Street and West Bank Expressway, Louisiana Street, and a drainage canal. The area had the look of a planned development built in the fifties, small two- and three-bedroom homes with picture windows and deep front lawns and carports. What made it look different than average American suburbia was that under most of the carports was a boat of some kind, fishing boats, flatboats, even an airboat at one house, the airplane propellor caged and mounted high for maximum propulsion through the marsh. Tied up close under several carport roofs were pirogues, mostly used down the river for duck hunting. Cars were second to boats in this community. If the car couldn't fit in the driveway it was parked on the street or pulled haphazardly up on the front lawn. One was a permanent lawn fixture jacked up on cinder blocks, a plastic garbage bag taped over one window. Maybe it was decorative, a Westwego variation of the colored globe on a pedestal or the virgin Mary framed by the manger, or maybe it was a sign of the times, a leftover from the Great Oil Bust.

Jackie's house was relatively plain, red brick, clipped grass, no landscaping, a compact foreign car under the carport, a Westwego cop at the large front window trying to get a look in between the curtains.

He turned around when I pulled up behind his car and waited for me on the concrete path to the front door.

"Something wrong, Officer?"

He was about my height, with a generous beerbelly stretching the black material of his short-sleeved uniform shirt. He had a large round head, fat doughy cheeks, and big sad brown eyes.

He smiled at me and said, just a shade away from apologetic, "Maybe you better tell me who you are and what you're doing here."

"Yeah, I suppose you might want to know that. Name's Neal Rafferty. I'm a friend of Jackie Silva's. I told her on the phone last night I'd come by this morning."

Big sad brown eyes don't do a hard cop stare very well, but his stayed on me a few seconds, weighing, appraising. Then, impulsively it seemed, he stuck out his hand.

"I'm Jackie's friend, too. Aubrey Wohl."

"Right," I said. "She's talked about you."

The wimp, she called him. The one who thought chicken drop contests were an okay way to make money.

"Won't she answer the door," I asked him, "or haven't you tried?"

He took that good-humoredly. "I don't usually peek through the windows first," he said. "I didn't think she'd be sleeping in this morning, not after the fire. I'm afraid something's wrong."

I didn't want to tell him how drunk she'd been the night before. She was probably passed out.

"Try the bedroom windows yet?" I asked

He said no and waited. I finally said, "I'm following you."

He still didn't move. He asked me point blank, "Do you know where the bedroom is in the house?"

"I've never been here before."

He trudged off across the lawn, down the left side of the house.

The screens on the windows were made of tiny slats that made it hard to see through them. It wouldn't have mattered because the shades behind the windows were pulled down tight.

Aubrey started pounding on the side of the screen with the bottom of his fist. A woman screamed in the house next door.

Aubrey whipped around. "Pam, is that you?" he called.

"Aubrey?" I could vaguely see someone behind the same kind of screen that was on Jackie's house. She unhooked the bottom and pushed the screen out. Her head came out, too, her bleached blond hair rolled up on beer cans, those half-can-size Budweisers.

"God-a-mighty, Aubrey! You scared me half to death. What's going on?"

"Sorry, Pam. Have you seen Jackie this morning?"

"I never see Jackie in the morning."

"Would you mind ringing her phone? I can't seem to get her up."

Pam ducked back inside and in a matter of seconds we could hear the phone ringing in Jackie's bedroom. After the tenth ring, Pam left the phone ringing and came back to the window.

"She's not there, Aubrey."

"Her car's there and this man has an appointment with her."

Pam looked at me and didn't quite know what to say.

Aubrey walked on to the back of the house. He tried the back door, but it was locked. The top part of the door was panes of glass, a cinch to break in.

Aubrey thought for a moment and pointed at the deadbolt above the doorknob. "I'm pretty sure it's keyed on both sides."

We went back to the front. Aubrey pulled at the door handle, being careful not to touch the top part of it where someone might have left a thumb print. The door moved fairly loosely in its casing.

"What do you think?" he asked.

"You're here," I said. "I don't have to think."

"I don't think it's bolted," he said.

He went off to the police car, opened the trunk, and came back with a crowbar. He slipped the flat forked part of the bar along the side of the door next to the door handle as far as it would go. Then he leaned all his weight on it. Wood splintered, the crowbar slipped a little farther in, and the door swung open into a small entrance hall.

Pam stood outside her front door, arms folded tight under breasts covered by a T-shirt that came all the way down to her thighs. She also had on second-skin turquoise pants, and white fluff-edged mules on her feet. She watched us go inside Jackie's house.

I knew it right away—death was in the house. I could feel its presence, smell its sweet stale odor, hear its palpable silence. Aubrey and I crept toward the living room and it rushed over us, seeking its release through the open front door so it could rush on to its next rendezvous.

She was on the living room floor, her head turned to the right, her face swollen and bluish, no longer Jackie, one leg, her thinner lame one, bent at the knee and twisted up beside her, her bare foot pointing away from her body, to the right, the same direction as her head.

She had on a lounging outfit, silky white material with gold thread, trimming, fitted legs, a long loose top pulled up showing a couple of inches of midriff. Her arms were at her sides, palms up, away from her body, as if she'd been laid out there, her pose almost whimsical, flighty looking.

She was obviously dead, but Aubrey bent over her anyway feeling for a pulse point. Above the scoop top of her lounging pajamas were bruise marks left by a strong hand.

And I'd been mad enough at her the night before that I'd thought I'd like to throttle her. I only wished now that it had occurred to me that someone else might have been angry enough to actually do it. She'd been wild and angry herself last night, belligerent, insulting. All in all, she could be an irritating woman, but somehow undeniable in all of her troubled vulnerability. People—men—

flocked around to do her bidding, to fall hopelessly in love with her. Yet last night I'd denied her need for company, for solace, a need to vent her anger over a tragedy in her life.

And someone else had denied her her life. Someone, maybe, who'd been drinking with her and smoking with her. There were two glasses with watered-down booze in them on the coffee table, an ashtray full of butts, two different kinds. The table lamps at either end of the sofa were still burning.

Aubrey stood up, his head bent down, as in prayer. When he looked at me his doughy face didn't seem so doughy anymore, clinched as it was with feeling, his sad brown eyes too shiny.

He held his arms out, palms up like hers were, his whole attitude one of disbelief.

He shook his head, letting me know he simply didn't understand.

"But everybody loved Jackie," he said.

10

Dangerous Men

The clop-clop of the hard soles of Pam's mules up the concrete walkway to Jackie's house jolted Aubrey and me out of our absorption and shock over Jackie's body. I was closest to the hallway so I rushed out to it and met Pam as she was crossing the threshold into the house, calling for Aubrey.

My arm around her shoulders, I turned her around and directed her outside again. She kept looking back, asking what was wrong.

"Jackie's dead," I told her.

Her face was bland, her eyes unblinking as her mouth opened to form the word *how*, but didn't quite get it out.

"Go on home," I told her. "Aubrey'll be over to talk to you in a little while."

For an instant—you had to be quick to catch it—there was a smirk on her face, then she cried, "Someone killed her, didn't they?"

I know people sometimes smile at first when they hear

of death or see an accident, but I always felt it was a reaction of disbelief for most of them, a way of saying to the bearer of bad news, "You must be kidding," or "This can't be happening." But Pam's reaction came a little too late, and it was no smile, I tell you, it was a smirk.

"Run on," I said, "Aubrey'll be along."

She took off across the lawn, her mules slapping hard on the bottoms of her feet, wailing, "She was my best friend," over and over until the storm door covering her front door banged shut behind her.

Aubrey joined me on the walkway.

"Pretty upset, is she?" he asked. I occupied myself lighting a cigarette. "I better go talk to her, and," he sighed, "call the Jefferson Parish Detectives Bureau. The murders are theirs." He started to go, but turned back, his sad eyes earnest. "You'll wait right here, won't you?"

I sat on the one step to the little concrete-slab porch, thinking that this Aubrey was a strange kind of cop. No swagger, no bull, no know-it-all attitude, no chip on the shoulder, not even that authoritative silence some cops of few words are so good at. Instead he was apologetic, almost sycophantic. Must be why Jackie called him a wimp. But I could see a watchfulness behind those sad brown eyes, and I didn't think it would be very smart to underestimate Aubrey Wohl.

Next door, Pam was hysterical, but Aubrey got her calmed down, made his phone call and joined me on the step to wait for the homicide detectives.

He nodded his large head toward Pam's house. "Those two were pretty close," he said.

"Close enough for a little competition?" I lit another cigarette. Waiting around turns me into a heavy smoker.

"How do you mean?" Aubrey asked, but not hostile or even wary. Again, rather apologetic.

There was a rusting bicycle with training wheels shoved into the bushes at the side of Pam's house, a soccer ball on her porch.

"Is Pam still married?" I asked.

"No, divorced." Now Aubrey sounded a bit wary, or maybe just puzzled.

"I thought so. Maybe she and Jackie were a little competitive about men."

Aubrey's forearms were resting on his knees. His hands were hanging over them. He turned them over. "I'm just not sure what you mean."

"I mean I left the telling to you, but before she ran off crying that they were best friends, she asked me if someone killed Jackie, and she smirked when she asked."

Aubrey dropped his hands, letting them dangle again. "Well, I know that a lot of times when men got frustrated with Jackie, they went to Pam for some comforting."

"In other words, she got Jackie's rejects, sometimes maybe angry rejects."

"I hate for you to put it like that. I've seen men so mad at Jackie they could spit, and the next day back in the hay with her again. I don't know how well you knew her, but it was mighty hard to stay mad at her."

I gave him a raised eyebrow, and he laughed softly.

"Oh no. We were good friends, never lovers. Can't say I would have minded, but it just wasn't like that. She was quite a gal, but I don't guess I need to tell you that."

And then I was telling him how long I'd known Jackie, about her friendship with my sister, and how she'd called me out of the blue about Bubba Brevna after so many years. Before long I was even telling him that Jackie and I were each other's first lovers, and that's when I knew for sure there was some art to Aubrey's apologetic demeanor.

I told him I was there that morning to take Jackie to the OCU, convinced as she was that Brevna had torched The Emerald Lizard. I asked him about the restaurant, the one Jackie kept talking about the night before, telling him that Jackie had said she could finger the person who'd done the job.

"No name?" Aubrey asked.

"No. Every time I asked her who it was, she'd say

something about Brevna, that Brevna had done it, and she was going to get him for it. She wasn't really making any sense, except what I think she was saying was that she knew who'd done the restaurant job, someone Brevna hired, and she could get Brevna by giving the cops that person. Maybe she thought the same person torched the Lizard, I don't know. Whatever, she said Brevna was behind both arsons."

"Could be," Aubrey said. "The Lizard was done the same way that restaurant was."

The restaurant had been owned by a woman named Kathy Thibodeaux. She divorced her husband and opened the place with money she got from the property settlement. The ex-husband was still loaded, but he ran around saying he'd been taken to the cleaners and was going to get even, so the police thought he'd given the order to have the place torched.

It was done with a plastic soda bottle, a piece of plastic pipe, and a rope, Aubrey told me. A hole was drilled in the walls of both the restaurant and the lounge, and the pipe was inserted with the rope threaded through it. Then the top part of a soda bottle was cut as a funnel and a mixture of gasoline and diesel fuel, added so the gasoline wouldn't explode, was poured into the pipe. The rope was used as a wick to ignite the mix.

But nothing was ever proved and, as far as Aubrey knew, the case was still open though probably not under active investigation anymore.

"Yesterday's arson will change that," he said.

Cigarettes are good stall tactics, so I lit yet one more before I told him what I knew: "You know, Aubrey, Jackie told me something else. She told me she went to you first about Brevna. It was only after you told her to go ahead and make some money off the chicken drop contests that she called me."

He gave a one-blow-through-the-nose sardonic laugh. "Because I wouldn't take on Bubba Brevna? Well, you know what? I'm not paid to take on Bubba Brevna. I'm just a Westwego patrolman. I give out tickets to anyone who speeds through our fair town, I give the town drunks a nice clean cell to sober up in, and if an armed robbery or a murder or anything important happens, well, I call the Sheriff's office. Bubba Brevna doesn't even live in Westwego. Jackie knew that."

Maybe I'd sounded too much like I was the one doing the questioning because then Aubrey said, "I hate to bring it up, but I know Detective Dietz will." He pointed. "Those scratches on your face and neck."

Involuntarily, my hand touched the side of my neck. Diana had gotten quite vicious on Sunday night and done some fresh damage, but I knew it wasn't fresh enough to worry about. I gave Aubrey a *cherchez-la-femme* routine.

He shook his head. "A real hellcat, huh?"

11

The Khaki Room

Detective Delbert Dietz of the Jefferson Parish Homicide Unit didn't like me at all. He didn't like that I was a private cop, he didn't like that I'd shown up at the scene of the murder, he didn't like that I'd been in the room with the victim, that I was her friend, that she'd called me, or that I claimed to have been taking her to the Organized Crime Unit. He seemed to like even less the reason I said we were going. In fact, he so little liked anything I had to say that I didn't try to explain to him all I'd told Aubrey, and I didn't hear Aubrey filling it in, either. I kept it all real simple: I told him about the loan, the contract on Jackie's tongue, my visit to Brevna, and Jackie's phone calls after the Lizard had been torched.

The kind of cop Dietz was could be pegged as easily as the taste of Glenfiddich. He was a combination of the know-it-all cop and the cop with a chip on his shoulder. He was ticked off all the time except when he got a laugh off getting the better of somebody. Anyone who wasn't a cop was automatically an idiot, and undoubtedly most cops made the category without halfway trying. Aubrey was small fry, but he got Dietz's approval (and a large measure of indifference) because he knew his place, which was on the phone immediately to Dietz and on guard in front of the murder site.

It made Aubrey sweat, though, when Dietz put him through an intensive explanation of why he'd broken into the victim's home. Two times of going through his concern for his friend because of the fire, her failure to answer her phone, his subsequent visit to check on her, and my arrival got Aubrey a quick affirmative jerk of Dietz's head, which had a bald spot the size of a beanie that he tried to cover with strands of hair almost the same color as his pale slick scalp.

But Dietz was going to have the most fun with me. The first thing he did after my initial explanation of my presence on the murder scene was make me cool my heels while he questioned all the neighbors. Aubrey went with him. Lots of them were at home because they were unemployed. Forty-five minutes of listening to the birds whistling to each other in a quiet suburban neighborhood made me antsy. Also, I was running out of smokes. There was half a pack or so in my car, so I started to go get them, but the deputy posted outside Jackie's house stopped me. He was one of those cops of few words and he didn't care what I wanted, I had to wait for Dietz. Right then I began to get an uncomfortable feeling that I was going to be the chief suspect until somebody else got available.

Dietz came back, more short-tempered, more abrupt than he had been.

He looked at his notes.

"At exactly what time did the victim first call you?" he demanded, though I'd already told him. I was also getting sick of his constant reference to Jackie as "the victim." I didn't like thinking of Jackie as a victim.

"Jackie Silva," I said, "called me at about seven-thirty. I told you I can't be any more exact than that."

He looked up from his notes. "Try," he said nastily.

My jaw tightened. What I tried to do was keep my voice as even as possible. "At about seven-thirty," I repeated.

"The second time," he snapped, like a drill sergeant.

"Like I told you, before ten o'clock. The ten o'clock news came on while we were still on the phone."

He got in my face. "The only name she mentioned in either of those conversations was one Bubba Brevna?"

"The one and only."

"Again," he snarled. His breath shriveled my nostrils.

"The one and only name she mentioned was Bubba Brevna." My jaw was locked.

"Take him in," he said to the deputy.

"For what?" This erupted with some fury.

But Dietz didn't have to listen to me. "Get a statement," he said to the deputy. He went on into Jackie's house.

The deputy, the authoritative-silence type, indicated his car with a finger and stood aside so I could walk in front of him.

Aubrey walked alongside me. "I'll bring your car around," he said quietly. I fished out my keys and passed them to him. The deputy chose to ignore this. I chose not to tell Aubrey I assumed he was under orders from Dietz to search my car.

At the Detectives Bureau in the old Gretna Courthouse, which is no longer a courthouse, I gave my statement and smoked my last cigarette while I waited for the statement to be typed so I could sign it. I was sitting in a dingy khaki room, the color a banana leaf turns when it's dead. They could pretend it was some kind of waiting room, but it looked like an interrogation room to me with its one table and chair, hanging light fixture, bare walls, and no windows. I wanted out.

The strong and silent deputy brought me the statement, I signed it, and got up to leave. He pushed me back in the chair.

"Wait for Dietz," he said. So far this was the only thing he'd said to me, twice now, except for "Start talking," when I was to give the statement.

I waited, with no cigarettes and nothing to do except tell myself to calm down and not act riled in front of Dietz or I wouldn't make it home till long past bedtime, and when I got there I'd be too sore to sleep. I tried thinking about my phone conversations with Jackie, about what she'd left out, not what she'd said. Then I remembered that the very first night she called me, after sixteen years, when she was also tying one on, she'd told me Brevna was a stupid man, stupid and cheap and dangerous because of it. He had a small-time operation and he hired people, probably stupid and cheap people, to do his dirty work. Jackie had known at least one person he'd hired and I would have, too, if I hadn't been so intent upon staying home last night. Dietz gave me plenty of time to be irritated with myself, until I started thinking Jackie hadn't acted like she thought Bubba Brevna was stupid and dangerous, she had acted as though she thought he was nobody's fool and dangerous. I decided she'd meant he was stupid about how to live well, cheap because of his small-time operation. Stupid, too, because he didn't know how to be anything other than cheap and small-time, but he was effective on his level. No Peter Principle problems for Bubba Brevna.

Dietz swaggered into the khaki room at two-thirty in the afternoon. He'd shed his jacket and loosened his tie. One button of his cream shirt was popped over his gut. He threw my statement down on the table.

"We got discrepancies in your statement," he informed me, except in that tone of voice he could just as easily have said, "We found the murder weapon in your car." Though of course the murder weapon in this case was attached to somebody's arm.

I waited.

"In her statement to the arson unit, the victim never said she asked you to talk to one Robert G. Brevna of Marrero."

I nodded. "Yes, she told me . . ."

"The victim never mentioned you at all in her statement to the arson unit."

This time I didn't bother to say anything.

"Robert G. Brevna of Marrero says you never came to see him, he doesn't know you."

I stared straight ahead, noticing that the khaki paint was peeling to show a light yellowy beige underneath. Too cheery for this chamber of tortures, but a little imagination and I could make the light beige splotch into a palm tree.

"Robert G. Brevna says he never threatened the victim, he asked for a show of faith on money he loaned her by this Friday."

I was getting attached to my palm tree, but a little more flaking and it would turn into a mushroom cloud.

Dietz's voice about shattered my left eardrum. "You have a comment?"

"No," I said calmly, in a moderate to soft tone, "I have a suggestion."

This Dietz was an animal. With his foot—and quick, too—he knocked the chair out from under me. I caught myself on the table, scraping it forward a couple of inches, and slowly lifted myself up. Every muscle was tensed for a working over. But Dietz righted the chair. I sat down.

"What might that be?" he asked in a cloying, sappy voice, his mouth curled with disgust, his nose wrinkled, apparently from my stench. Looking at his monochromatic coloring, the shirt almost the same sickly bland color of his face and hair, and his fleshy distorted lips without a drop of blood in them, made me want to puke. Or at least look as if I wanted to puke.

"Talk to Jackie Silva's bartender Jeffrey Bonage. He

knows about the threat Brevna made and he was in The Emerald Lizard the day she asked me to go see Brevna."

"That's not in your statement," Dietz said. "Are you revising your statement?"

"No."

"Maybe you'll change your mind. Let's talk about that second phone call allegedly made by the victim to you on the night of the murder. Were you aware that there was anyone with her?"

"No."

"She mentioned no names . . ."

". . . other than Bubba Brevna," I finished for him. I could feel my nerves starting to snap like rubber bands.

He put his foot on the rung of the chair, his gut grazing my shoulder. I braced myself for another fall. Instead he grabbed my hair and jerked my head back as if he were trying to break my neck.

"Just how good-a-friends were you and the victim," he said, changing his speech pattern, showing his versatility. "Good-a-nuff for a few fucks? She scratch your back up like she got your neck? Or'd she git you before you crushed her trachea?"

I was looking down the bridge of my nose. I kept on looking down the bridge of my nose. He let go of my head.

I shrugged and rolled my head then turned to face him, not moving away from his distended stomach, which was right on top of me.

"Get your gut out of my face, Dietz." I had a strong urge to bare my teeth, growl, and snap at his rolls of flesh.

He waited long enough for me to think he would already have made some sort of retaliatory move, then he used the foot on the chair rung, his gut against my shoulder, crashing the chair to the side. When I reached out for the table he toppled it, too. This offensive use of the gut must be big time on the West Bank. For that matter, guts themselves must be big, so to speak. Everyone there seemed to have one, or else they were sickly thin like Jeffrey Bonage and Larry Silva.

I got up. "Press charges or I want out of here, Dietz." I stepped away from the chair in case he had any other fancy moves.

The door opened a crack and the deputy rolled an eye over the situation and started to close the door. Dietz waved his arm, motioning for the deputy to come in.

"This asshole has trouble sitting in chairs," he said. "You better walk him to the door so he doesn't break his neck."

He flung himself out of the room.

12

Funeral in Never-Never Land

For the next few days I let the police do their work on Jackie's murder while I did some of the kind of work that makes me some money. After all, I had to pay for the Thunderbird.

There are several lawyers around town who consider me unbeatable at questioning witnesses to auto accidents, personal injuries, robberies, occasionally a shooting, and so on. I get witnesses to remember details they thought they'd forgotten, the kind of details that build strong cases, or sometimes I get them to question what they saw, put doubt in their ability to recall those same kinds of details. It depends from whose perspective I'm building the case. There are always several different possibilities, several different "truths." In fact, for every person involved, there's usually a slightly different truth. Once you've grasped this concept, that in most cases there is no single absolute truth, just varying and occasionally vehement opinions of the truth, the job is easy.

This kind of work pays well and doesn't usually give me a lot of headaches. Unfortunately, it is not the kind of work I find most interesting.

I gave Aubrey a call the day before Jackie's funeral to see if there was anything new on either the arson or her murder. Aubrey was not exactly privy to Dietz's every move, but that way he had of being apologetic, a bit servile, appealed to a guy like Dietz and got Aubrey some information. And Aubrey wasn't adverse to passing it on to me: the pathology report stated that Jackie had died as a result of a blow to the throat which had crushed her trachea at the voice box. She had not been strangled. Aubrey had talked to the pathologist, who'd told him that the blow looked as if it had been delivered by a powerful hand, but the possibility of a weaker person, even a woman, who'd struck out in intense anger couldn't be overlooked. As of the day before the funeral there was still no arrest, but Dietz was looking hard at Larry Silva. Some neighbor had told Dietz she'd seen Larry's car parked outside the house about ten. So Larry had been there at the right time, the second glass on the coffee table was his, and the cigarettes that weren't Kools were his brand. He said he was gone before eleven, at which time he drove down to Lafitte where he was temporarily staying on a friend's houseboat.

That statement put him on the scene when the coroner said the murder occurred, between twelve and twenty-four hours before he saw the body, which was after it was brought into his office. Since there is only one pathologist in Jefferson Parish, he rarely goes to the scene of a murder. So that put the time of death anywhere between ten o'clock, when I last spoke to Jackie, and midnight or a little past. Unless anyone else had spoken to Jackie after Larry left and anyone in Lafitte could corroborate his story, he'd picked a lousy time to visit his estranged wife.

Well, you could've fooled me. That day at the Lizard Larry had come off as some kind of peacenik, with his beard and his shabby clothes, bending over Clem Winkler, complaining about the violence in the lounge. That's not to say he didn't have a motive, what with his wife kicking him out of his own house when he was down and out and didn't know whether he was going to live or die, while she was blatantly seeing another man. People have killed for less than that. Not too long ago the New Orleans racetrack bugler was killed for eleven bucks.

The day of Jackie's funeral was a clear November day, sky like a glazed enamel tile. There was something like the snap of fall earlier in the morning, but by eleven o'clock, the time of the funeral, it was getting warm enough to want shed your jacket and roll up your sleeves. Winter was unthinkable.

I picked up my mother and sister. The old man is always up for a wedding, but no way was he going to a funeral. He'll go if it's family, and I guess he'll go to Roderick Rankin's, a New Orleans homicide detective and the old man's best friend, if he outlives Rankin.

The three of us took off for Canal Street to one of New Orleans' long-established funeral homes. My mother was up front with me, my sister in the back of the car. My mother is small, barely five feet, but somehow I never think of her as being that small. Maybe it's because she moves so fast. At home she always seems to be everywhere at once, in control of everything, efficient, competent, talking incessantly. Altogether, she seems larger than life, maybe because she's so full of life, fairly bursting with it as she moves and talks and does several things at one time.

But next to me in the Thunderbird that morning she was small in a navy blue dress with a collar of what looked like old lace. She probably looked small because she was weepy, a state she's rarely in, dabbing at her eyes with a thin white handkerchief, calling Jackie "that poor girl." To her Jackie was still a girl, at her eldest a young blushing bride.

Ma didn't ask any questions about Jackie's murder or make any speculations. My mother is the least judgmental person I know. That's probably because the old man makes enough judgments for the two of them. Instead, she tries to find something redeeming in everyone. On the way home from Jackie's wedding reception she made a big deal over what a nice wedding it was and what a polite, nice boy Larry seemed to be while Reenie was practically gagging over Larry's tattoos and the old man was being sour because they served some cheap bourbon instead of Jack Daniel's.

On the way to Jackie's funeral Ma reminisced about the poodle skirts—whatever the hell those were—she and Reenie and Jackie had made, and about the time Jackie, envious of Reenie's reddish-brown hair, had tried to put auburn highlights in her own dark hair. Instead of highlights, she got bright orange streaks which Reenie and Ma helped her cover with dye before Jackie's father saw her and brained her. I remembered that episode, a Saturday night, the three of them over the kitchen sink for hours, Jackie's hair stinking of chemicals when we made love later on.

I thought about making love to Jackie, about the first time, and I was back in the living room of my parents' house, and sixteen years old again.

Jackie crossed the room in her slow, sensuous way, over to the front door so she could peer through the curtain. I was intrigued. How could a limp, a leg that was a little shorter and just the barest bit thinner than the other one, be sexy? I watched her walk and she caught me watching. She gave me her sidelong look out of eyes shaped into Egyptian cat eyes with black eyeliner, and that seductively crooked smile that ended in two crescent-moon lines at the left side of her mouth, one moon a little smaller and nestled inside the other.

She and my sister Reenie were waiting for their dates to the Redemptorist football game. Reenie was a couple of months shy of fifteen, but Jackie was roughly my age, so my parents had agreed to let Reenie go on a car date if they went straight to the game and back.

The old man and I were watching the Friday night fights. Actually, I was waiting until the girls got off before I went over to Acy's Pool Hall to shoot a few games with Murphy—no football game for us, we were going to be pool sharks when we grew up. The old man was waiting for the girls' dates with his police .357 Magnum on the table next to his easy chair. I knew he was going to pull something, and I wanted to be there to see it.

Reenie was in the next room, in front of the mirror over the mantel, putting on eye makeup, wiping it off, putting on more. My mother was standing behind her telling her she was putting on too much, then telling her to put a little more on over here or over there. Periodically one or the other of them would call out over the noise of the boxing match to Jackie, "Are they here yet?" They both were nervous as cats.

The doorbell rang and Jackie moved in her slow, deliberate way to let the guys in. They strutted over the doorsill, cool cats in their shirts with pointed collars, shoes with pointed toes, and high-waisted trousers. They smoothed the sides of their Brylcreemed hairdos with their palms.

Jackie introduced them to the old man and then to me.

That was another thing, that voice of hers, husky and breathy all at once, the words slipping quickly, effortlessly, over the tongue, coming out like an expensive whiskey goes down.

I said hello to the dates like any regular person would. Not the old man. He didn't say a word, just scowled harder at the television set, which put those guys on edge right away. The little crescents at the side of Jackie's mouth nestled closer to each other.

Reenie came in, everyone said goodnight, and the guys, more relaxed now, told the old man it was very nice to meet him, snickering a bit, as if they thought he was deaf or dumb. They nodded at me and started to swagger out. Just as they got the door opened, there came a roar like the side of a mountain falling off. Those boys' pants fell from just below the rib cage to down around their hips. Even the cool and confident Jackie jumped.

The old man nailed them in the doorway with what was actually a watered-down (by Dixie beer) version of his famous Rafferty Laser Eye, meant to cut the confession out of the most hardened murderer. He turned thunder into words—"Not one second past eleven"—and the laser eye came to rest on the Magnum. The second boy out the door scuffed the back of the first one's shoes. The girls were mortified beyond belief. Reenie looked as if she was sure she'd never have another date.

Several hours later, in the dead silence of the night, Jackie appeared next to my bed, and without a word we began our dangerous liaison. In all that silence, our deep hot breaths were like two dragons breathing fire; the catch in her throat was as loud as the beating of the telltale heart; the creak on the stairs froze me, my hand over her mouth.

But it wasn't a creak on the stairs, it was in the bedsprings. We moved to the floor and started all over, and there was nothing like the thrill of all that passion forced to be silent, or the fear that we might be discovered. Danger and desire make strange and exciting bedfellows, especially for a sixteen-year-old boy being seduced by his sister's best friend, with his old man's eagle ears almost directly below him—uh, her.

It was almost too exciting, too dangerous. Almost. Every time we did it, I swore I'd never do it again. After all, I was a good Catholic boy, and maybe I wasn't doomed yet, not unless the old man caught me. Then Jackie would slip into my room in the middle of some lusty teenage dream and I'd think about the nuns at catechism saying I was born guilty and I'd figure I might as well know what I was guilty of, so I'd move over and hold the covers up and she'd get in beside me. It was funny—we'd always start in the bed, until the first spring squealed—just calling out to the old man, an entirely different sound than when you turned over—then we'd freeze, excited as much by terror as anything else, before we got down on the floor.

Danger was the taste and smell of Jackie.

Ma twisted in the car seat and said to Reenie, "We sure had some fun, didn't we?" She lifted the handkerchief to her eyes. "You two were such good friends."

Reenie tried to smile. She'd answered in monotones every time Ma had asked her something. Otherwise she was staring at me. I could feel her eyes boring into the back of my head. Reenie and Jackie were good friends all right, but that's not to say they had remained good friends. You see, twenty-two years ago, in the deepest dark of a hot night on my bedroom floor, it wasn't the old man who'd caught us, it was Reenie.

The funeral home was a sprawling pale terracotta-colored half mansion–half castle with a turret and gables and archways bordering a veranda, and a lot of decorative tile work. It was like something out of a Disney fantasy. Or the result of a millionaire's whimsy.

We got out of the car, from behind the shield of its tinted glass, and even with my shades on the day was too bright, too beautiful, the funeral home too never-neverlandish. It was all unreal. I had this peculiar feeling I used to get when I played hooky from school, a feeling that because I wasn't where I ought to be, where I was wasn't real. I wasn't supposed to be here at this strangely whimsical funeral home. Jackie wasn't supposed to be dead.

For a few moments as my mother, sister, and I made our way to the side door of the funeral parlor, I was dislocated. My legs moved but were not part of me, though my body was following. Any second now something would go Pop! and none of this would be happening. However, the sight of the Impastato twins arriving, dressed in their black suits, with skinny black ties, confirmed that all of this was indeed happening.

Both of them had their hair slicked in place—I'd seen them using combs when they got out of their car, both with the same mannerism, combing with one hand, the other hand sliding over the hair after the comb had gone through it—hair that was shiny with some kind of grease. But as soon as the smiley one nodded at me as he was going in through the door I held open, his front hank of hair fell forward on his forehead. By the time we walked to the parlor, where a short visitation was being held before the funeral, the other one had a matching 'do.

From the relentless brilliance of the blazing sun we passed into a wide, softly lit hallway muted by thick carpeting and flocked wallpaper. There was brilliance here, too, in the gold flocking, the beveled mirrors in gilded frames, polished brass sconces with electrically lit white tapers, and red carpeting that flowed into a parlor furnished with satiny upholstered Victorian chairs and sofas, and small highly polished occasional tables with marble tops. It occurred to me that the whole place was a lot like Diana's apartment, except on a much larger scale.

None of us spoke as we went through the hallway to the parlor. The hushed quality of the air forbade it. But I expected the usual murmur of voices in the parlor as people stood around waiting for the service to begin.

Instead there was a hush in the parlor as well. It was a double parlor with an elaborate archway of heavy decorative molding at its center. Large sliding pocket doors that came together under the archway were pushed back into the walls now. Dainty Victorian chairs and loveseat-size sofas were lined up along the perimeter of the big room, equally dainty tables separating them every now and then.

On one side of the room sat Jackie's parents and people I assumed were relatives. Squared off on the other side were Jackie's husband and friends, among

them her next-door neighbor Pam, Jeffrey Bonage, and
Bubba Brevna. The group was split the same way it had
been at Jackie's wedding, with the addition of some new
faces.

Bubba sat on a chair the seat of which was half the size
of his. He had his arms crossed over his chest, his legs
open and his feet planted securely in front of him to keep
his balance. He was directly across from Jackie's father.
They both had deep frowns imprinted on their foreheads.

The East Bank side and the West Bank side were
divided by a sea of red carpeting. My mother went straight
across it to Jackie's parents without hesitation. Reenie
hesitated, then followed her. I was actually more interested in the West Bank side.

Larry Silva was sitting fairly close to the doorway. I let
my hand rest on his shoulder. I started to tell him what
you're supposed to tell bereaved people, but I didn't. He
looked away from me before I could, his mouth strug-
gling to keep control within his beard, his eyes brimming.
I tightened my grip on his shoulder a second and let my
hand slide off, then went after Reenie to pay my respects
to Jackie's parents.

Mrs. Guillot, Jackie's mother, kissed Reenie and took
my hand, but all the time her other hand was on Ma's
arm, not letting her go. She and Mr. Guillot were on a
loveseat, but she squeezed over and pulled Ma down
next to her. I felt sorry for her. She looked old and faded
and alone, getting no comfort from her husband, whose
only reaction was to set his permanent disapproving scowl
deeper.

Mrs. Guillot introduced us to her sister and her husband, who were sitting next down the line. The sister had
a relatively unlined face, made-up flawlessly. I guessed
she'd made a happier marriage than Mrs. Guillot, and
judging by the jewelry she wore and the way both she
and her husband were dressed, a more affluent one as
well.

But remember how I said this story really began the

morning before Jackie called me, in Maurice's office? Remember I told you that the reason for this is because New Orleans is really just a tiny town? This is something I can go on about at length—about how sometimes it seems not more than a couple of hundred people live here and they all seem to be related; about how if you should happen to go somewhere and meet someone new, given fifteen minutes' worth of conversation, you find out your second cousin's wife is the new acquaintance's niece's husband's sister-in-law or something.

Well, here it was happening again, at Jackie's funeral. But nothing so far removed. Mrs. Guillot's sister and her husband were Mr. and Mrs. Greene, and next to them sat their daughter Nita, Jackie's first cousin.

I hadn't noticed her when I first walked in—I was too busy checking out the talent on the other team. Not only that, she looked different, all dressed up in a dark green dress with a white collar, white stockings, patent leather shoes with grosgrain bows, her hair pulled back with barrettes.

Her eyes were red and swollen behind her tortoise-shell glasses. We murmured something to each other, at about the same time, about it being a small world, then I walked with Reenie to the end of the parlor where we stood slightly away from another group of people who'd just arrived.

I assumed they were people who had frequented The Emerald Lizard. That's because, a couple at a time, they went over to Jeffrey Bonage, though a few of them stopped in front of Larry. One, a woman of ample build, braved a walk down the middle of the room to the casket, which was closed. She stood for a few moments with her head bowed and walked back. Mr. Guillot didn't seem to like her. Maybe it was the penciled-in beauty mark high on one cheekbone and the bright red hair done up in a beehive, or the way her shoulders were thrown back and her chest thrust out. Bubba, however, followed her walk with his eyes until he would have had to turn his head. His eyes snapped back to Mr. Guillot, who glowered at him.

Into the middle of this face-off strode a newcomer, a man in a dove-gray suit with Western details and a ten-gallon hat. It was Clem Winkler. He went right up to Jackie's parents, stood before her mother and took off his hat.

"Ma'am," he drawled, "sir," with a nod at Jackie's father, "I sure am sorry about your girl Jackie. I loved her."

Larry Silva let out an audible sob and Clem turned on the heels of his cowboy boots, which looked as if they'd been kicking cowpies all morning. He went off to do some time in front of the casket. Bubba and Mr. Guillot stopped staring each other down and had a fast, dead heat draw to see who could shoot the angriest glare at Clem's back. I noticed that Jeffrey Bonage was in on the action, too, glaring at Clem, but Clem was wearing his glare-proof vest. Impervious, he situated a chair so he was closest to the casket and sat his slim hips down on its slippery, rose-embossed upholstery.

Nobody seemed to like all this very much except one of the Impastato twins, the one who did all the talking, smiling and nodding while the other followed along. He elbowed his brother and the two of them stood up and crossed over to Jackie's parents where he said, "We're sorry, too. We are Frank and Vincent Impastato and we both were very good friends of your daughter's." He emphasized "very good friends" and led his brother to the casket. Together they mumbled a prayer.

Now all of this was very interesting and I, frankly, was on tenterhooks wondering what was going to happen next. Jackie's mother had been very polite, thanking both Clem and the Imps. Jackie's father, however, had taken on a perceptibly reddish hue about the neck and lower face. I think the appearance of Rodney Nutley at that moment would have sent him into a seizure. But I didn't imagine that Bubba thought Godzilla was presentable enough to let out of his cage to attend a funeral. I was thinking that everyone else was here, though. Then I took it right back—Aubrey Wohl wasn't.

The Imps were sitting down and Reenie was putting her hand on my arm. She looked distraught. "Should we?" She nodded toward the casket. I shook my head.

It was Bubba's turn. He stood up looking extremely hostile, bypassed the speech to the parents and headed straight to the casket. Not to be outdone, he plopped himself down on the prayer rail that had been placed alongside it. His rounded shoulders seemed to heave a bit.

Jackie's father could stand this no longer. He seared his wife with an accusatory eye as if to say this was all her idea, got up and left the room. Bubba got up and reclaimed his seat. Mr. Guillot returned a couple of minutes later with a priest. The priest began the service, cutting the visitation short by nearly fifteen minutes. From what he was saying, he obviously didn't know Jackie, but still he referred to her, at least once in every sentence, as "Jackie," as if that made her more familiar to him. I don't know why it irked me. I guess it always irks me the way they talk about someone they didn't even know.

"Wouldn't you think he'd call her Jacqueline?" I whispered to Reenie, thinking the occasion called for at least some formality.

"No," she whispered back, "that wasn't her name. *He* named her Jackie." She meant Jackie's father. "He wanted a boy."

13
An Arresting Interment

I spotted the car as soon as I pulled out on Canal Street in the tandem of cars going to the cemetery. It was a pale putty color, unmarked. Apparently everything he owned, even what he drove around in, was the same nondescript color he was. That isn't really fair since most unmarked cars are beige it seems, but I don't consider it unfair to accuse Dietz of being monochromatic or monomaniacal. not after what he did.

The deputy was with him, at the wheel. I wondered what the hell they were doing—tailing someone in a conspicuous line of hearse, limousines, and cars on the way to an interment? Sure enough, the car started up, made a U-turn, and joined the procession.

Jackie was being buried in the St. Louis Cemetery Number One, which is downtown just off the French Quarter. It's the oldest cemetery in the city, hundreds of crumbling, whitewashed tombs like tiny buildings, standing above the ground, safe houses for the dead so they're kept high and dry in a city that barely keeps itself above sea level.

Two police escorts, New Orleans police that is, on motorcycles, got us through the traffic in one unbroken line all the way to the cemetery. I wondered what they thought of the tail end of the line.

Once we got to the cemetery, though, the police stuck around instead of taking off as they usually do. I figured Mr. Guillot had given each of them a twenty to make sure the mourners weren't mugged during the service since the cemetery is in one of the roughest, most dangerous neighborhoods in town. All manner of trouble happens around there, including every now and then, a voodoo murder. Marie LaVeau is supposedly buried in St. Louis Number One, near the Basin Street entrance where we were entering. Gris-gris potions, bones, hair, dolls—you name it—are left at her tomb. And once in a while, nearby, a body will be found with some kind of gris-gris on it or next to it. Most of those murders are never solved.

The unmarked car hung back about half a block from the cemetery entrance. I followed the group, smaller than it had been at the funeral home, through the maze of tombs with crosses and angels on top of them. They were all very close together, and the sun dazzled them in a white heat.

Nita had separated herself from the group. I went and stood with her. Her eyes were hidden behind large, very dark sunglasses. When she spoke she didn't turn her head toward me.

"How well did you know her?" she asked, and the way she asked carried something of an accusation with it. It seemed to me she was asking me if I'd been sleeping with Jackie, but maybe that was just residual teenage guilt on my part, or the fact that every other man there seemed to have had some sort of intimate relationship with her at one time.

"Not very well anymore," I said to Nita. "She and my sister were best friends when we were all in high school."

"That was a long time ago," Nita said bluntly.

"Are you reminding me that I'm an old man"—I admit I said this pointedly— "or are you wondering how I happen to be at her funeral?"

One thing about Nita, she was not slow. And in her grief I suppose she had no use for subtlety.

"I don't think of Maurice as an old man," she said just as pointedly.

I half expected her to go on, to accuse me of not being much in favor of their relationship (I had no doubt that she'd picked up on my wariness the night we had dinner), but she stopped as if she'd lost heart. I found I didn't want her to think I was against them.

"I know you don't think of Maurice as old," I told her. And I told her about Jackie calling me; I pointed out Bubba Brevna to her, gave her the lowdown on the Impastatos and the chicken drop contests; I explained how the Lizard was torched, that it was torched the same way as the restaurant. I wanted to let Nita know I wasn't thinking she was a child, that I respected her intelligence.

She turned her head toward me, pulled her sunglasses down a bit and looked at me over the rims.

"What are they all doing here?" she asked incredulously.

"Well, strangely, they're all her friends."

"Geez," she said, pushing her glasses back on, staring ahead again.

The priest began his litany at the gravesite, some of the mourners making responses. As the coffin was slid into its slot on the bottom tier of the tomb, Larry Silva broke down. Jackie's best friend Pam was at his side and, I now noticed, all dressed up in a tight black dress and high heels. Her arm was around his waist, holding him up, and he was letting her, one of his arms across her shoulders, weeping into her blond hair.

Everyone started to disperse, but slowly. Bubba was in conference with the Imps. I thought I'd follow him out and try to have a few words with him concerning why he was lying to the cops about me. But I didn't want to leave Nita too abruptly. She hadn't moved.

"So how are you coming along with your photographs?" I asked her.

"Fine."

"Working hard?"

"I was."

Bubba and the Imps started moving in the direction of the exit. Behind them was the woman with the beehive hairdo. Before they reached us, I stepped slightly aside and put a hand at Nita's waist. I barely touched her. She moved out into the pathway and we walked toward the cemetery gate well ahead of Bubba.

I went on with our conversation. "I guess this slowed you down." She nodded.

We were walking over some tiny white shells now, our shoes crunching on them. I had a wave of déjà vu and then realized that the cemetery was oddly reminiscent of the trailer park where Bubba lived. White hot, little foliage, everything huddled together. I felt the need to talk, to make some noise other than that crunching sound. Just to have something to say, I told Nita I was sure she'd manage to get back to her work in a few days.

She said, "I pretty much have to, don't I. I have a deadline, remember?"

"I wasn't sure you'd decided to have the show."

"Diana didn't tell you?"

"No, but we've both been pretty busy lately. We haven't been seeing each other every day."

"I didn't mean for you to apologize," Nita said. "I thought she'd tell you right away because I thought she'd be . . ." She trailed off, unable to find the right word.

"Smug?" I asked. She shrugged. "Look, Nita, Diana was an ass that night and I told her so. But it's a good opportunity for you, and I'm glad you're taking it." I also wondered if she suspected I was glad the wedding was postponed. She walked on, not answering, looking at the ground; her hair, caught up high in the barrette, swung down over her cheek. She looked young and vulnerable.

We were at the gate. I moved off to the side just in front of the high wall surrounding the cemetery and stopped.

"Hey," I said, "how about a game of pool one night soon?" I grinned at her. "I'd like to show you off over at Grady's.

Bubba and his entourage had caught up with us. Nita was shrugging at me again and starting to say something when the woman sporting the beehive touched her shoulder lightly. Nita looked around and the woman said, in a kind, rather maternal way, "Hi, honey, how're you doing?"

"Hi, Mave."

Mave? Mave Scoggins who ran the Gemini owned by the Impastatos? How the hell did Nita know Mave Scoggins? *Why* did Nita know Mave Scoggins?

I didn't get a chance to ask. There was a blood-curdling scream on the other side of the cemetery wall from where we were standing. I looked around it, one arm reaching back, a protective barrier so Nita wouldn't follow.

Out on the sidewalk, Dietz was pushing Pam, who was screaming, and his deputy was pulling at Larry Silva. Pam was clinging to Larry's jacket. Now she was screaming, "No! Leave him alone! Stop it!"

Dietz put one of his thick sluglike arms between Pam and Larry and elbowed Pam out of the way. One of Pam's legs bent under her and she fell against the rough cemetery wall. As soon as he had Pam off Larry, Dietz flung him up against the side of the unmarked car and began cuffing him and reciting Miranda. At one point Larry tried to back away from the car and Dietz batted the back of his head with his palm. Larry's face smashed against the roofline of the car. I started running toward them, but the deputy stepped out, blocking my way. The two New Orleans cops had the small area around the car on the street side cordonned off with their motorcycles, arms folded, faces inscrutable behind aviator sunglasses.

So that's why they were here, so Dietz could make his showy arrest. He was on their turf—they had to be here.

Larry was turning his head, trying to look in our direction. He was calling for me.

"Just go with them, Larry. I'm following," I called back to him.

He got his head turned. There was blood running out of the side of his mouth.

At that moment I think I could have killed Dietz, I felt such rage. I stepped forward and so did the deputy. I put my shoulder up against his sternum and yelled, "Don't hurt him, Dietz." It carried a threat—I couldn't help that. But I knew better than to outright threaten him in front of witnesses.

His putty-like lips smiled at me. "Don't rush," he said. "He's got to be booked, stripped, and deloused." He opened the back door of the car and, his hand on Larry's head, shoved Larry down on the back seat.

14

Reenie

By the time the funeral party came out of shock, Dietz was laying rubber down Basin Street.

Pam was standing next to the cemetery wall, crying. Her arm was scraped where she'd fallen against the brick overlaid with cracked concrete. The reason she'd fallen was because the heel had broken off her shoe when Dietz pushed her. She held it and cried. It was hard to tell if she was crying over the shoe or Larry or everything.

I looked around for Bubba, but he was gone. He must have been the only one who kept moving during Dietz's stop-the-show performance.

Meanwhile, Jackie's mother was coming unglued. Ma helped Mr. Guillot get her back to the limousine and asked him if he wanted her to ride back with them, but Nita's mother came up and said she'd ride with them.

I drove across town to the Irish Channel, which is where my parents own the camelback double I grew up in. They live on one side, my sister and her family on the other. It's like that in New Orleans, especially in the Channel—whole families live in the same block for generations. It's also one of the reasons I got out. This town is claustrophobic enough being as flat as it is and shrouded with trees, without having to live under your family's nose. This, however, is another subject, as you've probably guessed, that I can go on about at length.

I suppressed my anger, waiting until I got Ma and Reenie home. The day had been upsetting enough without me raging all the way to the Channel. Anyway, I needed to cool down and ask myself why I was feeling so protective toward Larry Silva. I guess I just didn't buy that he'd killed Jackie. It was all too convenient, Larry's glass and cigarettes and his terrible timing. All that, though, was something a good defense attorney could use to some advantage. But that was another thing. Could Larry afford a good defense attorney? As far as I knew he was practically indigent. I let out an involuntary sigh of resignation. Neal Rafferty takes on yet another nonpaying client. Not having any idea what I was sighing about, my mother reached over and patted me on the arm. I smiled at her.

She'd had enough sadness for one day. When I pulled up in front of the house, she practically leapt from the car.

"I've got to run, darlin'," she said. "Your father's had that baby for almost two hours now." She meant my sister's baby, Reenie's third, a boy. She leaned back into the car and lowered her voice as if the old man was listening at her back. "You know that two hours' worth will send him over to Norby's for the rest of the afternoon." Norby's is a neighborhood bar near Audubon Park where the old man, in his retirement now, likes to while away the afternoons so he can get out of the house and away from shrieking kids (my sister's other two), the wailing baby, and the women's chatter. The second there is any kind of crisis he's off like a shot.

Ma started to pull back, but she stopped and said to me, "I hope you can help that poor man, Neal."

"I think I can," I told her. "If he didn't kill his wife."

"Oh"—she was surprised at what I'd said—"I'm sure he didn't do that." She shook her head, negating the possibility. "I'm sure he couldn't have done that."

Of course she was sure. Ma couldn't believe anyone would do that. I didn't want to believe Larry had done it either, but I also hated Dietz and wanted to prove him wrong.

"We'll see," I said.

She shook her head once more and was off with her usual speed and zest. Inside the house there were babies to tend to, life to nurture. For a few seconds I was overcome by a peculiar feeling—I envied my mother.

Reenie, however, was not in such a hurry. She climbed out of the back seat and took Ma's place leaning into the car. She had dark circles under her eyes and in general didn't look well.

"I guess you're in a hurry," she started.

The motor was idling; I cut it off.

"Not particularly."

Hell, it was Friday. Dietz would stall around long enough to make sure that Larry spent the weekend in Orleans Parish Central Lockup, so that he couldn't be arraigned and bail couldn't be set until after he'd been transported to the JPCC—Jefferson Parish Correctional Center, in Gretna—on Monday. For someone like Dietz it was fun going out of his way to make another person's life miserable.

I said to Reenie, "Wanna talk?"

She got in the car. We both rolled down the windows. It was November, and we were still riding around in air-conditioned cars.

"I do," she said, "but I'm not sure what I want to say."

I turned toward her in the seat, getting comfortable, and lit a cigarette. "I think you want to talk about Jackie."

She nodded, but she didn't speak right away. Finally, she turned in the seat, too, and got comfortable. We were all knees in the space between the bucket seats. Reenie folded her leg nearest me, tucked it partially under her, and smoothed her skirt printed with autumn flowers around her legs. She let the flowered crook of her knee rest against my kneecap. We settled in.

"Where do I start?" she asked, not looking for an answer. Her fingers drifted through her long hair, picking up one strand and twisting it 'round and 'round. "I loved her."

"I know you did."

"I mean, I really hero-worshiped her." She let the strand of hair fall, combing it back into her reddish-brown waves which shone against the black blouse she was wearing. "A lot of girls didn't like her, but they were just jealous. I didn't expect to have as many boyfriends as she did. I was just glad to get to hang around with her and be seen with her." She smiled. "I thought maybe some of her reputation would rub off on me."

"You wanted to be known as fast?"

"No! You see, that's what you don't understand because you were two grades ahead of us and you didn't hang out with us after school. The boys didn't think she was fast. They thought she was indifferent, and she was. She was completely aloof, she didn't care about any of them and that made them more crazy about her. Of course, they wouldn't have been if she hadn't looked the way she did and walked the way she did. And everyone knew she was older and that didn't hurt either."

Yeah, I thought, that walk of hers had gotten to them, too. But I didn't say anything. Reenie was starting to wade into some deep water here, and I hoped she'd back out. We'd never discussed her finding Jackie and me together. After a few months it just passed and we began acting toward each other the way we always had.

Reenie made a sudden move, sort of hitting my knee

with hers, straightening herself angrily in the seat so we were no longer touching. "Jesus, Neal, how can you say that, about her being fast? You were screwing her, right? So doesn't that make *you* fast? Or are just girls fast? What is it—guys are exempt?"

"Here we go," I said. "I didn't know what you meant. I didn't think you wanted to be known as fast. I may have been two grades ahead, but I heard guys talking. They talked like she was a pretty hot number."

"So what did you think? That she was screwing all of them, too? How could she, she was always at our house. She stopped going out with anyone at all after a while. What's the matter, don't you remember?"

She was quite furious with me. Apparently she'd never stopped being furious.

"Come on, Reenie, of course I remember. But what's the deal? We're talking twenty years ago, twenty-two to be exact. Why are you so upset?"

"Because I never forgave her." She started to cry. "All those years and all those times she called, trying again to be friends, and I never once called her. I wouldn't forgive her and now I *can't* forgive her."

She was filling buckets. I prodded all of my pockets—no handkerchief. But I remembered Diana putting a small pack of Kleenex in the glove compartment one night. I got it out and handed it to Reenie.

She snatched it out of my hand. "I forgave *you*." She hurled the words at me. Then she took out a Kleenex and sobbed into it, "But I wouldn't forgive *her*."

"Oh boy," I said to myself, but not out loud. I stared out the window a few moments, until she got herself more or less under control, then I said, "Look, Reenie, you *had* to forgive me eventually. I'm your brother. We lived under the same roof. You had to look at me every day."

It sounded pretty good to me, but no reaction from Reenie.

"You felt betrayed," I went on blindly. "You had to

be angry at someone, and you just couldn't stay mad at me forever. Ma would have finally made us sit down and tell her what was up." She still wasn't convinced. "Say what you want to about the unfairness of girls being called fast, but, face it, guys are expected to be raunchy. It's easier to forgive them."

I didn't know if I'd just made new inroads into psychobabble or if Reenie would start screaming at me again. I waited.

After a while she looked at me, disgusted. "That's about as enlightened as Dad gets." She knew that would hurt. "But you're right about one thing." She'd stopped crying so much, just a few drips she was catching with the Kleenex. "I felt betrayed. I felt like Jackie had never cared a thing about me, that the only reason she was coming over all the time was because of you. And to get away from that miserable father of hers. Do you know what he used to do to her?" I didn't. "He had this little leather strap, and when he got mad at her, he'd make her pull her blouse down, you know, so it was around her elbows and he'd hit her with that strap on her upper arms. She said it was humiliating, standing there in her bra. She started wearing slips all the time. She said he punished her that way because he liked looking at her. Isn't that disgusting? Her own father?"

When Reenie told me that I thought of something I hadn't thought about since one night when I'd felt what must have been the welts from that strap on her arms. I remembered whispering, asking her what it was. She'd made some deep sound in her throat and hadn't answered, but moved my hand somewhere else to take my mind off her humiliation. It now made me feel terrible.

"I wish I would have forgiven her, I really do," Reenie said, "but the next morning she cried and said if I stayed mad at her then she couldn't come over anymore and not only would she lose her best friend, but she wouldn't be able to see you. She said you wouldn't go out of your way to keep seeing her and she didn't know if she could stand it. Everything she said just made me feel more used and betrayed."

It was true, I hadn't gone out of my way. I'd missed her, but part of me was also relieved. I'd never really thought about how she must have felt, if I'd hurt her.

Reenie's laugh cut into my delayed misgivings. "Do you know what she used to say about you, before I found out? She used to say she didn't know how I could stand living in the same house with you all the time, the way you hung around, always watching us, spying. She called you *the voyeur*." She gave it a dramatic French accent.

"She did?"

"She did, and I never suspected a thing. Never would have. You know, Neal, now that I'm thinking about it, Jackie was really sly. You know, maybe there was another reason I didn't forgive her, and I'm not trying to make excuses because I really wish I had, but I just remembered something she did once that didn't sit at all well with me. Something I just had to forget about if she was still going to be my friend. There was something she wanted badly, some dress she'd seen at a department store downtown. She was dying for it, but her father wouldn't give her the money. One afternoon we were in the kitchen with Mom and all of a sudden Mom pulled a wad of money out of her apron pocket. She couldn't believe it. She said she must be losing her mind to have put that money in her apron. She'd gone to the store the week before and got in the checkout line, and when she went to pay, she didn't have any money in her purse. Mom was really kind of upset about it—well, I guess because Dad had a fit—but she couldn't believe she'd put the grocery money in her apron. Later on Jackie told me she'd taken the money out of Mom's purse, bought the dress, and the next weekend when she came over, she'd put the money back in Mom's apron. She said she was getting worried Mom wasn't going to find it. She never did tell me where she got the money to replace what she'd taken. And I guess I didn't want to know. I told her not to do that ever again. I don't think I felt quite the same about Jackie after that. I mean, think of it, poor Mom in the store with no money."

Yeah, think of it. I was thinking of too much. I was thinking that one minute a person could be crying over not forgiving Jackie and the next minute ticked over something she'd done twenty years ago. One day angry at her for calling me out of the blue and involving me in her sordid life, the next day feeling terrible over the way her father abused her. And the way I had used her.

Reenie was saying something about feeling a lot better and being glad we'd talked. She kissed me quickly on the cheek and said she'd better go take care of her baby. She ran up the steps to the double, the skirt moving prettily around her legs and her reddish-brown hair swinging as she turned to wave at me. The black blouse pulled out of her skirt at the side of her waist as she lifted her arm and revealed a small triangle of flesh.

I cranked up the T-bird.

Voyeur, indeed.

15
▪

Born Again
to Die

After I left Reenie, I went by Maurice's house, which isn't but a few blocks on the other side of Magazine Street from my parents' house. I was hoping to catch Nita. I wanted to ask her about Mave Scoggins, how she knew her, how well Jackie knew her, that kind of thing. But she wasn't there, probably still with her family.

"So I can't get you out of here, Larry. You can't be arraigned and bail can't be set until you're transferred to Jefferson Parish on Monday."

I was a little glassy-eyed from all the waiting around as I explained to Larry that, just as I'd figured, Dietz had made sure Larry missed the last pickup from Central Lockup to JPCC. But that bit about stripping and delousing was only more of Dietz's showing off. Larry still had on his own clothes minus his belt, tie, and jacket. Stripping him of those essentials, however, and taking his mug shot and fingerprints had managed to take over three hours.

We were in a small interrogation room that I'd had plenty of time to arrange with some old police buddies so Larry and I could talk privately.

He was sitting at a metal table roughly twice the size of a doormat, his arms stretched out in front of him, his fingers clasped. I stood on the other side of the table.

"It's all right, Neal. I got no money for bail and nowhere to go anyway. I might not even be alive by Monday."

I turned my back to him so he couldn't see my eyes rolling. It was a little pious, a lot self-indulgent. I paced two steps and turned around.

"Well, I don't suppose we should act on the assumption that you're going to be dead."

"Whether I'm dead or alive doesn't matter. I want you to find out who killed Jackie. Poor kid." His voice caught. He turned his head sort of into his shoulder, you know, as though he were going to burst into tears. "She didn't deserve to die like that."

He lifted his hands to his face and pressed hard on his eyeballs. The tattoos on the backs of his hands were faded, though the **X** full of smaller **x**'s was holding up better than the bird in flight. I found myself wondering about the rest of his body and got irritated.

"Look, Larry, we don't have time for you to have a breakdown. They could kick us out of here any minute. What can you tell me that might take the heat off you and put it on somebody else?"

His hands fell away from his eyes and he held them palms up toward me. It was reminiscent of a pose that shows up in a lot of religious paintings. Supplication, I believe it's called.

"Why would I leave a glass full of fingerprints and an ashtray full of butts if I killed her?" he asked.

"Your lawyer will ask the same question, but the D.A. will probably drop the charge to second degree murder and say you were so filled with rage and passion that you forgot about the evidence." He looked sad, sad and saintly. "Concentrate on someone else. Who did she talk about while you were with her?"

"Mostly me, that I'm an idiot about money, which is true, that I'm self-righteous enough to make a nun puke, which depends on how you look at it, and that everyone else was in love with her so why should she stay married to some poor self-righteous idiot who might croak in the saddle?"

"Did that make you angry?"

It made *me* angry to hear about it, but Larry said, "How could it? She was right—I could keel over any second. Anyway, you know how Jackie was. When she was drunk that tongue of hers was sharp as a razor."

"You know about Bubba Brevna threatening Jackie?"

"The contract on her tongue?" For the first time he smiled. No, he grinned. "Yeah, but I didn't pay any attention to that either."

"Why not? Didn't she tell you that I was supposed to take her to the Organized Crime Unit about Brevna the next day?"

"No." He drew his eyebrows together, perplexed.

To tell you the truth, so was I. Jackie hadn't seemed to hold her tongue about much. It made me wonder if she'd been serious about going. After all, we'd apparently been on the phone just before Larry arrived at the house.

"Nevertheless," I said, "Jackie seemed to take Brevna's threat seriously."

"But he was in love with her."

"People kill for love, Larry, especially for unrequited love. That's what they're going to say you did." His frown deepened. "Who else was in love with her?" I asked. I wanted to know his view of Jackie's love affairs and how angry he was about them.

"Well, Clem Winkler for one."

"She told me on the phone the night she died that she was through with Winkler. Do you believe that?"

"Hard to say. She told me he was over there earlier,

before I was, but she kicked him out. But Jackie liked to play that kind of game. It didn't mean much."

"Maybe it does this time. He told the cops he hadn't seen her since the night before, and he had an alibi, too." This was more information from Aubrey, though he hadn't told me who Winkler's alibi was. "Maybe he went back after you left."

"Aw, I don't think so, Neal. I don't much like Clem, but I don't think he'd've killed her."

"What about Jeffrey Bonage?"

"Jeffrey? Naw, forget Jeffrey. He didn't do it."

I turned away again for another bout of eye rolling. Larry was the only person I'd ever met who I thought could rival my mother for refusing to think ill of people. He didn't think anybody could have killed Jackie, not even Bubba Brevna, but Jackie was dead and someone had done it. I asked him if there was anyone else besides Brevna, Jeffrey, and Clem on the scene. He said he didn't think so.

"Do you know how Brevna got the money he loaned Jackie?"

"Brevna's loaded."

"You don't know about the case he was supposed have fixed for the ten grand he gave to Jackie instead?"

"That's news to me. Brevna makes a lot of money fishing."

"Larry, the man runs prostitutes and he's apparently not above a little arson on the side."

"Well, I know *that*, but *case* fixing . . ."

"Wait a minute. Are you trying to tell me he burns things down, but wouldn't fix cases?"

"Not 'wouldn't.' Couldn't. I don't think he has those kinds of connections."

"Wouldn't, couldn't—it doesn't matter. Apparently he didn't. He gave the money to Jackie."

"I don't know about all that. I mean I know he loaned her the money, but Jackie didn't tell me everything. I guess she really didn't tell me very much."

"Did she tell you about the restaurant Brevna had burned down? The one owned by Kathy Thibodeaux?"

"Bubba did that, did he?" He shook his head sorrowfully.

"Never mind," I said. This was getting too tedious. It was time to get down to what counted here—money. "How badly in debt are you to your bookie, Larry?"

"Jackie told you that?"

"No, Brevna did."

"What a bitch," he said without much heat.

"Jackie?"

"No, my bookie. She must have told Brevna."

"She? Who's your bookie?"

"Now look, Neal, I don't want you giving her any trouble. She's got a heart of gold. She never would have pushed me on it. I mean, she won't take any more bets, but she knows I'm good for it so I don't want you hassling her or anything."

I was beginning to feel wild. Patience, patience, I told myself as I let each word out with control: "And who is she, Larry?"

"Mave Scoggins."

Ah, Mave Scoggins. Old Mave kept popping up with the regularity of toast in a roadside diner at six A.M.

Larry was running on about not understanding why Mave would have told Bubba he owed her five grand. "She knows about the trouble between me and Bubba."

"The trouble over the fishing boat?"

"Yeah. You know about that?"

"Some. I'd like to hear it from you."

"Well, Bubba got his eye on this boat, a nice rig for shrimping out in the Gulf. He either didn't have all the money or he didn't want to use it. He asked me if I wanted to invest in the boat. I put up a lot of the money and Aubrey Wohl put up some, too. We were bound to get a return during the brown shrimp season, and I figured the white shrimp would get us a really solid profit. Till then, though, the boat had to be maintained. Then the wing nets had to be replaced. By that time I was out of money. Bubba said if I was out of money, I was out of the deal. There wasn't much I could do about it. There was a clause in the contract, but I hadn't bothered to get a lawyer to read the contract. It was my own fault, so I ate it, but a couple of months later, the boat burns up, right out in Turtle Bay. Bad wiring or something. Bubba's insurance pays off and he gets himself an even bigger boat, calls it *My New Flame*."

That Bubba, what a sense of humor. No wonder he'd gotten so jovial when I asked him about Larry's investment in the fishing boat. Quite a scam. No wonder, either, that Bubba didn't count on Larry giving Jackie the money to pay off her debt to him.

"So," I said, "your investment burned up, you've got no money for bail, no money for a lawyer, and no money for a private investigator."

Remember how I mentioned that the kind of work I'm most interested in usually wasn't the kind that made me much money? Here was a case in point.

But Larry was protesting, "Oh no, Neal, I'll be able to pay you, if you can hang on till the insurance company pays off on the lounge. It shouldn't take too long."

"Larry, I believe you're forgetting about payday for Mr. Brevna."

This time when Larry grinned he wasn't looking at all saintly. A little of the tattooed, street-smart guy we all thought Jackie had married was coming through. "There was no paperwork on the loan. No *signed* paperwork. Jackie never quite got around to it. And for a while there, she managed to make Bubba forget he cared, if you know what I mean. The insurance money is mine."

"Maybe it's just as well you can't make bail, the way Bubba likes to put contracts out on people's body parts."

Larry was still grinning. "It's hard to scare a man who could drop dead any second."

"That's true," I said dryly. "I forget you have this

basic advantage over other people. But what's Bubba's excuse? He's not even afraid of the IRS".

Larry, I could tell, was a very literal person. He said, "I keep telling you, Neal, Bubba's a fisherman. Even the IRS can't audit fish."

16

Drawing Conclusions

So Larry wasn't very angry at all about Jackie's affairs. The fact that she slept with other men didn't seem to make him angry, jealous, or cause him to love her any less. Maybe Westwego was like a lot of small towns I've heard about where screwing is the favorite sport, the preferred leisure time activity because there's nothing much else to do.

Or maybe Larry was just screwy. I could buy that without much trouble. I believed that Jackie was afraid of Bubba because she believed he'd burned down the Lizard. I thought it was possible Bubba had killed Jackie or had her killed. But Larry didn't think so because he believed Bubba was in love with Jackie.

None of this made much sense if you tried to think about it logically. Look at it this way: If Jackie had never signed the paperwork on the loan, but she was afraid enough of Bubba to pay off the loan, then it didn't make sense for Bubba to kill Jackie. On the other side, though, was the possibility that the money itself meant very little to Bubba or that Bubba thought Larry was enough of a sap to pay him the money Jackie owed even if she was dead. Or he thought he could scare Larry into paying. Larry may have been given a death sentence, but he hadn't been given a date. Or the king of the trailer park didn't like Jackie making a sucker out of him and burned her place down, then killed her. What really didn't make any sense was trying to figure it out without more facts. Whether Bubba had killed Jackie or not, it seemed to me he was the logical person to begin with. So far everything had either started with or come back to Bubba.

I was ready to have another talk with the West Bank kingpin.

However, it was almost four-thirty, and no sane person gets on the Greater New Orleans Mississippi River Bridge going to the West Bank during rush hour. Especially not on Friday.

Maurice's office was over on Tulane Avenue not far from Central Lockup. In the old days, before Nita, he would almost certainly still be there.

The office was a single-story building that had once been a double. Maurice had knocked out a few walls, removed a kitchen, added a lot of bookshelves, desks, conference tables, and computers and turned it into his law office.

Through the front French doors I could see a light on in the outer office, but Pinkie wasn't behind the desk. Instead her chair was tucked neatly under it and its top cleared and straightened.

There was no point checking to see if his car was in the back; Maurice never drove to work. He never drove at all if he could help it, though he still had his father's 1969 faded blue, dented Mercedes garaged at home. He took cabs everywhere. The reason for this is because whenever Maurice got behind the wheel of the car, he invariably plowed through street blockades and cone markers (the streets of New Orleans are always undergoing repairs because of the shifting mud underneath them), side-swiped parked cars, and demolished garbage cans. While he was still driving he replaced his own garbage cans about eight times, I think, and backed into his neighbor's cans across the street about four. But it was the night he creamed a St. Charles Avenue streetlight while backing out of the way of a streetcar that made him give up the car for good. He avoided the streetcar, all right, but the light pole fell on it after wiping out the electrical trolley lines above it, and before the damage was repaired the accident caused a backup of some eight cars of angry riders.

I knocked on the French doors and before long Maurice emerged from his back office. He was still looking very uptown preppy, wearing khaki slacks, a white Oxford shirt, and penny loafers. The next step, I feared, would be Madras bermudas and Top-Siders for weekend attire. I had a rush of nostalgia for the Western-suited, cowboy-booted Maurice, my friend the eccentric lawyer, Nita's high plains undertaker. Then I realized I was doing what I accused New Orleanians of always doing, never wanting anything or anyone to change, the way many of them had never changed out of khaki slacks and Oxford shirts.

"I thought it might be Nita," Maurice said, opening the door.

"Yeah, I'm glad to see you, too."

Maurice takes most of what I say quite seriously. "Oh no," he said, "I meant I was expecting her. I'm always glad to see you, Neal." He hung an arm over my shoulders for a moment as we walked toward his office.

Now I ask you, who wouldn't want a friend like Maurice? I grinned at him. "Thanks, but I really can't blame you for preferring to see Nita. She's okay, Maurice."

We hadn't had a chance to talk since the night of the disastrous dinner with Diana. Admittedly, I hadn't been so sure Nita was okay, and I guess I was feeling sorry that I hadn't called Maurice and let him know I was glad for him.

But Maurice didn't appear to be worried about my lapses. Here was one of the most feared lawyers in town, reddening from the neck up just because I'd said his girlfriend was okay.

"As a matter of fact, I talked to Nita for a while this morning," I went on.

He was clearly surprised. "At her cousin's funeral?"

We settled down in Maurice's office, each of us slinging our feet over a corner of his mammoth desk, and I told him a bit about my relationship with Jackie Silva, near and far past, then about Jackie's problems with Bubba Brevna, The Emerald Lizard fire, and the typical New Orleans-type coincidence that Nita Greene was Jackie Silva's cousin.

This coincidence interested Maurice least of all now.

He looked at me intently. "Do you think Brevna killed Jackie?" he asked.

"I don't know, but her husband's been arrested for her murder and I'm pretty certain he didn't do it."

I gave him the story on Larry, the good-hearted born-again who might possibly drop dead at any moment and showed no anger or jealousy, only sadness, over his wife's extra-marital affairs. I asked Maurice if he had either the time or inclination to represent Larry.

"Oh, sure, sure, I'll be glad to," he said, but he was distracted, thinking about something else. His eyes drifted over to a window and held. I waited, wondering what he was going to come up with and, as usual, he asked a question I least expected.

His eyes came back to me. "Do you know if Brevna has an interest in any other lounge, either ownership or financing or any other kind of backing?"

"No. I asked Jackie the same question, but she didn't know, and Larry keeps telling me Brevna's a fisherman. Any reason?"

"Just find out. I'll go over and see Larry tomorrow. I'll call you afterwards."

"When's Nita supposed to be here? I'd like to talk to her."

Maurice glanced at his watch. "Not for a while, actually. When I'm waiting for her it's always earlier than I think."

Maurice has such a way of saying things.

"Now there's a definition of love," I told him. I pushed myself out of the chair. "Well, I'm off to the West Bank. Mind if I use Pinkie's phone on my way out?"

Maurice was in an intense state of thought, his usual state, before I was across the threshold.

Out in the reception area, I pulled the chair out and sat behind Pinkie's desk. In back of her name plate was a pink and gray pen set with a memo pad of pink paper imprinted with "From the desk of Pinkie Dean" and a head sketch of a girl with spiky hair and a turned-up nose, wearing a pair of cat-eye glasses.

While I waited for Diana to answer the phone I started drawing a monster with walleyes and lightning bolts around his head on the top sheet of the memo pad.

The princess was getting dressed for our date.

"Sorry, princess. I've got to work." I gave the monster an apelike body.

"That's absolutely no fair," she protested. "I think if I don't get out of here tonight I'll go crazy!"

I started drawing curlicues of hair all over the ape's body. "Call that lawyer—what's his name?—Wylie St. Cyr."

There was a moment of silence after which I expected a scathing remark. Instead I heard a remarkable thing—sniffling. The princess, it seemed, was crying. I stopped drawing.

"Diana?"

"I really wanted to see you, Neal. We haven't been together all day."

This had never bothered her before. "I'm sorry, princess. I didn't expect to have to work."

"What do you have to do?"

"Oh, just some regular ole gumshoeing across the river. I could come over afterwards." I decided to put a see-through suit on the ape's hairy body.

While I was coloring in the tie, Diana said, "I have a much better idea." Indeed, she sounded much chirpier. "It's five o'clock—you can't go across the river now. Let's meet at K-Paul's and have dinner. It's so early we won't have to wait in line, and then I'll go across the river with you."

You could say I was stunned by this suggestion. "I don't know, Diana. It may take a while and you'll probably be bored. Not only that, you'll hate the places I have to go to. They're places I'm not so sure you *should* go to." I was thinking chiefly of the trailer park and the Gemini lounge. I put a pair of aviator sunglasses over the monster's walleyes, blocking them out.

"I'll wait in the car if you want me to, and I promise not to complain."

"I don't know . . . " I changed the monster's mouth into a roguish grin.

She spoke quickly. "You're the one who says I always want to do the same things, go to the same places. Please, Neal. I won't get in your way and I'll do whatever you say, no questions. Say yes," she finished breathlessly.

"Well, no questions, no complaints . . ." Behind my now rather rakish-looking ape man, I penned in a silhouette of the T-bird.

"I promise! At K-Paul's in twenty minutes?"

I was still in my funeral suit, which is also my power suit and my going-to-court suit. "I've got to change," I told her. "Meet me at the Euclid."

I hung up the phone, added a couple of touches like watch and shoes, and wrote under my drawing, *LOW-LIFE ABOUT TOWN.*

17

The Operative

Diana was telling me, informing me, she would be my operative for the evening. She was wearing a black turtleneck, black slacks, and over that a fuchsia jacket made of raw silk. On her feet were a dainty pair of black flats.

"And that's what you think an operative should wear?" I asked her as I tucked a plain white dress shirt into a pair of jeans.

"Without the jacket, of course," she said. "That's to go to dinner in."

"I see." I tied the laces on a pair of Converse low quarters. "And do you think that as an operative you're worth the price of a dinner at K-Paul's?"

"Without a doubt," she answered without pause. "Don't you?" She wandered over to the bedroom windows.

"On experience, I couldn't say. On sight, I'd say absolutely."

She turned to give me a come-hither smile and return the compliment. "You know, you look very sexy dressed like that. There's almost nothing sexier than a well-built man dressed in a white shirt and jeans."

"I'll remind you of that next time you demand to be taken to a fancy restaurant," I said and responded to her smile by walking over to her and putting my arms around her waist.

She ran her hands over my chest. "Especially a man with a sexy scar dressed like that." She circled her arms around my neck and the way she kissed me could have made me forget all about going over to the West Bank if I wasn't such a responsible guy.

There were lots of things I liked about Diana. Besides being gorgeous and great in bed, especially lately, she thought the scar on my face was attractive. I don't think I'm particularly vain, but for a while after I was cut, I was self-conscious partly because the scar was red and swollen, but mostly because it caused my eyelid to droop, which I thought made me look mean and ugly. I began wearing sunglasses a lot. Gradually the redness went away, but there had been no improvement in the eyelid. Then along came Diana who didn't want to mother me because I'd been hurt and marked for life and wasn't repulsed for the same reason, who thought the scar enhanced my looks, made me look, as she said, dangerously glamorous. I began wearing sunglasses only when I was out in the sun.

I pulled her toward me by the hips, then finally pushed her away, saying, "Time to go." I grabbed my navy blue sportscoat and her hand and headed out.

We went down to the lobby in a different elevator than we'd come up in. It appeared as if someone had slashed the wall covering on one side of this elevator.

Diana pointed at the rip. "What's going on around here, Neal? Is it vandals? Is the place deteriorating? I noticed from your window that the canopy out front is all ripped up, too.

"Nobody's bothering to fix anything anymore. They're

turning the place into a hotel. Everyone's got to be out by the first of the year."

"Good. Maybe you'll find a decent place to live." By that I had a feeling she meant a place more like hers.

"What? I like living at the Euclid. I wish I didn't have to move."

She looked at me with some disgust. "I hope you won't move into one of those horrible apartment complexes."

"I swear, Diana, you are so *uptown*." Actually, it was one of the things that, for the most part, I liked about her. It was part of her allure, her hauteur, her self-confidence.

She now looked at me with some alarm. "You haven't already rented an apartment in one, have you?"

"Yes, out in the suburbs, in Fat City." Alarm turned to horror. "No," I told her, "I haven't had time to look for anything yet."

"Good," she said again. "I'll help you look." By this time we'd hit the lobby. We walked out through a back door into the garage. The spring hinge at the top of the door was bad and the heavy door raced after our heels behind us. Diana moved out of the way without appearing to rush. "In fact," she continued as we headed over to the T-bird, "why don't you come stay with me until we find you a place?"

"Thanks, princess, but we'd probably kill each other."

"Hmm," she said, with a sidelong, highly suggestive look at me out of those chocolate-drop eyes, "sounds like fun."

Our next stop was K-Paul's, down in the French Quarter.

"This is ridiculous, Diana. I don't know why we couldn't just grab a burger across the river."

"Because I'm craving a Cajun martini and blackened redfish."

"Well, I don't give a damn about either one of those things. Once again you've conned me into taking you to a fancy restaurant even if it isn't exactly a fancy restaurant." What I meant was the prices are fancy even if you don't have to dress up. Diana fingered the hair on the back of my neck and smiled a Cheshire cat smile. "If more than two people are waiting, we leave," I told her.

Chef Paul Prudhomme's restaurant is so popular people line up clear down Chartres Street to get in. K-Paul's has become almost exclusively a tourist restaurant. Most locals don't go anymore unless they're with someone from out of town. That's because K-Paul's won't take reservations and sometimes you wait an hour or more to get in. If you want a drink while you wait, you have to walk down the block to the Napoleon House. But Diana loves Cajun food and she knows almost everyone who works in the place, which means we usually don't wait long and we're treated like royalty, the part the princess loves the most.

When Paul Prudhomme invented blackened redfish, which is not burned as some people joke, but black with pepper, it became such a national craze that redfish catches have had to be limited. Fisherman were going out into the Gulf of Mexico with closed-at-the-bottom nets called purse seines that they threw over huge schools of "bull" reds, the spawners. Sometimes the catches were so big they couldn't haul all the fish into the boat, so they dumped them back into the Gulf. Unfortunately, fish die in purse seines, so tons of dead redfish were washing up on the barrier islands. The Wildlife and Fisheries got worried about the brood stock. The Feds made purse seines illegal, imposed strict limits on offshore catches and, later, inshore fishing as well. But blackened trout just didn't sound as good, I guess.

Anyway, people were already waiting at the door of K-Paul's but they were moving steadily into the restaurant.

"Let me out and I'll have a table by the time you park," Diana said.

I didn't object too strenuously because she probably would have jumped from the moving car if I hadn't stopped and also because K-Paul's gets people in and out fast, sometimes seating two couples who've never seen each other before at the same table, which I *do* object to strenuously. However, Diana knew that.

I parked around the corner and by the time I walked back, she was sitting at the only table for two in the restaurant, sipping a Cajun martini out of a Mason jar, which is how they serve them, a Scotch and water in front of my place. I'd often kidded Diana, telling her to get off this Parisian French bull, when she can sit in K-Paul's and slurp down two of those fire-hot martinis without shedding a tear.

"God," I said, mentally scaling the latest price hike on blackened redfish, "I bet someone could make a killing if they marketed blackened fish sticks in the frozen food department at the supermarkets."

"Fish sticks?" Diana said incredulously and rinsed her mouth with another sip of Cajun martini.

Forty-five minutes later I had the princess fueled on enough pepper to blast us across the Mississippi River Bridge.

18.

Mave

The evening of gumshoeing began uneventfully.

I told Diana a bit about Jackie's murder as we drove to the Marrero Trailer Court. She waited in the car while I trekked across the oyster shells to Bubba's trailer. No lights were on, and the Lincoln and the flatboat were gone. The trailer court wasn't quite so depressing in the dark, but only because you couldn't see as much of it.

The next stop was the Gemini. The Gemini, like the Lizard, was located on 4th Street, but the part of 4th Street that runs through Marrero. It was also in a pretty unsavory neighborhood, another lounge across the street, a lot of litter, and several ramshackle clapboard buildings that could have been unoccupied. A woman leaned on the front wall of one of them. In a neighborhood like this you might have expected her to be a bag lady with stringy hair, tennis shoes with holes, and a dress hanging together by the last of its threads. But she had platinum blond hair, cherry red stiletto high heels on her feet, and a dress to match that was sewn to her skin. A siren in the slums. She was interested in the car until Diana stepped out of it. Then she gave a giant yawn and began sucking at one of her fingernails.

As we walked to the Gemini a very dirty pickup truck came speeding up the street, its empty bed slamming on the chassis as the wheels bounced in and out of potholes. It screeched to a stop in front of the woman, who was able to get up into the truck cab only because of a slit in the front of her dress, almost to her crotch.

We watched as the truck roared off. Aside from the pickup action, the street was relatively quiet for a Friday night. Inside the lounge, though, was the beginning of a good crowd.

The Gemini itself was a smallish red brick building, nothing fancy, but the newest construction on the street. It was set back so five or six cars could park in front. I guess I expected the inside to be done up in the Lizard's kind of style, all dark and plush with carpet. I was surprised by the simplicity of the place: a gleaming wood bar stretched across the back of the room, tables and chairs on a short-napped, red-mottled-with-black carpet in front of it. On the walls were carriage house-type light fixtures lit with chandelier bulbs. No intimate levels, no candle-light, no parquet dance floor. Who needed any of that when you had Mave?

She was fixing drinks behind the bar, her red hair shining in its elaborate beehive, her penciled-in beauty mark dramatic against peaches and cream skin. She had on a white blouse cut so low that I held my breath when she bent over to scoop some ice into a glass.

She went to the cash register where she rang up the drink she'd just made and got change for the waitress who was waiting at one end of the bar. She returned to the register and stood there several more seconds. From behind she seemed to be counting money. It was in her hand when she turned around and took it to the other end of the bar.

There were only two patrons, both male, sitting at the bar, but not together. One of them was at the end Mave was approaching now, standing to the side on the part of the bar that was perpendicular to the wall. Mave put the money down in front of him. Then she sat on a high stool facing him, so her profile was to us, and rested a foot on the edge of the bar. She wore a pair of cut-off jeans and her thigh coming out of that faded blue fringe was smooth and shapely. She sat forward, her forearm across her knee and watched as Clem Winkler counted the money.

He didn't have his cowboy hat on, but even from across the room I could see the dent left by it in his thick brown hair. His leathery hands moved fast as a card shark's counting the money.

Luckily there were enough people in the lounge and the jukebox was loud enough that neither Clem nor Mave noticed our entrance. But the real stroke of luck was finding the cowboy and the bookie together, exchanging money yet.

As I inched forward, I said to Diana, "The papers for the lounge will be posted somewhere behind the bar. See if you can read the names off them." Somehow it made no sense that the Impastato twins owned this place. One thing, there was no chicken drop board.

Diana nodded and we bellied up to the bar on little cat feet as Winkler pocketed the money and drawled, "Well, then, Mave, I'll see you 'bout this time next week."

Clem started to leave and Mave started to ask what she could get me, then they both realized I had a familiar face.

"Well, I'll be goddamned," Winkler said.

"I hope not," I told him, "not after such a nice payoff. Horse come in?"

Clem was ready to turn nasty, but Mave intervened. "Something I can do for you, mister?" She had a drawl that sounded like Texas, like Winkler's, but more refined than his.

"I hope so, Miss Scoggins. I was a friend of Jackie

Silva's. I'm investigating her death." I told her my name and gave her a card. I introduced Diana as an agency operative.

Clem snorted at that. "Don't take you long to mourn the dead, does it?"

"I wouldn't be so cocky if I were you, Winkler. It's just a matter of time before the cops figure out you were over at Jackie's the night she was murdered."

"I wasn't anywhere near there."

"Sure you were, hours before she was killed. What I'm wondering is why you lied, why you were afraid to tell the truth, unless you went back there later."

His wiry body tensed. If I hadn't already knocked him out once, he would have pounced.

But Mave didn't know our history of duking it out, and she wasn't taking any chances. She reared up over the bar so her hairdo was in between us and said in a low threatening voice, "I don't want any funny business in my barroom. You boys got that?" Clem let the balled-up fists at his sides relax. To me Mave said, "I don't know where you get your information, mister, but Clem was with me the night Jackie was murdered. The cops already know that."

"You sure about that, Miss Scoggins? You sure you didn't come in to work that night, or go to the grocery store, or out to dinner? Eyewitnesses have a bad habit of showing up when you least expect them. If Winkler's a murderer, lying for him makes you an accessory."

It's hard to say whether Clem was defending his own honor or Mave's, but he tried that right hook on me again. I blocked it and jabbed at his chin with my left, all in one movement. My jab didn't hit him hard enough to move him except that he was off balance to begin with. He staggered back a couple of steps.

"Enough!" Mave commanded, slapping the bar. We were attracting attention. Mave gave Clem some kind of eye action and he took his cowboy hat off a bar stool, jammed it on his head and let the heels on his cowboy boots dig his way out of the Gemini.

"Okay, Rafferty. I can tell you're a persistent kind of guy, so we might as well have a talk." The waitress was waiting for Mave at the other end of the bar. Mave called out to her, "Can you handle it, honey?"

"Sure, Mave." She let herself behind the bar through a flip-top opening and began mixing the drinks herself.

Diana, who had moved down the bar away from the action, drew alongside now, smiling up at me.

"Why are you protecting him, Miss Scoggins?"

"Clem doesn't need any protection, Rafferty."

"No he doesn't, not if he didn't kill Jackie."

Mave gave me a soft, almost motherly smile. "Why would Clem kill Jackie? He was in love with her."

What was it with these people? I asked myself that question. I asked Mave, "And what about Larry Silva, her husband. You know, the one they're holding for her murder. Don't you think he loved her, too?"

"Yes I do, but," she shook her head sadly, "Jackie didn't love him anymore. Anyone can tell you how cruel she could be when she told a man to get lost."

"Ah. I see. Maybe Clem didn't tell you that Jackie told him to get lost, too. The night she was killed."

Mave stared at me. There was no expression on her face, but her silence spoke for itself.

"Clem didn't tell you the truth, Mave," I said.

"And who told you?"

"Jackie did." Well, not technically. She'd told Larry, but I let that slide.

"So then it's your word against Clem's the way I see it."

"Unless someone in the neighborhood saw him around and decides to say so."

"That's right, but no one has, so I'm gonna keep right on believing Clem, Rafferty." This Mave stuck to her guns and to her cowboys. Must be that heart of gold Larry was talking about.

"Is Clem a heavy gambler?" I asked.

There was some more of Mave's expressionless yet meaningful silence.

"I know you're a bookie, Mave. Larry told me he's in debt to you. I have no intention of using it against you. I'm just trying to clear Larry."

"And I hope you do. I like Larry. That's the only reason I went to the funeral today, but what Clem does isn't really any of your business, is it?" She didn't say this unkindly.

"It is if it affects Larry in any way, or if Clem killed Jackie."

"I wish you'd just take my word he didn't."

"I wish that's all it took, Mave."

About this time Diana walked around the part of the bar where Clem had been standing. She went up to a pay phone on the wall at the end of the bar. The ownership papers were framed above it. Mave looked around. Diana started putting a quarter in the phone.

"What's it say, princess?" I asked.

"Frank Impastato and Vincent Impastato," she read. She got her quarter back, pocketed it, and came around to where I was standing at the bar.

"Where are the Impastatos?" I asked Mave.

"Gone fishin'," she told me. I would have laughed, but here on the West Bank there was a good chance that's exactly where they'd gone.

"Those Impastatos," I said. "An unpredictable pair. Hard to imagine them owning a place like this when they seem to be into such tasteless shenanigans as chicken drop contests."

"I have no idea what you're talking about," Mave said.

"Over at The Emerald Lizard," I added to help her out.

"I still don't know what you're talking about, and I don't much care either."

"You and Jackie weren't very good friends, were you?"

She put her hands on her rounded hips which strained

the seams of her cut-offs. She didn't deny it, she said, "We weren't enemies either. I think you've asked plenty enough questions for right now. I've got customers to take care of."

Her loyalty to her friends, her caring for her customers, her kindness to strangers while standing her ground, the bosom, the hairdo—yep, except for the cut-offs, I could see why Jackie had tagged her Miss Kitty.

"Just one more question," I said, "about Nita Greene."

"No," Mave shook her head. "That's just one question too many."

One question too many, or the wrong one? Was Mave protecting Nita, too? Why? What was Nita up to?

19

Prostitutes

See you 'bout this time next week, Mave.

Something like that was what the cowboy had said to Mave as he was getting ready to leave, after he'd counted his money.

That didn't sound like a gambler. He'd been too businesslike. And, anyway, what gambler takes his winnings and counts it out like a bank teller? Well, okay, that may be stretching the theory, but it was gnawing at me that Mave was paying the cowboy for something other than a bet he'd won, as if he'd come in to collect his weekly pay.

I was trying hard to imagine that Clem Winkler worked for the Impastato twins, but I was diverted by Diana getting into the car and immediately beginning to laugh.

"What?" I asked.

"Nita Greene."

The key was in and I was ready to turn it. I let my hand fall away. "What about her?"

"You know how secretive she's been about her proj-

ect. Well, I figured it out. It's the prostitutes. With
Mave's help she's getting into their hearts and minds.
With them she's experiencing another 'slice of life.' Re-
member how she talked that night?"

A creeping sense of alarm came over me. "What do
you mean? I thought she took pictures."

Diana could get very exasperated with me when she
thought I was being dense. "She does, Neal. She's a
photographer. In order to take good photographs, to
make the camera *see* the subjects, the prostitutes in this
case, she has to strip them down, if you'll forgive the
pun, to their vulnerabilities—their sadness, their gro-
tesqueness, their funniness. Don't you remember how
she talked? She has to understand how they experience
life. She has to *become* one of them. That's how some
photographers work."

"She has to 'become' one of them? Nita?"

"No, no. I don't mean that literally. She talks to them,
she gets them to tell her how they feel about what they
do, about themselves, so that they *expose* themselves to
her, then to the camera." She put her hand on my thigh.
"Oh, Neal," she laughed, "just imagine Nita, preppy
receptionist by day, turned Marrero prostitute by night!"

"I just did," I said. "It was not a pretty picture."

Diana thought this was uproarious. "She's an *artiste*,
Neal, not an adventuress!"

I was not nearly so amused. After all, if it concerned
Nita, it concerned Maurice. And if it concerned Maurice,
it concerned me. I felt about Maurice the way I would
have felt about a brother. Odd, really, if you considered
that we came from such entirely different backgrounds,
his father a graduate of Harvard Law School, mine of the
New Orleans Police Academy, yet we became friends,
good friends, immediately. Our friendship, though, wasn't
the typical male friendship, getting together to play sports
or watch sports or take in some action. When we got
together we talked, mostly about our work, sometimes
about our fathers, less often and only if it was important,

about women. Nita was important. It bothered me that I didn't know exactly what Nita was up to. It bothered me even more that Maurice probably didn't know either.

Following 4th Street over to Barataria Boulevard, I headed south, down-river direction, though we were not on the highway that follows alongside the river. I was on my way to Lafitte, which is separated from the river by a lot of marshland, bays, waterways, and bayous. These are a part of the wetlands that are endangered, fragile as they are and constantly changing, eroded away by natural causes such as hurricanes, and man-made causes such as dredging by oil companies. There are people who know the waterways so well, boating, hunting and fishing on them all their lives, that they can point out changes in the coastline as they happen. Then there are other people, like me, who could get lost forever in these waterways, like the man who never returned.

Diana got very quiet, and when she finally spoke I thought she'd want to know where we were going, but there was something else on her mind.

"What did that cowboy mean, you don't take long to mourn the dead?" she asked.

"Who knows."

She'd left her hand resting on my thigh as I drove, but she took it back now.

"Were you and Jackie lovers?"

I considered this question in all seriousness, but finally I had to answer, "Yes."

She was quiet again before she followed up with, "For long?"

Again I considered before answering, "For a while." For the better part of a year.

Part of Diana must have been thinking she shouldn't be jealous of someone who'd been murdered, but I knew she was jealous nonetheless. You see, she always let me know she had dates when we weren't together, but I never told her what I did when I wasn't with her unless I was working. I guess she'd been thinking all along that if I wasn't with her that's what I was doing, working.

I enjoyed torturing the princess all the way to the Lafitte LaRose Highway, then I finally told her Jackie and I had been lovers years ago.

No, Jackie had not been my lover when she was murdered. She'd been my client, the only client I'd ever had who'd been murdered.

I didn't like that.

20.

Pirates

"He was a violent man," I said. "He controlled his own men with violence."

Diana and I were discussing Jean Lafitte, the pirate. We were past the subdivisions at Barataria Boulevard and on the part of the Lafitte LaRose Highway that is flanked on either side by dense woods. We were approaching Crown Point and the only national park in the state of Louisiana, which happens to be named for Jean Lafitte. I had remarked that it was typical Louisiana to honor a pirate this way, a smuggler who increased the slave population of the state almost a hundred times during the first part of the nineteenth century.

Diana was arguing that he was a patriot because he turned down the British offer of thirty thousand dollars and helped Andrew Jackson win the Battle of New Orleans instead. It was obvious to me that thirty thousand, even if it was an enormous sum of money in 1814, was a drop in the bucket when Lafitte could get a thousand dollars a slave. His finances might not have continued to flourish under British rule, I told Diana.

She dismissed that, saying it was a way of life that was too deeply ingrained. "Anyway, Lafitte was known to be a gentleman. He was stylish, charming, and glamorous. He was friends with many aristocrats in the city; he was accepted by them."

"Of course he was, but that's nothing to be proud of your ancestors for. He sold them slaves and got rich off it. They probably liked him because he was richer than they were."

"The only people who consider it a cardinal sin to be rich are those who don't have any money," Diana replied.

I won't go on repeating this ridiculous argument. I'm only telling you about it because we were en route to the little towns of Barataria and Lafitte out of which the pirate conducted his marauding and smuggling and where the intricate waterways he knew so well made it easy for him to hide, and escape. And I also tell you because in a strange way, the story of Lafitte ends up having some bearing, if only peripherally, on the story of Jackie's murder.

Not only that, but you can see that Diana and I obviously loved to argue.

We got to Crown Point and came up over the high rise of the Intracoastal Canal Bridge there. Once you're over the bridge, the woods end and it's nothing but flat marshland all the way to the Gulf. It is only from a promontory like the bridge—the only kind of promontory around New Orleans, unless you want to consider skyscrapers—that you can fully appreciate the beauty of the terrain. It's a quiet beauty. It doesn't shout at you and announce itself from the hilltops, because there aren't any hills. It's not flashy; it doesn't titillate you by changing colors much. Its colors are infinite shades of green, from emerald to gray-green, which quietly change to a yellowy brown. The color change usually signals the very end of fall, not the beginning of it. Out in the marsh there isn't even much flowering in the spring, and most of that is hidden, for the benefit only, it seems, of the creatures who live there.

Its beauty lies in its apparent sameness, mile after indistinguishable mile stretching out, offering itself to the destructive waters of the Gulf. Even if you are out in the marsh, which I was only a couple of times in an uncle's boat, it all seems the same, confusing in its sameness because one cut of water looks much the same as another, a labyrinth of cuts, grassy islands, and mud lumps which only ends by presenting you with another expanse of another shade of green, the coastal Gulf water.

The marsh is formidable land if you don't know it, but it is, as I said, fragile, constantly in danger of disappearing before your very eyes. I remember my uncle saying every time he went out in the marsh to fish or hunt, which was usually every weekend, that he could see more changes—they happened that fast. All I knew was that being out there had made me very uncomfortable, once because there was nowhere to get away from the sun and intense heat, another time because there was no shelter from the dampest, iciest wind I'd ever felt. It was a weird kind of open-air entrapment. I much preferred to view the marsh as I was viewing it now, illuminated by the full moon, a misty and eerily lit mass of spectral gray with pillowy patches of fog shining whitely, a kind of low-forming cloud bank, penetrated by soft lumpy forms.

I was awed by it. There are times when New Orleans can seem like the end of the earth because it is so isolated, so different from other cities, so far away, but New Orleans is the center of the universe compared to the feeling I got from the marsh. The princess, however, was only mildly interested in any land mass uninterrupted by signs of civilized life.

Crown Point, Barataria, and Lafitte are so close together that you barely know you're out of one before you're in another. There are many bridges over small waterways running from the Intracoastal Canal to the lakes. We went over one and were in Lafitte.

We were on the Old Lafitte Road. Lights from houses appeared through the branches of oak trees whose trunks had been twisted by the prevailing weather—wind, rain, and storms. Moss hung thickly from the trees here; in New Orleans most of it has been killed off by pollution. We passed a cemetery, one where coffins had floated up once, set loose by a hurricane, tiny vessels carrying the dead across the water as if they were crossing the River Styx. My uncle had told me about that and it had left a deep impression on me. I told Diana about it now. She said nothing, but folded her arms tightly across her breasts as if she were cold.

I had no idea where Bubba kept his boat. In many places along the road you could see clear to the water. I slowed to a crawl and rolled down the windows, hoping to catch a glimpse of *My New Flame*. The only reason to think I might was that parked along the edge of the bayou like cars in a parking lot, were shrimp boats, one after the other, their big wing net frames folded up to tower over the boats themselves, the nets hanging in black graceful swags like so much mosquito netting. I didn't understand why they all weren't out. I'd always heard the full moon meant good shrimping.

Every once in a while I could see the name of a boat written across the bow, but only if it was docked beside a lighted pier. Lafitte isn't very big; in fact we were soon at the end of it and could drive no farther without a boat, but there were far too many boats in the little water town to be able to pick out Bubba's even if it had been there.

We stopped at a barroom with no name we could see in a building shaped like a large trailer. We knew it was a bar because of all the beer signs out front.

Inside were lots of fishermen, maybe fifteen or twenty, and a handful of women. You could tell the men were fishermen because most of them had on the white rubber calf-high boots that the fishermen around those parts wear. The women were dressed as if they were at home, some with backless terrycloth slippers on, one with her hair up in foam rollers. All of them were watching a football game on cable TV, laughing and talking, getting riled up over a play every now and then.

No one looked at us with hostility as we walked in, but they did look at us. They looked at Diana—especially the women. The bartender was a woman. She was small and plain with nondescript brownish hair held back off her heart-shaped face by a pair of bobby pins. She didn't ask what we wanted, she just stood there staring at us until I asked for a gin and tonic and a Scotch and water. She made them, took the ten I'd put out on the bar, and laid the change down where it had been without a word. I had a feeling that a lot of talk in the form of questions wasn't going to be welcomed.

We sat watching the game with the rest of the crowd, but I couldn't tell you who was playing. I had homed in on a kid, about thirteen, wearing the same kind of white rubber boots as the rest of them, off to himself in a corner playing a video game. I waited until I figured everyone had forgotten we were there, then I went over to watch the kid play. It was some kind of Space Invaders game.

He glanced at me out of the corner of his eye, which was shielded by a sweep of long black hair sliding across his forehead, but kept his concentration on the game. If anything, my presence seemed to help him concentrate more. The longer he played, the faster the Space Invaders filled up the screen. He dodged several invaders, his body movements becoming more animated, but finally his last man was caught and disappeared with the computerized whine of disappointment. The kid slapped at the machine, but he wasn't really angry.

"Pretty good score," I told him. He seemed a little shy, and smiled slightly, but didn't answer. "Aren't you going to play again?"

"Out of quarters." I strained to hear him, only realizing what he'd said after a few seconds.

I dug into my pocket and handed him one. He hesitated before taking it, then shoved it fast into the slot. Once again, his concentration was high, but he didn't do so well this time. I dug for another quarter, taking my time.

"How's the shrimping?" I asked. I pulled out two nickels, spent a couple of seconds inspecting them while he shrugged in answer to my question, and went back to digging. "The full moon's out," I commented.

He shrugged again, but said, "Tide's wrong. It's gotta be falling."

The kid took the quarter I offered him. I waited until he finished the game. This time his score was higher so I waited awhile.

"When will you go back out?" I asked after he finished.

"Maybe midnight." He was waiting for more money. I used to wait for someone to pay for a pool game the same way, eyes darting around as if I didn't care one way or another whether I played, but hugging the side of the pool table.

"Hang on," I told him. I got five dollars worth of quarters from the bartender.

That got me a gratified, "Wow!" He started to turn back to his game. I put my hand on his shoulder. "Do you know where Mr. Brevna keeps his shrimp boat?" I asked him.

The joy drained from his face. He let his fingers hang by their tips from the machine. I don't know why, but somehow my asking him that had made him sad. "No," he said.

I gave his shoulder a friendly pat and wished him luck.

Now here was a funny thing—I finally asked the bartender where I could find Brevna's boat. While the kid had been sad, the bartender was amused.

"I'm sure I couldn't tell you," she said. Without bothering to wait until we left, she called out to a fisherman—I think she called him "Boo"—who was straddling an old chrome and vinyl kitchen chair near the TV, his beefy back, from hauling those shrimp nets, to us. He got up, came to the bar and listened as the lady bartender whispered in his ear. His head with its limp, greasy, blondish hair swiveled in my direction.

Just to finish up that business about Lafitte the pirate, legend has it that he had quite an incredible network of spies. I suppose such a network is useful to any criminal who moves contraband under cover of darkness.

21

A Lot in a Name

I thought Boo might follow us out, but he didn't.

We drove to the end of Lafitte again, and then started back slowly, taking one last look before giving up. For all I knew, Bubba had returned to his mobile home to wait for the tide to change.

We were about a quarter of a mile before the turn to get back on the Lafitte LaRose Highway when I spotted the Lincoln. It was pulled up into some trees off the road toward the water. The land between the road and the water here was wider, and the bayou curved out and away, flowing into Turtle Bay.

The Lincoln was in a small clearing between two groves of oak trees. The road down to the water was just another clearing obviously used by heavy vehicles that had made some deep ruts. Directly ahead of where the double row of ruts ended was a dock. No boat was tied up to it. The T-bird bounced over the ruts as I pulled up into the trees next to the Lincoln. From here the dock wasn't visible.

To the left there were more oaks, trunks twisted painfully in an effort to get away from the beatings they got from the storms. Behind those was an old rusting corrugated metal garage. To the right was a clearing of maybe twenty-five feet and then a dense thicket and more trees.

I turned off the motor and sat, waiting, watching.

"What are you doing?" Diana asked.

"I'm not sure. I guess I'm trying to figure out why Bubba's out and no one else is. The kid in the bar told me the tide isn't right for shrimping."

"Maybe he's fishing for something else."

"Maybe, but the money's in the shrimp. Maybe he's out early to get a jump on everyone else. Or he's throwing one of those boat parties Jackie told me about."

I reached over Diana, opened the glove compartment, and took out my Smith & Wesson .38 snubnose.

"What are you doing now?" Diana asked.

"I'm going to take a walk down to the dock and see if there's anything on the other side of those trees over there." We both started opening the car doors. "Stay here," I told her. "It might be muddy." She closed the door.

I got out, stuck the gun down in the waistband of my jeans, and leaned back in the car.

"Move over here, Diana. Keep the doors locked. If anyone tries to bother you, take off. Okay?"

"What if someone blocks me in?"

"If anyone drives up, lean on the horn. I won't be far away."

She got out and came around to the driver's side. I hit a button and locked her in.

I moved out of the darkness of the trees and headed for the dock. Luckily there hadn't been much rain lately so the ground wasn't too mucky.

A fishy smell grew stronger as I approached the dock. It was a wide dock, very sturdy, fairly new-looking. I walked out on it. A large brush with a long handle was lying on one side. Its bristles were wet. The dock, I could see, had been cleaned fairly recently, but even so a fish scale glinted here and there in the moonlight. Other than these tiny flashes of brilliance, the only thing to see was a locked dock box.

I paused and glanced back toward Diana and the T-bird, but the view was obscured by the trees. Facing the direction of the car, I could also easily see that the thicket and trees now to my left continued unbroken for quite a distance, a good hundred yards, where there was another dock with a small Lafitte skiff tied up to it. Much farther away were several more docks with boats secured to them, easy enough to see because the land jutted out and around. Beyond it was Turtle Bay.

In the other direction it was much the same. There was a long pier on the other side of the corrugated garage. It was a rickety structure that had taken a great deal of abuse from the weather. A lone flatboat, the one I'd seen next to Bubba's trailer, was tied to it.

The still damp dock and the flatboat tied to the pier made me think we were not necessarily alone here. I turned around in the direction of the car again, straining to hear or see anything. Everything was still and quiet. I stayed tensed like that for a few minutes before I relaxed enough to give my attention to the dock box.

It was a good-size box, say four feet by six feet, about two feet high. It was fastened with a very cheap padlock. If Bubba was stashing anything of value, surely it wouldn't be here. A racoon could break into this thing.

Leave no stone unturned. I lifted my foot and came down hard on the lock. It popped right open, loudly. I laid it on the dock as if it were a bomb, listening hard again. Then I began lifting the top. A godawful stench came up and I almost closed the box at once, but I stifled my gag reflex and kept going.

Inside was a mass of stiff black netting. There was also a long stick, which was there to prop open the top. I put it in place and stared at the nets. I guess they smelled so bad from being contained. I poked around at them, lifting them at the edges. I could see a couple of trawl boards underneath. And the white bellies of a few small rotting fish. I removed the stick and let the top down.

I was leaning over to wash off my hands when Diana's voice came to me clear and sharp.

"What do you think you're doing?" she demanded.

My head jerked up and I looked toward her, but couldn't see her.

Then she said loudly, very sternly, "You get away from this car." She paused a beat. "Do you hear me? Now!"

I was off before she finished, grabbing my gun out of my waistband, slipping slightly on the dock before my feet got going in a fast sprint toward her. I was bounding over the dried-mud ruts and I could hear someone else bounding into the thicket, branches cracking, leaves making a swishing sound. They were still trembling where he'd entered the thicket when I came around some high shrubbery, but I didn't run into the thicket. I ran into the grove across the way where the car was parked.

My heart was pounding like mad. If anything had happened to Diana, I'd never forgive myself, but she was standing in front of the car looking toward the last trembling leaf.

"Who was that?" I asked, out of breath more from the adrenaline rushing around my system than from running.

"I have no idea."

Well, of course she didn't. "What were you doing out of the car?"

"Looking at the garage." She pointed at it.

I was irritated that she hadn't followed my instructions. I motioned for her to get back in the car. She went to the passenger side and had to wait until I released the lock. My door was wide open. I got in the car, one foot still on the ground. The glove compartment was open—he'd been rifling through it. But something else bothered me more than that.

There was no buzzing sound. The car door was open, but no buzzing. I felt for the keys. They weren't there.

"Where are the keys?" I held out my hand. Diana just looked at me, eyes wide. "Shit!"

I put the gun on the console in between us and opened the trunk with the lever inside the glove compartment. I told Diana to get out of the car.

"You just told me to get in," she said.

"And now I'm telling you to get out."

I got the tire iron from the trunk and went around to her side. I put the edge of the tool in the key slot, cursed silently at he damage I was about to do the car, and hit the tool with as much weight as I could. The cylinder popped out. I went back to my side to fool with the wires.

Diana slipped back into the passenger seat. "Are you hot wiring the car?" she asked.

I stopped and turned my head toward her. "Do you have any other suggestions?"

She didn't answer.

I went back to work. "Did you see him?"

"It would have been difficult not to. He was as big as the side of a house."

Again I stopped. "Yeah? Black beard, long hair, silent?"

"He didn't say anything if that's what you mean."

I was having some trouble seeing the wires in the dim car light. Diana snapped on a flashlight. She had certainly come prepared.

So Godzilla was on the scene in Lafitte tonight instead of farming out shady ladies. Big break for them. He must have been waiting for Bubba to get back. Nutley the Faithful.

With a pocket knife, I scraped the covering off the wires. I started laughing. Diana was about to say something, but I put the wires together and she jumped as they sparked and the car started.

"Calm down, princess. It's only a couple of wires. You just scared off the biggest, baddest guy on the block and

didn't flinch." I mimicked her: " 'Get away from this car
. . . Now!' and the giant scampers off into the forest like
a scared bunny."

It occurred to me that Godzilla might be a brute, but
Rodney Nutley was a coward. It made one think there's a
lot in a name. That turned out to be an incredibly stupid
thing to think.

22

Nightly Rituals

Diana's big work for the evening had been to explore the perimeter of the locked, windowless corrugated garage in Lafitte, and dirty the knees of her expensive slacks when she found a rusted-out section of metal at ground level. She had peered through it and the beam of her sleek gold-tone flashlight had found the large wheels of a truck.

She told me this as we had drinks at the bar of the Barataria Tavern, a large seafood house on Goose Bayou.

"But I told you to stay in the car," I reminded her, "and you promised to do whatever I told you to do, no questions, no complaints—remember?"

"So?" She dropped the lids over her brown eyes for a couple of seconds. "What are you going to do about it?"

Far too many drinks later we found our way out to the parking lot where I looked upon the T-bird with extreme fondness and realized I was too drunk to drive. So was Diana.

Across the lot, situated on the bayou, was a boatel, a strip motel the front of which was a long dock. It angled out perpendicular to the road following the curve of the bayou. On its narrow end facing the road a sign was tacked up that stated simply, NIGHTLY RENTALS, the only name the place had.

So in answer to Diana's question, what was I going to do about her not doing what I'd told her to do, I was going to do precisely what she wanted. Before the night was over we'd renamed the boatel "Nightly Rituals."

I woke up the next morning with a strange sort of hollowness inside me that I couldn't blame entirely on the hangover I had. I was thinking about what was going on between Diana and me, how it had all come about by accident. Hadn't it? Not really. I had reacted to her meanness, and apparently that is what she wanted me to do. This meanness; was it some sort of atavistic anger felt by all women, directed against all men, that Diana was somehow closely in touch with, which directly affected her sexuality?

Last night she hadn't told me she loved me, she'd told me she loved my scar, that it made me look brutal and dangerous—and mean. This was going beyond her "dangerous glamour," and it didn't make me feel good. Every time we made love now, she turned the act of love into an act of violence.

I have a lot of theories about violence, for instance that witnessing an act of it can train your future reactions more precisely than any amount of purposeful training, just as it can also produce fear, alienation, or isolation. Or, if it's bad enough, it can break you. But I had no theories to cover what was going on between Diana and me. All I knew was that there has been and is enough violence in my life that Diana's penchant for it was getting me down. I guess I'm just a romantic guy.

I looked at Diana sleeping peacefully, her head on my shoulder, her body snug against my side. One of her legs lay across mine; my arm was around her. She looked young and innocent with a strand of her dark hair across her cheek. It reminded me of Nita on the day of Jackie's funeral, her head bent, her hair falling across her cheek.

I wanted to make love to Diana with no show of force, no act of violence, but an act of romance. I put my hand on her breast and caressed it. Her leg moved down over mine a bit. My hand drifted along her skin, into the hollow of her waist, up over the rise of her hip, along her thigh. It went to the inside of her thigh, coming back up, but the moment I touched her pubic hair she made a small sound of irritation and turned away from me.

Well, so much for romance.

23
Winkler's Alibi

The sun shone so brilliantly off Goose Bayou that I stumbled like a blind man toward the car to get the sunglasses that were folded up in the visor. A soft breeze ruffled the surface of the water, and Lafitte skiffs and other fishing boats were tied up to the docks, picturesque as a post card. Barataria that November morning was a Caribbean paradise where there was never any winter.

I left Diana sleeping at the boatel, a note on my pillow that I'd gone back to Lafitte to check out the garage.

Bubba's car was still pulled up under the oaks, but this time I didn't park near it. I found a place down the road and walked back, checking behind each bush for a lurking hulk.

There was a clearing in front of the garage for the big double doors to open out into, and a rutted driveway, part mud, part shells, that was lined by oak trees, the kind of oak-lined drive you see in front of antebellum homes along the river. The garage itself was padlocked with a lock about as sturdy as the one on the dock box. All it took was one blow with a rock that fit in the palm of my hand. Either Lafitte was populated with the most trustworthy people in the world, or Bubba's network of spies was extensive. I'd put my bet on the latter.

I opened the door enough to get in and closed it again. Inside the garage, with the help of Diana's flashlight, I could see plenty enough space for two trucks. At present only one was there, though I could see marks on the dirt floor of the garage where another had been.

It was an insulated refrigerated truck, the container part about twelve feet long. Its sliding back door was propped open. A slanting metal ramp led to a dark interior where I could see the dim outlines of a lot of boxes. I went up the ramp. The boxes, collapsible wooden crates reinforced with wire, were for transporting sea-food. I poked around a bit, but there was nothing else except a fish smell that kept my nose wrinkled. It wasn't a bad smell really, because everything was clean and being aired properly, but it wasn't a place to spend a lot of time either. I went down the ramp and outside, glad to be breathing fresh bayou air again.

Larry Silva had told me Bubba made a lot of money fishing and indeed he must have to be able to afford even one of those refrigerated trucks. But in this part of the world plenty of fishermen with large boats made good money and had refrigerated trucks. I could see nothing particularly unusual about this part of Bubba's setup, but I reminded myself that Bubba's illegitimate activities could easily have paid for the trucks.

When I got back to the boatel Diana was dressed and wanted to get back to town. She had a command perfor-mance society ordeal to attend that evening and needed the afternoon to get ready for it.

We didn't talk much. I figured she was thinking about what to wear while I wondered if she was going with the lawyer Wiley St. Cyr. She needed both of us, I was telling myself—not without a twinge of jealousy—because

I could never be part of her high society life, so it surprised me considerably when we pulled up in front of her apartment and she invited me to her parents' annual soiree to kick off the holiday season the following Saturday night.

Diana, it turned out, was getting ready to make a statement. And a proposal.

Maurice and Nita seemed to have vanished. No one was at home, and Maurice wasn't at the office. I went back to the Euclid, shaved, showered, changed, and tried again. When I still couldn't get them, I called Aubrey Wohl. He told me to meet him at his boat around four o'clock. That gave me time to go see a guy I knew in the Channel who put the key cylinder back into the steering column of the Thunderbird.

Aubrey kept his shrimp boat at Happy Jack, which is on the road to Venice, Louisiana—the very last town before the mouth of the Mississippi.

Aubrey had a sprightly looking Lafitte skiff about twenty-five feet long, rigged with wing nets and electrical winches to move them. When I got to Happy Jack, nothing but a small fishing village, I spotted the boat right away, because Aubrey was standing on the fan tail coiling a heavy yellow line. He had on the regulation white boots.

Right off he gave me the long tour of the boat, proud that he could man it all by himself, but explaining that he preferred to have someone with him, especially if he made a big haul. He offered me a beer and asked if I'd like to go out with him. I told him I wanted to talk to Jeffrey Bonage that evening and got him to tell me where Jeffrey lived.

Aubrey unfolded a couple of lawn chairs and we settled in them to drink beer.

"So how's the shrimping?" I asked.

He balanced the beer can on his big stomach. "Oh, on again, off again," he said. "Mostly off. I just like to be out on the water so I push for a little while 'most every night."

"Push" is a shrimper's term for putting the nets in the water and slowly driving the boat against the current.

"I guess this warm weather's no good for shrimp."

"Oh no, it makes 'em grow. Then when we get a good blow, they'll start running and it'll be payday."

"So why does Bubba Brevna go out for two days when no one else is doing so good?"

"He's probably out in the Gulf. When you go out there, you stay for a while, but you gotta have a big boat."

"Yeah, *My New Flame*. I understand the old one burned up. That he burned it up."

Aubrey shrugged and took a long pull at his beer. He seemed more relaxed out here, not so sad, his white-booted legs stretched out and propped up on the console of the boat. He didn't seem too worried about anything, least of all Bubba Brevna.

"I thought you owned part of that boat," I said.

"I did, but after the first brown shrimp season, Bubba bought me out. Helped pay for this baby."

"That was the plan, for Brevna to buy you out?"

Aubrey nodded. "We were lucky the shrimp ran good that season."

"Larry Silva didn't make out so well."

Now Aubrey turned those big sad eyes on me. "Yeah, I know."

We both knew why, and there didn't seem to be too much to say about it.

"You missed Dietz in a real funeral-stopping performance when he arrested Larry yesterday."

Aubrey started to speak, stopped, puffed up his cheeks with air and expelled it. Then he said, "I stopped going to funerals about five years ago."

We sat in the boat and watched as twilight began to creep out of the marsh grasses around us. Activity increased on neighboring shrimp boats; a couple started up and pulled out into the canal.

"About time to get going," Aubrey said, somewhat happier. He made motions toward getting up, dropping his feet from the console to the deck.

I leaned forward and put my hand on his arm to stop him. "Aubrey, I watched Mave Scoggins pay off Clem Winkler over at the Gemini last night. Only it didn't look like she was paying off a bet. It was more like a regular pay check he was picking up because he told her he'd see her same time next week."

"He probably books with her on a regular basis." He slid his feet under his knees so he could stand.

"Could be, but if that's all, why is Mave giving him a phony alibi for the night of Jackie's murder?" Aubrey stopped trying to leave—I had his attention. I answered his unspoken question: "Jackie told Larry that Clem had been over there earlier, much earlier. She said she dumped him. He's acting guilty as hell and for some reason I want to put Clem and Bubba together in this."

"You mean Bubba paying Clem to kill Jackie? Mave as the middle man?" Aubrey was fascinated by this theory.

"Maybe. Or Bubba paying Clem to torch The Emerald Lizard."

"You think whoever torched the Lizard killed Jackie?"

"It's a good possibility."

"But Clem has an ironclad alibi for the night of the fire."

"What's that?" I asked.

Aubrey said, "He was in the clink all night. I caught him driving drunk through Westwego."

24

Down and Out on Urbandale

So much for great theories.

I jumped off the skiff onto the dock.

"Sure you don't want to come along?" Aubrey asked. "If the shrimp don't run, we can always do some night-time fishing. I know a great floundering spot."

"I'll tell you, Aubrey, I've had two unforgettable fishing experiences. One started on an Audubon Park lagoon one summer when I was a kid. We left home early in the morning and fished all day, a buddy and myself, sweating in the heat, getting soaked in the afternoon rain and bitten by hundreds of mosquitoes. Come five o'clock we had a respectable string of perch between us. I thought my mother would be really pleased when I showed up with dinner. We were too young to think about anything so practical as an ice chest, so in the five o'clock rush, we got on the St. Charles Avenue streetcar carrying our string of perch. Nobody was particularly anxious to sit by us, but one old lady got bent out of shape when the streetcar lurched and the tail of a perch sort of slipped down her blouse. We got thrown off the streetcar. By the time we walked to my house, dinner was over, my mother took one whiff of the perch and threw them out, and my old man was so ticked that I'd been gone all day without telling anyone where I was that he made sure I didn't sit down to eat leftovers."

I let Aubrey chuckle a bit before I went on. "The second time I went fishing it was with my uncle on his boat in the dead middle of the winter. It was so damn cold that when I went to bait my hook with a shrimp I baited it with my finger instead. I didn't realize what I'd done till I saw the blood. We had to go back and get the hook cut out. Needless to say, I wasn't asked again, not that I wanted to go, you understand. So thanks for the invitation, but I think I'll pass."

"Okay, Neal," Aubrey laughed, "but this is a great escape. There's peace and quiet and no hooks, just nets and gigs for the flounder."

"I'd probably gig my foot."

He assured me my foot looked nothing like a flounder. "If you change your mind," he said, "just call. I'll be here every evening until I go on the nightshift next week, and sometimes I even go around midnight after I get off. It's real relaxin' after a long day."

"Listen," I told him, "if I ever call and tell you I want to go fishing, assume it's a mayday call." I took a pack of cigarettes from my shirt pocket and reconsidered. "I don't know, maybe if I solve this case I'll be ready for some relaxing."

I untied the last line for him and stood there smoking a cigarette as I watched him slide off into the night.

Jeffrey Bonage lived on the first floor of an apartment complex on the Westwego-Marrero line, a street with the oxymoronic name of Urbandale. Most of the apartments on the side of the complex where Jeffrey lived had aluminum foil covering the windows instead of curtains. The place looked as if it had been deliberately built to fall down in exactly fifteen years and this was year fourteen.

I knocked several times and was about to give up when I heard noises inside that sounded like somebody kicking things out of the way.

"Who is it?" he called.

"Neal Rafferty."

"Who?"

"Friend of Jackie's."

He opened the door cautiously. It was six o'clock on a Saturday night and I must have just awakened him. He had on a pair of jeans but no shirt and no shoes. His wiry hair stuck out at odd angles. He rubbed an eye with his fist. The other hand he stuck in his pocket, his arm closely guarding his body.

"What do you want?"

"I want to talk to you about Jackie."

I pushed on through the door and he backed away.

The living room, lit only by the light from the hallway, was in complete disarray. There were a couple of large cardboard boxes over in a corner.

"Moving?" I asked.

He glanced around the room as if the question perplexed him. "No."

As my eyes adjusted to the dim light, I could see that the disarray was clothes dropped on the floor, dishes used and left, record albums, books, newspapers, and so on. In short, Jeffrey Bonage lived like a pig.

"How about some light," I said, but he stood there, apparently unable to wake up entirely.

I pushed a nylon duffle bag out of the way with my foot, encountered phone books, both white and yellow pages, avoided a pie pan, crumbs glued to it by sticky-looking reddish stuff, and switched on a table lamp. I took in the sofa and waited until Jeffrey rubbed his eyes some more before I said, "How about if we sit." Frankly, I wasn't up to tackling the sofa alone.

Reluctantly he pulled his hand from his pocket and

cleared off the sofa by picking up everything on it and dumping it all on the floor, giving us barely enough room to put our feet down in front of us.

Jeffrey sat heavily, his shoulders slumped, his chest caved in. His eyes were dopey. He kept rubbing them, trying to wake up. I didn't see evidence of a lot of booze or empties around and Jeffrey didn't smell like a distillery. My guess was he'd been knocking back downers.

I told him I was trying to clear Larry Silva, that I didn't believe he'd killed Jackie even though Dietz seemed determined to make a case against him.

He stopped mauling his eyes. "You put that creep Dietz on me." Not a statement with much fervor, but I'm sure his system was too depressed to get fervored.

"No, I told Dietz you heard Jackie tell me Brevna threatened her and ask me to go see him for her. Did you tell him?"

"Yeah, I told him, and after he practically broke my arm I told him I didn't know for sure if you'd gone either."

That got me riled. Somebody ought to put Dietz out of his and everyone else's misery.

"Does that suggest anything to you about the relationship between Dietz and Brevna?" I asked.

"What do I know," Jeffrey said, "I'm just a bartender out of work." With that he scrunched down farther into the sofa.

"Well, you must know something about the relationship between Jackie and Brevna," I suggested.

"I know it was like all the others."

"How's that?"

"He comes in swaggerin' and talkin' loud, she flirts, he decides he wants to possess her, she gives him the big kiss-off." His tone of voice was bored, but his eyes seemed a bit more focused now.

"But Brevna didn't kiss off so easily," I encouraged him.

"None of them do. Jackie went for the macho types.

She wanted to be swept off her feet, but she didn't want anyone to tell her what to do. She wanted to be possessed, but then she wanted to be in control of everything. She wanted a wimp in a gorilla suit," he finished.

"So what happened when she tried to get rid of Brevna?"

"He started sending over his goons and threatening her."

"I thought he was doing that because of the money she owed him."

"Well, sure," Jeffrey said. "Whenever they had trouble it always became an issue over the money."

"You don't believe it was the money, though."

"The bottom line wasn't the money, no."

This, of course, was Jackie's theory, that what Brevna was mostly upset about was getting shot out of the saddle, as she put it. Jeffrey might have been mouthing what Jackie had told him.

"So maybe Jackie wasn't as afraid of Bubba as she said she was. Maybe it was all part of a game they were playing." That was *my* theory.

"That's not so," Jeffrey said with as much heat as he could muster in his semi-soporific state. "She was actually talking about putting the lounge up for sale and getting out of Westwego to get away from Bubba."

I wasn't impressed. "I don't know, Jeffrey. Jackie was the big fish here, this was her scene. I can't imagine her letting Brevna scare her away."

"You don't think so, huh? Well, let me tell you how bad she wanted to get Brevna off her back. You remember she told you the lounge was broken into and mostly booze was stolen?" I nodded. "Twice that happened, twice when she needed to pay Brevna. She paid him with the insurance money. But when she replaced the bottles, it was with the same ones, some with a jigger or two missing, others half empty."

"You're telling me Jackie swindled the insurance company?"

"Maybe I shouldn't, but what does it matter now? I

never let on that I knew." He laughed bitterly. "She must have thought I was real idiot."

"Or else she thought you'd understand and wouldn't say anything." I guess I was feeling sorry for Jeffrey. "What you're mainly telling me, you realize, is that she loved the place enough to go to some extremes to save it."

"Yeah," he said and seemed lower than he had when I walked in, "I guess you're right. Jackie loved The Emerald Lizard."

And almost everybody loved Jackie.

25
Pam

I stuck around Jeffrey's a while longer, asking him about the people who'd showed up at the funeral, if anyone was among them who might possibly have wanted to kill Jackie. He didn't think so. Bubba Brevna still looked like the suspect of choice to me, but for the second night in a row, he wasn't around. Neither were the Impastato twins. I thought I'd go spend some time with Jackie's friend, Pam.

Pam was so glad to see me she could have fainted. She was so worried about Larry she was practically crazy. She was so nervous her stomach was one big knot, and she hadn't eaten a bite in two days.

She told me all this while she slapped around the kitchen in her white-fluffed mules, fixing both of us a couple of stiff drinks. A little boy about eight or nine appeared in the kitchen doorway and whined that he was hungry. Pam's voice traveled up the scale an octave as she yelled at him to get out, that the kitchen was closed until further notice. The kid let out a wail but took to his heels when Pam went after him with a raised hand. The noise from the shoes on the kitchen tiles would have been enough to turn a herd of cattle.

"Excuse me," she said after the boy had disappeared, her voice back within its normal register, "I'm so wrought up I'm about ready to kill the kid."

Lucky kid.

She finished mixing the drinks and suggested we move out to the living room. We sat on the sofa across from a gigantic television set in a fruitwood cabinet decorated with scrollwork. It was about the ugliest thing I'd seen since Rodney Nutley. On top of it was a doll braced on a stand. If asked to describe it I would have to say it appeared to be a Scarlett O'Hara replica.

The TV was ugly, but it was probably the nicest thing in the room, not that there was much. The sofa was a dull gold that looked as if a cheetah had been using it as a scratching post. The coffee table was blond wood-grained Formica missing the strip along the front edge and pitted with several cigarette burns. There wasn't any other furniture in the room, just the wall-to-wall carpet, which had large irregular stains on it. The cheetah must not have been house-broken.

We'd just gotten settled, our drinks on coasters—for what reason I can't imagine—and Pam had put out an old Saints ashtray with a schedule of that year's games printed on it. I lit a cigarette for her, and the kid appeared in the living room doorway and whined that he wanted to watch TV.

Pam opened her mouth and my eardrums flinched. I put my hand on her shoulder. "Why," I said too loudly, "don't we sit in the kitchen?"

"Oh, okay." She was totally irritated. "You just have to be a pest, don't you, Jason?" She picked up her drink and walked over to where Jason was making himself comfortable directly in front of the TV screen and bent down to grab him by the arm. His shoulder jerked up toward his neck. So did mine. "I don't want to hear another word from you, do you hear me?" she shrieked loud enough to be heard in Crown Point.

Jason nodded. I picked up my drink and the ashtray to follow Pam, but I stopped and said to Jason, "What's on?"

He cut his eyes toward me, but wouldn't meet mine, then said sullenly, "I dunno."

Eight years old and already an angry young man.

Pam was furious, practically throwing dishes off the kitchen table into the sink. She started talking slowly, but then got wound up telling me how she tried to go see Larry but they wouldn't let her and told her she wouldn't be able to until they moved him out of Central Lockup and he was arraigned. But then they wouldn't tell her when that would be. She said she didn't know if Larry could even call his lawyer, and to top if all off she'd been trying to reach Aubrey Wohl.

"He's just like every other damn man around here," she said. "Whenever you need them they've gone fishing."

I waited a second to see if she'd realize she'd just said that to a man. She didn't. I told her she'd probably be able to see Larry late Monday or Tuesday and assured her I'd gotten him the best criminal defense lawyer in town.

She thanked God and said she'd been praying, and she knew God would take care of Larry. I didn't mind giving God the credit, but I would love to have known if Pam was born again the day Jackie died.

I asked her if she'd been home the night Jackie was murdered, apologizing for asking questions I knew the police had already asked, but that it might help Larry.

"I don't mind at all," she told me, "especially if it will help Larry. I was here all evening with Jason, except around dinner I went over to Jackie's to see if she wanted to come eat with us."

"What time was that?"

"About six."

Before Jackie called me. "Did she eat with you?" I asked.

"Oh no. She was far too upset to eat, she said."

"Did she tell you Clem Winkler had been by?"

The question seemed to affront Pam in some way. "No," she answered shortly.

"Did she tell you he was going to come by?"

"No, she didn't. Look, Neal—you don't mind if I call you Neal, do you?—she was pretty drunk." She had switched into a confiding mode, leaning toward me, her voice hushed as if Jason might be trying to tune it in on the TV set. "I don't know if you knew this, Neal, but Jackie was an alcoholic," she said in an it's-so-tragic tone. "You know, she could be very abusive when she was loaded. It wasn't easy being Jackie's friend." She sat back to let this important piece of information penetrate my brain.

I let my face register nothing. "Did you see Clem Winkler's car over there?" I persisted.

"No," she said with the slightest edge of aggravation.

"Anybody's?" She shook her head. "Not Larry's?" Another shake. "Your houses are pretty close—didn't you hear anything?"

"I was asleep. My bedroom's on the other side of the house," she said, not quite so friendly as before.

"How do you know you were asleep while Jackie was being murdered?"

With the look she gave me, her attitude could have changed into open hostility in a flash, but she managed to control herself.

"Because I'd already gone to bed by the time Larry left. He told me he would have come by, but all my lights were off."

"Did he usually come by?"

"What exactly are you trying to imply?" she snapped.

"Nothing. What do you think I'm trying to imply?"

That made her very nervous. Her legs were crossed

and her foot was jiggling so fast that she lost its mule. It clattered to the floor. The sound seemed to freeze her.

I left Pam while I had her off balance. I didn't really think she'd killed Jackie, though the way she'd jerked her kid's arm I'll bet she was strong enough to have done it. And she'd have had about the best motive in the world—she coveted another woman's husband, and the man was getting ready to come into some bucks.

26

The Hustler

Maurice had taken Nita to the Gulf Coast to help her over the trauma of Jackie's murder. Nita was taking Jackie's death fairly hard—it seemed Jackie had been quite good to Nita when she was a child. In the early years of Jackie's marriage, during the long spells when Larry would be offshore for weeks at a time, and before Jackie began to drink so much, she would take Nita to the zoo, on picnics, to movies, sometimes a short trip to Texas or Florida. I remembered a tiny girl preceding Jackie up the aisle at Mater Dolorosa. That had been Nita.

It was mid-afternoon on Sunday and Maurice said Nita was taking a nap. He said she'd been sleeping a lot during the past week, which was not like her.

"I can't seem to snap her out of it," he told me.

"It'll take time," I said, trying to be reassuring. "but I would like to talk to her, Maurice. Do you think she's up to it?"

He considered this and came up with an idea. "Are you free tonight? Could you take her out for a few games of pool?"

"Will she go?" I asked.

He thought she would since he was tied up the rest of the day preparing for a trial. I told him I'd call back in a couple of hours, then I went over to the old man's and hit him up for a substantial part of the track winnings I know he has stashed around the house in places where he thinks my mother won't find it. He actually still believes she doesn't know he bets the horses.

Thus bankrolled, Nita and I were going to have some fun at Grady's tonight.

It was a bit tense at first. I didn't know if Nita was only going with me because Maurice had asked her to even though she wasn't up to a crowded bar or becoming a pool hustler. Or answering a few questions.

I asked her if she'd ever read *The Hustler* or seen the movie. She thought she'd seen the movie—she vaguely remembered Paul Newman—but it had been a long time ago. So I told her the story of Fast Eddie Felson, how he did a lot of small-time hustling until he got a match with the best pool player in the country, Minnesota Fats. He lost to Fats not because he didn't have the eye but because he didn't have the smarts, then spent a lot of time and paid a lot of dues, including having his thumbs broken, before he got a rematch with Fats and won. At the end of a long night Fats told Eddie he was quitting because he couldn't beat him.

"But the best line in the book," I told Nita, "is when Fats pays off and says to Fast Eddie's manager, " 'You got yourself a pool player, Bert.' " Murphy Zeringue and I used that line for everything. If one of us won a game over at Acy's the other would say, " 'You got yourself a pool player, Bert.' " If there was a good-looking girl watching us play, we'd say, " 'You got yourself a pool player, Bert.' "

I told her how *The Hustler* became the Bible to Murphy and me. We read it so many times and gave it away so much that we each must have bought close to ten copies.

Nita liked my talking about all this. She seemed to be snapping out of the boredom, depression, or sleepiness she was in the grips of when I picked her up. She told me her two older brothers had been pool fanatics, too, and they'd had a pool table in the basement of their house. That's how Nita had learned to play. Of course, she'd been born with the eye and the hands. She told me her brothers used to take her over to the University Center at Tulane and make pocket change off her by taking bets.

"If they'd been caught, they could have been thrown out of school," she said.

"Did they give you part of the money?" I wanted to know.

"No way!" She wiped the air in front of her. "They bought me Cokes and candy bars. I didn't care. All I wanted was the attention."

I asked her if she'd like to turn into a pool hustler for a night and explained that all the guys at Grady's were friends of mine and we could have some fun with them. I told her I wasn't going to lie to them, that I was going to tell them right off she was a terrific pool player. All I asked was that she lose the first game.

"You don't have to play too long either," I said, "just long enough to stir up a little action over at Grady's."

"Fine with me," she said. "I could use a little action."

Like she wasn't getting enough. Was Nita already getting tired of Maurice's work habits?

Grady's is buried deep in the dark and dangerous recesses of the Irish Channel. Most of Grady's patrons are blue collar workers, pool hustlers, or both. And most of them are men, although the women who go there look capable of wielding both a cue stick and a stiff uppercut to the mouth if anyone gets smart with them.

Grady's doesn't appear to be a very large place, crowded as it is with a bar, tables, chairs, and six pool tables. And people. All the regulars were in attendance. Murphy had his knife-edge of a nose about an inch from the felt as he eyed a tough shot. Murphy's whole face is so thin and sharp it looks as if it could slice straight through the cue ball.

Swain, Swyer, and Lobo, who are always together and affectionately but accurately called the Three Stooges, stood by—Murphy's silent cheering section. Murphy is the best pool player at Grady's.

George, who is actually better on the pinball machines than he is on the pool table, was, however, effectively wiping out someone I'd never seen before. It is rumored that George is the famous science fiction writer, George Alec Effinger, but he vehemently denies this, nearly every night.

I could get carried away talking about the characters at Grady's, not the least of which is Grady himself, who vaguely resembles Winston Churchill except for his thick salt and pepper hair which is curly all around the edges like a lasagna noodle. Grady is always chomping the end of a cigar butt. He doesn't say much, but he laughs a lot, though not always at whatever everybody else is laughing at. Grady seems to have a unique point of comic reference or else a large sense of the absurd. He was standing behind the bar now laughing his slow deep laugh as he drew beer into a pitcher. For all you could tell, the way the beer drew was the source of his amusement.

Nita and I got a beer and watched while we waited for Murphy to score a few bucks off Bob Carmine, who wears muttonchops, is a longshoreman, and works just to pay off his gambling debts. I told Nita that Murphy's strengths were patience and a reserve of stamina for the long haul. Other than that, he tended to make mistakes when he got too cocky or was intimidated, something not many pool players other than myself could manage, and me only because I'd known Murphy most of my life. I told her Murphy would give her the first break, but not to break too impressively that first time. Make it strong, but not the thunderbolt break she might as well have shot me with that night over at Robert's.

Murphy took enough money from Bob Carmine to keep Bob working another week and strolled over to where Nita and I were standing.

The Murph is a pretty cool customer with that patience of his and a face that registers nothing to those who haven't known him for thirty years. I, however, could see his eyes flicking at Nita and knew that curiosity was simmering behind them. Murphy, for all his inscrutability, is insatiably curious, though he considers it a great weakness to let it show. He was dying to know who Nita was since I rarely brought women into Grady's and with those girlish looks of hers, she wasn't my usual type.

I didn't do anything to satisfy Murphy's curiosity. I introduced Nita to him by name only, no other explanation as to who she was, and went on with the normal chitchat—who'd been coming in, what kind of money had been around, and so on. Murphy can keep up this kind of patter forever. Every ball in the pocket and every exchange of money is action to him. But he kept one eye on Nita. Nita just stood there saying nothing, looking innocent and shy.

At the first lull in Murphy's weekly pool news digest, I dropped it that Nita liked to play.

"Oh, yeah?" Murphy said, and I could see a smile trying to break out of the corner of his mouth.

I'd expected Nita, articulate as hell, to pick up here and toss in a few words, maybe something about the family pool table. Instead she looked down at her beer, more bashful than ever, almost embarrassed. And it was exactly the right way to play it. Murphy cracked a smile of indulgence. I felt an immediate surge of power.

"Yeah," I said. "Her brothers had a table. Nita grew up playing pool—when they let her play," I added.

Nita directed it straight at Murphy, a sardonic, my-brothers-were-a-pain-in-the-ass look.

"Hey," I said, nudging Murphy with the hand holding the beer can, "don't let me give you the wrong impression —Nita's a shark." I let that seemingly outrageous statement sink in, then said, "I've been promising to bring her to Grady's so she can play the best."

Murphy let a moment's worth of silent rebellion pass before he did the polite thing. "Would you like to shoot a game?" he asked.

"Sure," Nita replied with just the right amount of enthusiasm—too much. I felt great fondness for her.

She went over to the wall rack to pick out a cue stick. Murphy sidled up and jerked his head toward her. "Your latest?" he asked softly.

"Oh no, just a friend."

This deserved a dirty look and I got one before Murphy moved over to the table, picked up his stick, and stroked the end of it lightly with chalk.

Nita bent over the table, circled the stick with a forefinger and slid it back and forth over her thumb, eyeing down its length for straightness. Murphy wasn't impressed. He asked her what she liked to play. She asked him if nine ball was all right. Nine ball was fine. One of the Three Stooges arranged the nine balls in the front of the rack.

This really wasn't fair. I knew Murphy too well, and it pains him greatly to play a game with no stakes. He looked at me from across the table with that hang-dog expression he can get.

"What do you say, Murph," I said loudly, "ten dollars a game?"

From behind the bar, Grady laughed. Ten bucks was respectable for anyone but Murphy. Anyway, Grady's laughing sort of clued in a couple of people standing around. Bob Carmine was the first to ask if he could get in—ten on the Murph. Swain, Swyer, and Lobo followed— always in that order—but it wasn't until George tossed in his ten bucks' worth that the game became serious. George gets respect around Grady's. That's because they all think he's a famous writer. It's crazy because I doubt any of them could tell you the last book they read. Anyway, it wasn't long before I was going to be out a good hundred and fifty bucks. Murphy should have been ashamed of himself.

"You break," he said cavalierly to Nita.

She came around, put the cue ball slightly off center to the left and broke. It was strong enough to get a few whistles from the Stooges. Grady laughed long and low. If Murphy hadn't been so damn cocky, he would have recognized that laugh as prophetic.

Nita displayed some fine wrist action and got off a few nice shots, but she flubbed on the four ball. Murphy finished the game. I paid everybody off. When Nita said she wanted another game, a few more got in on the action.

The winner breaks in nine ball. Murphy hurtled the cue, spread the balls, and won with a combination of the nine on his third shot. I paid off again, over three fifty in the hole. With all that money floating around, Grady's was getting rowdy.

The only thing I had to worry about was running out of cash. I was good for maybe four more games. I had to count on Murphy's cockiness.

He didn't let me down. The third game, he hitched up his pants on his thin body, a habit he has, like a tic when he plays, and went for making the nine ball on the break, a showy but not always reliable shot. It wasn't this time. A chorus of "Aw shucks, Murph" went up, but nobody was worried. Nita ran down the balls and won with a beautiful Fast-Eddie-Felson shot bouncing lightly off the rail and coming down to slice the nine ball in the right corner pocket. Everybody was very complimentary as they paid off.

Nita caught my eye, a question in hers, asking me if it was time to let go. I nodded.

There it was, the sledgehammer break, slamming in three balls. Then with what can only be described as "a woman's touch," she put the nine in with the two ball.

What I cannot adequately describe is the look on Murphy's face. I knew he'd never seen a woman break like that before. I loved Nita for giving me a once in a lifetime chance to see the Murph baldly stripped of his inscrutability, unable to keep his mouth shut or his pants hitched. He stared at her with total disbelief.

Everybody paid off. I figured that would be it. I had no idea if Nita could sustain this kind of thing over the long haul; but Murphy wasn't the only disbeliever, they all wanted to see it again, sure it was a fluke. I told them if they wanted to see it again, it would cost them twenty to get in. They all put it up so fast I was mad at myself for not saying fifty.

Nita gave them their money's worth, sledgehammering the nine ball in on the break. It was a beautiful piece of work, and I must say everyone at Grady's was appreciative. After I replaced the old man's bank roll, I gave Nita all the money that was left, four hundred and fifty dollars. With a grin that was good to see on her face after the sadness of the past week, she called for beer all around.

Now I said everyone at Grady's was appreciative, but I wasn't including Murphy. I assumed he would be pissed enough to make sure I never played another game with him for less than a hundred bucks. I looked around, but didn't see him. I excused myself, though Nita was plenty busy talking to all the guys, and went to the restroom. Murphy wasn't there. I got a bit upset, thinking he'd left, and walked out into the night to see if I could catch him.

Murphy was leaning against the wall of the building smoking a cigarette, just outside a circle of yellow light thrown by the street lamp. We were alone.

"Uh, Murphy?" I stepped tentatively toward him.

He looked up at me with yet another amazing expression, if I was reading it right in the darkness—admiration.

"Neal," he said barely above a whisper, "did you see that sledgehammer break?"

"Yeah," I nodded.

"And that wrist action. A woman." I nodded some more. "And that Fast Eddie shot. I mean Jesus, Neal, she's amazing."

"Yeah," I said.

He pushed himself away from the wall and stood with his feet apart as if getting his balance. He dropped his cigarette but didn't bother to grind it into the pavement. I waited, braced, figuring now I was bound to take some abuse.

"Help me back inside," Murphy said. "I think I'm in love."

27

Nita

Murphy took it hard when he found out Nita was Maurice's girlfriend.

Once back inside Grady's, however, he still had to be pried away from her, and then only after she promised a rematch, a long night of straight pool, Murphy's best game.

I told Grady to pour me a shot of Pinch, which made him laugh, and moved Nita to the far end of the bar where it was less likely we'd be interrupted.

"I talked to Mave Scoggins Friday night," I said for openers.

Nita's face lit up. "Isn't Mave great?"

"I don't know, Nita. To me all those people are murder suspects."

The brightness vanished. "Oh."

"Jackie introduced you to Mave?" She nodded. "Why?" I asked.

"Because of the pictures."

"The photographs you're taking of the prostitutes who work out of the Gemini," I stated.

"Mave told you?" She sounded disappointed.

"No." I hesitated, then said, "Diana was with me. We saw one of the girls standing outside, and whatever it was you told her about the women you were taking pictures of, she figured it out."

I almost didn't tell her it was Diana, afraid it would irk her, but she hunched closer, staring at me out of those big tortoise shell glasses, anticipation widening her eyes.

"What did she think?" she asked, a child asking for approval.

"She thinks it's original," I lied. "She wants to see what you have."

She sat back, but straight up, not leaning on the bar at all. "Well, it's not *really* original. I mean, my photos will be original, but Bellocq did portraits of the Storyville prostitutes back at the beginning of the century. Have you seen them?"

"I think I have, a couple of them anyway." I vaguely remembered some pictures of the old New Orleans red-light district in the newspaper, but it was long time ago. "You're doing the West Bank version of Storyville?"

"No," Nita said, "it has nothing to do with the West Bank, it's the girls. These girls are *very* original, very different from the girls Bellocq photographed." She was warming to her subject, to telling me about it. I let her go. "When I first thought about doing this, I wanted to see how different the prostitutes today were from the prostitutes then, and how they might be alike, too . . . Neal," she said, putting her hand on my forearm, her youthful exuberance close to bursting from her in her rush to tell me, "the results are amazing. I had no idea what a *good* idea this was until I got into the darkroom and then put the photographs next to Bellocq's."

She pushed her straight silky hair behind her ears, her bangs touching the top of her glasses. "I did what I thought Bellocq had done—asked them to pose in whatever way they saw themselves, dressed however they wanted to dress, or nude, to show off what they were proud of, in whatever environment, with whatever props. A lot of Bellocq's women posed with dogs, a lot were dressed in their Sunday best, many were nude, but not very many were dressed like prostitutes. But the women I've been photographing—they don't dress to look like prostitutes, they dress up in outlandish outfits, very tight, very bright colors, clothes that make them tough and raunchy, not at all seductive or enticing. They also like lots of black leather and chains and whips. Some of them posed with animals, too, mostly big mean dogs; one with a pit bull, another with an ocelot. And one of them posed with a gun, sweeping her hair back with it." She stopped to show me, using her index finger, cocking her thumb.

She went on. "The photos of mine and Bellocq's that are most similar are two nudes, both girls stretched out in strange corpse-life positions, but Bellocq's girl looks mostly uncomfortable, stiff, not using the pillows behind her to get comfortable. My girl—her name is Candy Malone— just looks like she wants to *be* dead. There is this terrible vacancy in her eyes, her hands crossed over her breasts." She briefly crossed her own hands. "I felt so sorry for her."

She shook her head sharply, as if to jolt herself out of her sympathy. "Anyway, Bellocq's women are soft, femi-nine. Some are sad, some are haughty, but Neal, *these* women, except for Candy, are violent, their poses are violent, their dogs aren't cute, their dresses aren't frilly. They're hard, cold, cruel, and they're proud of it. But you know what? Underneath they're sad. Very sad. Much sadder than any of Bellocq's girls. They hide it under layers and layers of anger."

She stopped, incredulous, wanting me to see how in-credible it was, to share the surprise she felt. But I wasn't twenty-two years old and I wasn't surprised.

She put her hand flat on her chest, above her breasts,

just at her neckline, a hand with short fingernails, a no-nonsense hand. "I thought at first it was because I was a woman taking their pictures," she said, and I thought, a child-woman, "that for Bellocq they wouldn't have been so angry, but Bellocq wasn't exactly your typical man either. He was practically a dwarf, with a big, deformed head. Imagine those women letting him take their pictures, exposing themselves to him. And I don't mean just their bodies. Maybe it was easier for them because of the way he looked, so strange and deformed . . ." and she launched into more exclamations and fascinations, telling me about one poet's version of Bellocq's death, how he burned himself up, using a circle of chairs to make a ring of fire high on the wallpaper around a room, finally crashing through a wall of fire, and how that version of his self-destructive death had more truth in it than the real truth, that Bellocq simply dropped dead on Carondelet Street one day.

While Nita talked I thought about her intensity and her idealism and how all things are possible when you're young, and wondered how she'd lose that youthful exuberance. Would it be hard or would it come about naturally, part of the process of aging. I thought that with Maurice maybe she could escape doing it with too many hard knocks.

"Maurice doesn't want me to do it anymore," she was saying.

It caught me off guard. "Your photography?"

"Oh no. This project. The prostitutes. I think that's why he took me to the coast this weekend, to talk me out of it. And because he knows I'm really upset about Jackie." She looked depressed, but somehow, at this point in time, I thought it had less to do with Jackie.

"Did he talk you out of it?"

She flipped a hand and glanced over the bar at Grady, who was fooling around with something down at our end, his wide back to us. "I guess so," she said to Grady's back. "I think he's being way too cautious."

I tapped her shoulder to make her look at me. "Nita, the truth is that age and experience make people cautious. He's looking out for you."

"I know he is," she said, "but you have to admit that Maurice was probably a cautious two year old." She smiled. "That's just how he is."

"I think you have caution confused with wariness. He has some reasons."

"What?" she wanted to know, palms and eyebrows up.

"Well, first of all, your cousin was murdered. Second, those people over at the Gemini have some connection with a man who might very well have killed her." She started to interrupt me. "Wait," I told her, "some of those people might even have their own motives. I haven't finished looking into it yet. I think Maurice would like you to stay away from all that till we know who killed Jackie."

"What if you never know?"

"Hey," I said, fingertips against my chest, injury in my voice.

She smiled, but just barely. "Who do you think killed Jackie?"

"I said 'might have.' Do you remember Bubba Brevna?"

"That man at the funeral."

"Right. Well, he's the man really running the prostitutes. Do you know Rodney Nutley, known as Godzilla?"

"Godzilla—the girls call him that. He's their bodyguard."

"That's what they told you?"

She nodded, but slowly, as if she wasn't so sure. "They make jokes about him because he's so big and ugly and he never talks. Sometimes they call him their 'money-guard.' "

"That's what he does, he makes sure they turn all the money over to him. Then he gives it to Brevna."

"Oh."

"Have you ever seen him hit one of the girls or do anything violent to any of them?"

"No!" Quite horrified.

"And none of them have ever told you about him doing anything like that?"

"No! They tease him, to his face. Not mean, good-naturedly. It's not like what you're saying."

"Maybe not. Maybe you just haven't seen it."

"I think one of them would have told me by now."

"I'm not so sure they'd talk to you about those things, Nita."

"I think they would."

There was no point in arguing. "What about the Impastato twins, the owners of the Gemini. Do you know them?"

"I know who they are. I didn't know they owned the Gemini."

"Who did you think owned it, Mave?"

"No . . ." She drew the word out. "I guess I never thought about it."

"You've never seen the Impastatos work in there?"

"No. I've only seen them in there a couple of times." You'd think they'd try to put on a better front.

"Nita, where do you take the pictures?"

"Mostly in a back room at the Gemini, an office. Mave lets us use it. Sometimes I take the pictures at their apartments."

"Does Godzilla know you're taking the pictures?"

"Yes. Sometimes he's at the Gemini, but he waits outside with Mave."

"Did you know that Mave is a bookie?"

"No . . ."

"Look, I think it would be best if you stopped working on this for a while, until I find out what it is Bubba Brevna is up to, what *all* these people are up to—"

"But I'm almost finished! Just a few more sessions—"

"Why don't you give Diana what you have?"

"It's not enough. I only need a few more."

"Nita," I held her arm at the elbow, stopping her mid-gesture, "can I ask you something? I'm not trying to make you angry or anything, but why did you agree to do this show, let Diana goad you like she did, when you'd already decided you didn't need to do shows and all the stuff other photographers do to do your work. Why?"

Her eyes bored into me. I thought she was going to unleash a stream of vitriol, but she said in a most controlled, steady voice, "I know I said I didn't want to be like all those stupid, self-important people, and I know Diana goaded me, as you say, but none of that matters. It's the girls. That's what you and Maurice, nobody understands. It's those women themselves. *They* have something important to say, not me, *them*. I'm just a means for them to say it. They deserve to have their say."

All the serious, high-minded idealism of youth. So appealing, so full of contradiction. What could I say to her—who was going to see the pictures? And the miniscule number of people who would see them, would they know what the prostitutes had to say? Would they see all the violence in the pictures that Nita saw, or would they just see a bunch of flagrant whores and be fascinated or disgusted or titillated?

I put my hand on her neck, feeling great affection for her. "Nita," I said, "I wish you'd just concentrate on Maurice."

"I am," she assured me. "I love Maurice, and I have to make him understand. I've *got* to do this. I want to. All that other stuff, Bubba whatever-his-name-is—"

"Brevna."

"Brevna. I don't know about all that. I'm not involved in any of it. I'll take the pictures only at the girls' apartments if that will make you feel better . . . Neal"—she stood up abruptly—"will you take me home now? I've got to talk to Maurice."

I took her home.

28.

A Few Words with Maurice

Nita wasn't the only one who wanted to talk to Maurice; I did, too, but I had to wait until five-thirty the following afternoon.

Maurice had had a long day in court. I'd had a long day on the tail of a malingerer. We were both too tired to see trouble coming.

I met him at his office. He had on a light brown suit with a white shirt and his blue striped tie was loose around the unbuttoned neck of the shirt. So normal was this attire on other people that it seemed completely foreign on Maurice, much more so than the casual clothes I'd seen him in lately. Never had the black string tie he wore with his Western suit hung loose or the top button of his shirt been unbuttoned. Maybe talking to this new Maurice contributed to the problem, too.

The office, however, seemed the same as it had been on Friday evening. Pinkie's desk was neat, her chair tucked under it. One thing was different, though. *LOW-*

LIFE ABOUT TOWN had been affixed to a piece of white cardboard and was propped up on a cabinet behind the desk, leaning against the wall. I liked that.

I followed Maurice into his office. He didn't sling his feet up on the desk. Neither did I.

"Your boy has been moved over to Gretna," he informed me. "I talked to the D.A. I think the charge will be dropped to second degree."

"Good. Thanks." He acknowledged my thanks with a curt nod. I said, "I don't think Nita should be hanging around the Gemini and those prostitutes right now. Were you able to talk her out of it?"

He fixed me with eyes too stony to be boyish. "I *had* talked her out of it until she went out with you last night. She's over there now—for the evening."

"And you're blaming me for that?" I asked him, my voice rising as much in irritation as disbelief.

There was a long heavy pause before he said, "No." Another half beat, then, "Sorry."

"Look, Maurice, why don't you just tell her she can't do it anymore, period."

Now he was impatient. "Why don't you tell Diana to tell her the show is off?"

I picked up his desk phone and punched in Diana's number.

"Hello, darling," she said. "Are you on your way?"

"No." I was looking at Maurice. "As of right now Nita's show is off," I said to Diana. "As far as she knows, you called it off."

"I can't," she said. "It's too late to call it off."

"It's off," I repeated. "Canceled, got it? Find another photographer."

"Okay, Neal," she answered, resigned. "You certainly do make life difficult, darling. When will you be here?"

"Maybe not tonight. I'll call you." I hung up. "Done," I said to Maurice. "Tell Nita Diana called and said it's off."

"Nita will call her. What will Diana say to her?" The

impatient tone was gone. He was thinking, covering all the bases.

"I don't know, Maurice. She'll probably say I told her to do it."

"If she says that Nita will blame me as much as you."

"Think of a reason and call Diana." I jotted her number down on his desk pad.

"It might just make her more determined," he said.

"You know, you said it yourself," I told him. "You told me you and Nita are exactly alike. You know why you love her? Because she's just as driven and strong-willed and determined as you are."

"That's true, but if Diana hadn't dared her to do this show, she never would have pursued it this way. Not now, at least."

For some reason this made me feel a bit testy. "It's not like you to be blaming everyone in sight," I said.

He matched my tone. "I'm not blaming anyone. It's a statement of fact. It's why Nita is across the river and not at home tonight."

"Nita's doing exactly what she wants to do."

"I'm saying she didn't want to do this before Diana's offer."

Even though what he was saying was true, his blaming Diana for what Nita was doing made me mad. "And when you moved her into your house," I said, "you gave her everything she needed to make Diana's offer unrefusable."

This was as close as Maurice and I had ever come to having an argument. I stood up. "Call Diana," I said, starting out.

"Where are you going?"

"Across the river."

To fucking China.

29.

Straw Men

"Don't Mess With My Toot Toot" was playing to a practically empty Gemini when I walked—no, make that *strode*—into the lounge. Mave was behind the bar, two West Bank business types with their sprayed hair, gold chains and bracelets, and Sears Roebuck suits were at a table off to the side, and the Impastato twins were perched high on bar stools, drinking beer.

I was glad to see the Imps. Most likely, since I assumed they'd been out fishing with him, it meant Bubba Brevna was back, and the person I was most interested in seeing after the conversation with Maurice was Bubba Brevna. The first order of the evening was to check on Nita, however. I had to admit that on the drive to Marrero she had been reduced in my mind from strong-willed and determined to simply stubborn.

Mave, hair piled high and arms akimbo, watched as I strode up to the bar. On her face was a we-don't-want-any-trouble-in-here-Rafferty look. Or maybe it was just that silly song blaring out of the jukebox, but I imagined her saying that to me and, weight equally balanced on suddenly bowed legs, me drawling, "Trouble is my middle name, Mave." I was already irritated, and this piece of ridiculousness coming unbeckoned into my brain made me feel more irritated.

"Where is Nita Greene?" I demanded, too loud and belligerent.

"I really couldn't tell you," Mave said, her tone even, in control of herself.

"Couldn't, wouldn't, or better not?" I tromped over to a door at the side of the bar and flung it open.

The lights were off. Nita obviously wasn't taking any pictures back here, but I felt along the inside wall for the lights and switched them on. A sheet was loosely draped across a wall; in front of it was an old over stuffed sofa with mauve cabbage roses all over it.

I turned off the lights, thumped the door shut hostilely and returned to a face-off with Mave.

"If you know where Nita Greene is, you better tell me because if anything happens to her, I'll hold you personally responsible."

Mave's reply was equable and easy. "Rafferty, you can hold me responsible till the cows come home, but if there aren't any cows, what good will it do?"

Well, that statement both confused and defused me. I sat on a bar stool. "Do you know where she is, Mave?"

"No." She gestured toward the back room. "She isn't here, as you can see, and she hasn't been here."

"If she's with one of the girls, would you have any idea which one or where?"

"No idea at all."

I turned to the Impastato twins. With no expressions on their faces, I couldn't tell them apart, but the talkative one had trouble keeping the smile off the corners of his mouth. I directed the question at him.

"Is Brevna back?"

"Oh yeah, he's back." He shifted his smile to the side,

to his brother, who acknowledged him with a sidelong glance, a quick cut of the eyes.

The next question I directed to all of them, Mave included: "Does anyone know where Rodney Nutley is?"

"Oh sure," said the talkative twin, "he's unloading all those beautiful shrimp for the boss. Right, Vinnie?" This got a split-second smile out of Vincent.

Given the interplay between the twins, this statement was not a hundred percent reassuring, and I wanted to be reassured about Nita's safety.

"Well, Vinnie," I said, and he looked at me from half closed but not sleepy eyes, "and Frankie, how about if I buy the owners of the Gemini a drink?"

Frankie flicked Vinnie with the back of his hand. "Sure. Why not?"

I told Mave more of the same for the twins and a Scotch and water for me. I suggested we move to a table. Frankie jerked his head at Vinnie and the two stood up together and moved over to the table, where I put my drink down.

"You sure that goon Nutley is occupied for a while?" I asked the twins.

"Oh sure," Frankie said, tossing a grin in Vinnie's direction. "Lots of shrimp for him to pack."

"How come he gets to pack the shrimp but he doesn't get to go catch them?"

This was a tough question. Frankie shrugged, but not at me, at Vinnie. Then he turned suddenly, a big smile on his face, and said, "He's too big. Takes up too much space on the boat." I wondered if Vinnie was sending him psychic messages.

"He *is* big," I agreed, "and he doesn't seem to have much to say. Did Brevna rip out his vocal cords?" Frankie laughed. "Maybe he cut out his tongue," I suggested.

Frankie sobered up, checked in with Vinnie, and said, "Mr. Bubba brought him to lots of doctors when he was a boy," he told me. "They say he had a trauma." As in, he had the measles.

"Is he Brevna's son?" I asked, somehow finding this hard to believe.

"His nephew. He came to live with Mr. Bubba when his mama died."

"Is he stable?" I asked, and when Frankie didn't seem to understand this, looking at Vinnie with cocked eyebrows, I translated, "Does he ever get out of control, violent?"

Frankie grinned at Vinnie, then told me, "He gets out of control, Mr. Bubba gets out his bullwhip."

"Oh," was all I could say, stunned speechless myself. Yet another sign of the times, the Age of Violence. I felt vague stirrings of sympathy for Rodney Nutley. I trash-canned them fast. After all, enough abuse, and you turn the victim into a monster.

We sat for a few minutes, sipping at our drinks, then I looked at Vinnie and said, "Vinnie doesn't seem to have much to say either."

Vinnie's eyes turned into menacing slits. Frankie said, without his usual friendliness, "Vinnie can talk if he wants to. He doesn't usually want to."

"Sure," I said, shrugging indifferently. I let a few more moments of silence pass. Vinnie's eyes never left me. Frankie might be the talker, but I was beginning to sense that Vinnie had all the power. Finally, I let my eyes drift around the room. "Nice place you guys have here." The twins didn't go for this soft soap. "I don't see any numbers on the floor anywhere. No chicken drop contests here?"

"Not here," Frankie said.

"But you had them at The Emerald Lizard," I said. Frankie started to speak but stopped. Vincent glared at me; I felt sure he'd given Frankie some unspoken command. "Even though Jackie didn't want them," I went on. "But I guess you go wherever the boss tells you to go."

I waited but the twins had nothing more to say to me. Men of straw go up in smoke too easily.

30

Torch Song

I'd like to tell you that I went over to the trailer park and had a confrontation with Bubba in which he broke down and confessed to the murder of Jackie Silva and the torching of The Emerald Lizard. Instead, ten minutes with Bubba at his mobile home and I had to revise my thinking about both crimes.

He certainly wasn't what you'd call cordial when I arrived, but he did let me in without a fuss. He had overnight bags under his eyes, and he hadn't bothered to shave. He was wearing a pair of pajama bottoms, but he seemed too tired to care much about it, too tired to be very talkative dressed or undressed. The TV was on in the bedroom.

He sat on a creaky rattan stool on the living room side of his kitchen counter, the fat on his stomach fluffing over the waist of his pajamas as baking bread rises over the sides of the pan. I stood where I was, near the door, not that I was invited any farther.

I said, "Why didn't you tell Dietz I came over here to talk to you about Jackie Silva's debt?"

"I don't like talking to cops," he said. "That includes you."

"I can understand that. After all, you were threatening Jackie, you got ten grand off someone you were supposed to fix a case for, and you had no signed papers on the loan anyway. But what I don't understand is why Dietz leaned on Jeffrey Bonage hard enough for him to say he didn't know whether I'd come over here or not. That sounds like he might be helping you cover some tracks, doesn't it?"

If I thought that would get a spark out of him, I could forget it. He just sat there, looking at me, and not very hard at that.

"I don't guess it would do much good for me to ask where you were on the night the lounge was torched or the night Jackie was murdered." I waited but not for long. "I suppose Dietz gets his share to corroborate whatever you tell him." His mouth may have turned down a bit more, but it was already so inverted, I could have been wrong.

"You know"—I was undaunted—"Larry Silva knows Jackie never signed any papers for the loan. He has no intention of turning any insurance money over to you."

"So what?" he blurted with enough animation to make the rattan squeak. Then he laughed, his chest and shoulders bouncing, his upside-down smile righting itself briefly. "The poor sucker needs the money, doesn't he? He's welcome to it for all the good it will do him." The humor disappeared as fast as it had come. He thrust his face at me belligerently. "That's right, no signed papers. So where's my motive, scumshoe? Why should I burn down the lounge if there're no signed papers?"

"That didn't stop Jackie from thinking you did it, or had it done," I shot at him.

A look of shock disturbed the set of his face. He wiped it away after a fraction of a second, but it was genuine, and when he said, "That woman didn't know me very well at all," I could have sworn it was with some degree of sadness.

I stood there knowing full well Bubba Brevna hadn't torched The Emerald Lizard, though before that could sink all the way in, he startled me by suddenly reaching across the counter, the stool squealing with strain, and flinging open a drawer. I almost jumped him but, still stretched across the counter, he sailed something through the air at me. The keys to the Thunderbird landed with a metallic snap in the palm of my hand.

"You ever step foot on my property again," Bubba said, "I'll see to it both your legs are broken."

Bubba and I had several more vile things to say to each other, but that's not what I thought about or even particularly remembered after I left him. After all, Bubba threatening to have my legs broken if I ever stepped foot on his property again came as naturally to him as it comes to other people to say "Have a nice day." No, what I remembered was his unmistakable shock, and I still say sadness, that Jackie could have believed he would torch the Lizard. I sat in my car, pulled up on the oyster shells flanking the trailer park, thinking in the dark, that whether a person can love another is no gauge whatsoever of his humanity.

I was also thinking Jackie had convinced me that Bubba torched the Lizard. I thought that, and a few seconds later I felt the heat of being humiliated by my own gullibility on my neck and face as I sat all alone. I remembered Reenie telling me how sly Jackie could be, and two things that should have hooked up in my mind before stood out with crystal clarity now. One was Larry Silva telling me that Jackie had not mentioned going to the Organized Crime Unit to him. The other was Jeffrey Bonage telling me that Jackie had burgled her own lounge twice.

Every cop instinct I ever had was telling me now that Jackie Silva had torched The Emerald Lizard.

I wasted no time getting over to Jeffrey Bonage's Urbandale apartment.

There was no answer to my slugging it out with the door so I picked the lock and let myself in. Nothing was different. Even the pie pan with the red gunk on it was still there.

Jeffrey was in the bedroom on his stomach across the bed, his legs hanging off the end, one arm bent in what appeared to be an unnatural way, his hand trapped underneath him. He was clad the way I'd left him two days ago, blue jeans, no shirt, his thin body now looking agonizingly young and inert.

Next to the bed on a night table was an empty bottle of Seconals, a prescription for—who else?—Mrs. Jackie Silva.

Jeffrey could have been dead, but his mouth was open and I could hear him breathing, faintly and shallowly, but breathing.

I turned him over on his back, shouting his name at him and slapping lightly on his face, my fingers contacting a line of drool running from the corner of his mouth to his ear. His eyes started trying to open, but all I saw of them for a few minutes were the whites.

He finally woke up enough that I was able to get him off the bed. One of his arms across my shoulders, one of my arms supporting him by the waist, we got down the short hallway into the kitchen where I bruised us both considerably banging into counters and appliances as I tried to find a pot and some coffee. Once the water was on I walked Jeffrey up and down the kitchen, through the hallway, a couple of steps into the bedroom and back, the only relatively clear passage in the apartment. He was coming around enough that I considered it safe not to call an ambulance.

The better part of an hour later I had him sitting on the sofa, sipping at a second cup of coffee. All this Florence Nightingale crap had given me more time to think.

"Did Jackie help you burn down the Lizard or did she just tell you to do it?" I asked him.

I didn't mean to scare him—you've got to start some-where—but he jumped and sloshed coffee out of the cup. The saucer caught most of it, though some dripped on his pantleg. He set the cup and saucer on his thigh. His hands were shaking. He hiccupped and almost dumped the coffee over on the sofa. I took the cup and saucer away from him and put it down on the floor, where it would probably grow mold before it was removed.

"Let's have it, Jeffrey," I said. He hiccupped again. "Did you get your experience on the Thibodeaux restaurant?"

"What? No. Shit." He put his head in his hand, resting his elbow on his knee. When he hiccupped his head bounced. His elbow slid off his knee.

"Then how come the Lizard was burned down the same way the restaurant was?"

"I read how they did it in the newspaper."

"Christ." Why don't they just print a how-to section on crime?

I got the story through an onslaught of the hiccups. It seemed Jackie had complained regularly to Jeffrey about her high mortgage notes, the dropoff in business since the oil bust, and the money she owed Brevna. After she told him three or four times she wished the place would just burn to the ground, he decided she was telling him to do it. After she commented another couple of times that she ought to be as lucky as Kathy Thibodeaux, he decided she was telling him how to do it.

He stayed late one night after the lounge closed and drilled a hole in the side of the building under the raised level at the back, where it wouldn't be noticed. On Sunday, he and Jackie locked up, got in their separate cars, and left. Except Jeffrey returned, funneled gas and diesel fuel through the plastic bottle, inserted the rope, lit it, then hauled out as fast as he could.

He didn't talk to Jackie until she called him a few hours later, hysterical, and asked him to pick her up and bring her to the fire. In front of the still smoking remains of The Emerald Lizard, she wept and told him her life was ruined. At first he thought she was putting on a show for the cops, but he soon realized she meant it. And if her life was ruined, then he had ruined it.

"How could I have been so stupid?" he asked and hiccupped twice. "Even you knew she loved the Lizard." I decided he meant even someone who didn't know Jackie all that well. "I don't guess I ever could have told her," he said miserably.

Which meant she really did think Brevna had burned down the lounge. So maybe she had been serious about going with me to the OCU. So maybe there was still, somehow, a connection between the fire and Jackie's murder.

"What are you going to do?" Jeffrey asked me, his brown eyes big and scared, his hiccups cured for the moment. "Are you going to call Dietz?"

I didn't know what I was going to do. In one long minute, I tried to play out in my mind what would happen if Dietz got his hands on Jeffrey, if Jeffrey told him Jackie had burgled her own lounge, told him Jackie said she wished the place would burn down. He would become an accessory to Jackie's crime. Her fear of Brevna wouldn't play with Dietz or anyone else any more than it had played with me. She'd thought she'd outsmarted Brevna by not signing the papers on the loan, but what she'd done was remove him yet another step away from any involvement with her.

"Are you going to call Dietz?" Jeffrey asked again.

"No more pills," I told him. "If I ever come over here and find you in this condition again, I'll feed you to Dietz while you're unconscious."

He thought about it, making sure, I suppose, he understood what I was saying, then his hiccups started up again with a vengeance.

There was a pay phone in front of a convenience store on Urbandale. I stopped to call Maurice, both anxious to talk to him and more than a little apprehensive. It was closing in on eleven o'clock, and if Nita hadn't made it home yet—

"She's home," Maurice said. "She's in the darkroom." His tone was a bit clipped, as if he were aggravated. If he was, though, it was probably with me. I was feeling pretty bad about the words between us.

"Did you call Diana?" I asked him.

"Yes." A blast of expelled air rattled in my ear. "I told her the show's back on." He spoke over my protest. "If I call it off, it's going to become an issue between us, a power struggle. She says she'll be finished sometime next week."

I started to remind him that Nita would never know he'd called it off, but I let it go.

"Well, if it makes you feel any better," I said, "Nita seems to be pretty far removed from whatever sleaziness is going on here. Aside from seeing him at the funeral, she didn't know anything about Brevna."

"But she does now—you told her."

"True." Again, he sounded as though he were accusing me of something heinous. I didn't like that at all, but I liked even less these bad feelings between Maurice and me, so I let it go, too. I said, "I found out positively tonight that Brevna had nothing to do with The Emerald Lizard burning down. The truth is"—I was admitting this for the first time to myself as well— "I don't believe he had anything to do with Jackie's murder, either."

"The truth is, Neal," Maurice said, "even if you'd found out Brevna is a mass murderer, it wouldn't stop Nita now."

Here was the real truth: Maurice hadn't called off Nita's show because he didn't trust Diana not to tell Nita he'd done it. As I hung up with him I thought he had no good reason to trust Diana. It was just the sort of thing she would do.

31

Big Blows

The day after Thanksgiving I talked to Aubrey. All he really wanted to talk about was the weather.

"The big blow is coming, Neal. We're gonna catch shrimp tonight."

Outside my office window were other office windows, no trees, nothing to indicate that the wind was shifting and the temperature dropping except an overcast sky. But I'd felt it that morning when I left the Euclid—the first serious cold snap of the season.

"I thought you were going on the nightshift," I said.

"Not till Monday. I'll have to round up all the drunks early."

He asked me how Larry Silva was doing. Larry had done fine, taking everything in his philosophically fatalistic way, until Thanksgiving day.

"There's just something about the holidays, you know?" He must have said it three or four times, his shoulders slumped, his eyes downcast.

I'd spent part of the afternoon with him, feeling depressed myself because I had nothing to tell him, no hope to give him. I didn't want to tell him about Jeffrey and the torching of the Lizard, I guess because I was still thinking that Jeffrey's blind and stupid act of love and loyalty to Jackie had somehow caused her death, and I was frustrated because I couldn't figure out how. But I didn't want to tell anyone about Jeffrey's arson because I was afraid a case could be made, by the insurance company at least, that Jackie had done it herself. It would only be one more blow for Larry.

Aubrey had nothing encouraging to tell me. Dietz had long finished his investigation and the District Attorney's office was putting together its case. Unless I could come up with something, things didn't look too good for Larry Silva.

I wasn't being my usual talkative self. Aubrey tried to fill the silence.

"Yep," he said, "we'll have a blow and then over the weekend we can go catch those big reds." Redfish, the new Louisiana gold since oil prices had plummeted. "Aren't you ready to go fishin' yet?" he asked me, and I knew he thought Larry Silva's case was hopeless.

"Not yet," I said, "but this much I do know—Jackie's killer didn't torch the Lizard."

He asked me how I knew, but I didn't tell him, and we got off the phone.

The rain started in the afternoon. It whipped around the Père Marquette and slashed at my windows. And then it was gone, not as big a blow as Aubrey had thought, but enough to usher in some frost that night and make us feel that winter finally was at hand.

32
Nice Men

Diana got out of bed and slipped into a little black dress that was cut to Brazil.

I was in bed smoking a cigarette. "Why do we have to go out to dinner?" I asked. "I thought your parents had two different caterers doing this party."

She clipped on a pair of ruby and diamond earrings that nearly reached her shoulders. "They do, but I don't like to eat at parties."

She'd made reservations at an uptown restaurant not far from her parents' house on Calhoun Street where the holiday soiree was taking place.

We swished into the restaurant all fancied up, Diana having added black stockings, black satin very high heels and a mink jacket to her ensemble, me in my courtroom power suit.

It was definitely an uptown New Orleans eatery what with its white tablecloths and napkins, black-suited waiters, and a menu that demanded at least a reading knowledge of French. Mirrors above wainscoting and framed caricatures of patrons who were also local celebrities filled in an atmosphere of casual bonhomie.

Next to our table a bottle of Dom Perignon was on ice. The waiter popped the cork and filled two slender glasses.

I took a sip, wished it was Scotch, and said, "What's the occasion?"

Diana put those semi-sweet-chocolate eyes on me. "The occasion is a proposal. I want you to come live with me, darling."

"Diana, I thought we decided we'd probably kill each other."

"I certainly wouldn't call that any sort of decision. That was just talk. Now I'm serious. You can move your clothes tomorrow, then—"

"Hold it. There's lots more to this than moving my clothes." I said that, and didn't quite know what else to say. I turned my hands palms up on the white tablecloth. "I haven't even started thinking about moving."

That wasn't exactly true. I hadn't given it much thought, but the warehouse district, down around Julia Street, was most appealing, as if it were a brand-new part of town. Out of uptown, at any rate.

You could call her smile indulgent. "I understand, darling. You'd rather it be your idea."

"Maybe," I conceded, "but that's not it. I need my own turf."

"Of course you do. We'll fix up one of the spare bedrooms into an office—whatever you want."

"That's not what I meant."

"Oh. I see. Fine. We'll find another place. I'll start looking."

I shook my head.

She reached across the table and put her hand on my forearm. She wasn't smiling anymore. "Think about it." I started to speak, but she cut me off, her dark eyes shiny in the soft light of the restaurant. "Don't say no tonight."

"Okay," I agreed, "not tonight."

*   *   *

We pulled up next to a fire hydrant across the street
from her parents' house. It was a corner house fenced
with wrought iron. Tiny Chinese stone lanterns flanked
the walkway up to wide bannistered wooden steps. Around
both sides of the yard, lanterns on poles marked path-
ways through the trees and shrubbery. The shutters on
four French windows were open and we could see people
through all of them.

Diana had timed our arrival so we were a bit more
than fashionably late. Even so, a lone couple was just
then arriving, walking along the sidewalk from their car
to the house. I started to open the door.

"Just a minute," Diana said. She watched the couple's
progress. We waited until the couple was inside and we
were alone on the street.

Diana wanted to make an entrance and create a sensa-
tion. Which she did. Which she would have done without
being the daughter of the host, though that added to the
hoopla. A small black woman in uniform waited for her
jacket.

I admit to hanging back and trying to melt into the
crowd, searching for the nearest bartender, but Diana
kept taking my hand and introducing me to people faster
than I could catch their names.

The nameless people seemed entirely too interested in
me. Diana repeated several times that I was a private
investigator. I began to feel like a bull in the china shop,
conscious for the first time in a while of my scar, and that
my power suit didn't seem to be all the occasion called
for, and that I didn't talk with the same soft, genteel
accent that a lot of these people had. Their accent was
slightly Southern, though nothing harsh and twangy, nothing remotely like that flat, rather nasal sound some New
Orleanians make. I didn't mean to, but I kept thinking I
was sounding too tough. I thought a little Scotch would
slick up my tongue.

There must have been a hundred and fifty people

there, of all ages, laughing and easy with each other. Certainly it was a concentration of some of the best-looking people in New Orleans, but an average annual income of eighty grand in the ghetto would improve everyone's looks there, too.

Another maid in uniform passed with a tray of champagne, but I'd had enough of that. I tried not to be too obvious about looking over everyone's head for the bar while Diana talked to a woman named Kitsy or Bootsy or one of those uptown girls' names. Anyway, they were deep into a conversation about faux jewels, specifically Diana's earrings. I thought I could disappear unnoticed, but a very clean-cut, preppy-looking guy—nice-looking if you didn't consider his head too long and narrow—came up to us.

"Hello, Diana." He had a soft gentle voice.

"Wylie. How are you," Diana said in a peremptory tone and told her girlfriend she'd talk to her later. Wylie was shrugging slightly, but Diana ignored that and introduced us.

Wylie said Diana had told him I was a private investigator, that I'd once been a homicide detective. I said that was right. Diana for once said nothing but was overseeing the conversation, and was, it appeared, pleased with it.

Wylie frowned slightly. "Do you still investigate murders?" he asked.

"Sometimes."

Apparently this wasn't forthcoming enough for Diana. "He's investigating one right now," she told Wylie. "His sister's best friend was murdered a couple of weeks ago."

"That's shocking," Wylie said, "so close to your family."

I could have straightened him out, but after all, we were achieving a conversation here, awkward as it felt. However, I then found I had nothing to add to Wylie's assessment.

Diana did. "It's tragic, but how many people are there

at this party, do you think, who don't know someone who's been held at gunpoint or shot?"

She was referring to a rash of incidents uptown, robberies, muggings, a couple of murders of people coming home from parties, the grocery store, jogging in the park. I wondered if she meant it wasn't shocking anymore.

"That's true," Wylie said. "It disturbs me how many people have begun carrying guns around here."

"It may disturb you," Diana remarked rather offhandedly, "but it's a fact of life. Sometimes it's kill or be killed."

I said to Wylie, "It should disturb you."

"Have you ever killed anyone?" he asked me.

I was going to tell him about the one time I came close to killing someone, while I was still a patrolman, chasing a guy over fences, through yards, and into a cemetery in Mid-City after he'd stabbed and robbed an old lady who was walking along the street with her sack of groceries. I'd shot him in the hip.

But Diana answered before I started. "He's killed several people."

Wylie was frowning again. "You shot them?"

"No—"

"He killed them with his bare hands."

"There's my little girl!" A tall man with graying hair and Diana's dark brown eyes came into our circle and kissed her. "How's my baby?"

"Fine, Daddy. This is Neal."

He put out his hand. Wylie looked on, his face possibly registering some concern that I might crush Mr. DiCarlo's fingers. "I was about to say, this must be Neal, since I know Wylie." We shook. "What? No drinks yet? Follow me. Mother's waiting for you in the back," he said to Diana. "Join us, Wylie."

"Thanks, Peter," but after we began heading toward the rear of the house, Wylie moved in the other direction.

We passed one bar on our way to a room stretched across the rear width of the house. It had probably been another porch once, but was now closed in with three sets of French doors leading outside. One set was open. The yard was completely covered by a huge yellow and white striped tent and lit by more lanterns. There were tables around the patio-dance floor, yellow flowers on the tables, and ficus trees in large pots. At the far end a band was setting up.

Mr. DiCarlo led Diana and me down some steps into the tent where a couple of long tables were strung together and draped with white to form a bar and serving area. Not very many people had filtered out here yet. A woman, obviously Mrs. DiCarlo, was giving some instructions to one of the bartenders. She was elegant, with skin still as smooth as Diana's, and short shiny brown hair waved and pretty around her face. But her face had a slightly stern set about it, the face of a person who is in charge, competent and efficient, and expects the same from others.

Diana and her mother buffed each other on the cheek so as not to disturb their makeup while Mr. DiCarlo got the bartender working on our drinks.

"Everything looks wonderful, Mother."

"Thank you, dear."

I wasn't certain, but their tones seemed chilly.

Mrs. DiCarlo turned her full attention on me. "This is Neal Rafferty?" she asked, her eyebrows arched.

"Of course," Diana said.

"If you don't mind my saying so, Neal, you show evidence of being in a dangerous line of work." She looked at my drooping eye and the scar falling from it. Notice I was in a "line of work." Only doctor, lawyer, and CPA are professions in this set.

"Oh for God's sake, Mother."

"Diana thinks I'm too outspoken."

"Then I know where she gets it from," I said.

Mrs. DiCarlo liked that. When she smiled her face softened considerably. "An attribute she appreciates only in herself," she informed me.

"You might remember that I am here and a participant in this conversation, Mother."

"Of course, dear."

Mr. DiCarlo came up with drinks. As he handed me one, Mrs. DiCarlo said, "I believe you had something to tell your father."

Diana was clearly not ready for this. A moment of surprise, then narrowed eyes at her mother, a rather defiant look at me, she recovered, turned to her father and said, "Daddy, Neal and I are going to live together."

Her father clearly was not ready for that, but he recovered, laughed, and said to me, "Diana likes to shock us. You'll have to forgive me if I tend to react slowly."

"I suppose it would be more shocking if she told us she was getting married," Mrs. DiCarlo said.

"One life to live, Mother. One is all you get." The emphasis was on *you*.

Mr. DiCarlo was irritated now, but determined to keep his savoir faire. "I don't believe this is the appropriate time or place. Could we discuss this later?" He looked at all of us in turn, me last.

"I don't believe that will be necessary," I said. I took the drink from Diana's hand and put both hers and mine on the bar. "Excuse us."

I took her by the arm, tightly, and propelled her through an opening in the tent out to the side yard. No one was there. The weather had warmed since the night before, but it was still cold. I walked until we were out of any lantern's light, under a huge magnolia tree.

"What the hell are you doing?" I demanded. My hot breath fogged in the air.

She rubbed her arm where I let it go. "I'm not doing anything," she said petulantly.

"The hell you're not. If you were twenty years old I'd say you were trying to prove your independence, but you're too old for that. What you are doing is trying to prove how bad you can be. Flaunting it? No, worse, using *me* to flaunt it." I could feel a lot of anger boiling away inside. "Fact is, you think you can use a man any way you want to, hunt him down, use him, discard him. Tell me, how long do you think we'd last under the same roof? Until Mommy and Daddy stop being upset about it? How long?"

"Stop it. Please."

"No." I was furious now. "Another thing I want to know—when did it become trendy and glamorous to go around killing people? I've never killed anyone, and if I had it isn't something I'd go around bragging about. Have you lost your mind?"

"It was just Wylie," she said. She was rubbing at her arms again, cold.

"Just Wylie. Another poor sucker, another reject. How does it go—the more they love you, the more you despise them?"

"I won't listen to this!" She took off across the yard to the garage at the end of it. Since the house was on the corner, the garage emptied out on the side street.

I heard a car start and the automatic door of the garage lifting, sliding up on rollers. She backed out, rubber squealing, squealing again when she took off down the street. The garage door rolled down and clunked into place.

My hands were shaking as I lit a cigarette. I walked through the yard to the front of the house. I could hear laughter and talking through the closed windows. Behind me the drummer swished his brushes across the skins and gave the cymbals a couple of muted claps.

I was approaching the veranda when someone spoke.

"Where did she go?"

I stopped and looked up. Wylie leaned over the veranda railing toward me.

"I don't know," I said.

"She's a difficult woman." I nodded. He hesitated, then asked. "Are you going to marry her?" God only knows what she'd told him.

"No. I'm not going to be seeing her anymore."

"She was supposed to be here with me tonight." He said it sympathetically, and I realized he assumed she'd left me, too.

The band struck up a soft instrumental version of "Mack the Knife."

Wylie said, "Maybe she can't be with anyone. I worry about her. I'd be happy just to take care of her."

I took one more drag and flicked the cigarette out over the wrought iron fence into the street. "You seem like a nice man, Wylie, but let me tell you something, Diana doesn't like nice men."

33.

What If...

It was dusk the following Tuesday and I was still in my office. I wasn't staying late because of any work, but because I saw no good reason to be anywhere else. You might say I was brooding. The bottom drawer bottle was out and I had poured myself yet another two fingers.

There was no dearth of things to brood about, that's for sure. Maurice and I were okay with each other, but not quite the same as we usually were. I wasn't sure we ever would be the same again, not because we couldn't get over a few words, but because his marrying Nita would naturally change things.

Then there was the scene with Diana at the party. We hadn't seen each other or spoken since. It wasn't that I wanted to see her; I didn't. But the whole scene, with her parents and Wylie and what I'd said to her standing out in the cold under the magnolia tree, had left me feeling pretty low. And it wasn't that anything I'd said wasn't true or that I wanted to take any of it back either.

There was also Larry Silva. The poor bastard was still in the Gretna jail, still without a dime to his name to make bail, and condemned no matter how you looked at it. True, he was going to get the best defense money could buy, and true, all of us are going to die, but I hadn't uncovered a thing to make his defense any easier, and most of us don't have to go around thinking this very moment could be our last.

All that, and still the problem of where I was going to live. As I said, it wouldn't be much trouble to find a place, but I couldn't decide where in town to look. The afternoon before I'd gone down to the warehouse district with the full intention of looking at a place, but once I got there, I'd kept on driving, heading right back to St. Charles Avenue to have a drink at the Pontchartrain Hotel. All of a sudden I didn't like the idea of an old building with a brand-new interior. I didn't want old; I didn't want new. I wanted to stay at the Euclid.

Anyway, I was sitting there, feet up on the desk, glass to my lips, when the door to the waiting room opened. I wasn't expecting anyone so I didn't jump to attention. Through the pebbled glass of my office door I thought I could make out the form of a woman.

A light knock, I called out to enter, and Diana walked in. The overhead lights were off, so it wasn't until she got closer to the light thrown by the desk lamp that I could see the black smudges under her eyes, how tired and unhappy she looked. She tried to say hi but her voice failed, her mouth trembled, and her eyes filled up. She stood on the other side of the desk blinking hard so tears wouldn't spill.

I got up and went around the desk and she clung to me for a while, until the tension in her body seeped away along with her tears.

I asked her if she wanted a drink, but she shook her head, still not trusting her voice. I had no idea I'd made her so miserable, no idea, to tell you the truth, I could. I told her I'd take her home.

The bottle put away, the Scotch drained, and the glass rinsed, I took my jacket from the coat rack and switched off the lamp. I closed the office door behind us and the phone began to ring. I almost went back for it, but Diana had the door to the hallway opened and was going through it without even looking over her shoulder. I decided to let the answering service get it and followed her.

I'll never know whether going back would have changed anything or if what was going to happen was irrevocably set in motion and it was already too late. If it would have changed anything, I'd rather not know.

34

Gone Fishing

I left my car in the Père Marquette garage and drove Diana home in hers. When we got there and she realized we weren't going to make things up and carry on where we'd left off, all those tears she'd tried so hard to hold back broke. She wept a great deal. Part of me felt guilty for hurting her so badly while another part thought she was devastated mostly because she couldn't have what she wanted, couldn't exert her usual control over everything and everyone around her. I also had to come to terms with blaming her unfairly for the trouble between Maurice and me.

So I stayed with her for a while, out of guilt and also because I was trying to sort out my own feelings, all of which could have been dealt with later, and none of which served any other purpose than to cause more delay before I hopped a streetcar back to the Euclid and got the message that Pinkie Dean had called and said it was an emergency.

*   *   *

The answering service also had two other messages. The first was from Mave Scoggins at the Gemini, the second from Maurice. So when I heard the third was from Pinkie saying it was an emergency, it put fear into my soul because the number she left was the same as the Gemini's.

I called it immediately. The woman's voice that answered was definitely not Mave Scoggins'.

"Pinkie?" I could hear country music playing in the background.

"Oh Neal, thank goodness . . ."

"What the hell are you doing there? What's going on?"

"Stop yelling. I'm not sure what's going on. I'm not even sure it's an emergency. The bartender here at the Gemini—Mave Scoggins?"

"I know her," I snapped.

"She called Maurice and told him she didn't know where Nita was but the girl Nita was with got beat up and then Nita was gone and then Maurice tried to call you—"

"Christ, Pinkie, slow down. Where's Maurice?"

"I don't know, but he cranked up that old car of his and drove it across the river."

"Jesus." For Maurice to drive across the river, it must be an emergency. "Look, Pinkie, don't move. Stay right where you are until I get there. Is Mave there?" She said Mave was. "Tell her not to go anywhere either. I'm on my way."

Only my car was downtown in the Père Marquette garage. Another delay. And again, as I called a taxi and scrounged around the apartment for a flashlight, I found myself blaming Diana, the same way Maurice had blamed her, except I'd taken her side then.

It wasn't until I was downstairs waiting for the taxi that I realized how cold it was getting. The wind picked up and I swear the temperature dropped a couple of degrees while I stood there. I still had on the same medium-weight suit I'd worn all day. I was about to head back upstairs and grab a coat, but the cab arrived and I blew it off.

Once I got to my car, I double-checked to make sure all cylinders of my revolver were loaded and put the speed loader with its extra five bullets in my coat pocket. All that was left now was to pray that the Mississippi River bridge wasn't backed up. I did. It wasn't.

The street in front of the Gemini was lined with cars. I had to park nearly a block away. Mave was doing a pretty big business for a Tuesday night. All the tables were filled, Ricky Skaggs was coming out of the jukebox at top volume, and the cowboys were rowdy. Mave drew another round of beer and they all started singing "Happy Birthday." Pinkie had stumbled into a theme party.

She was easy enough to spot among the cowboys in their shit-kickers and their buxom girlfriends in their flounced denim skirts. She was sitting at the bar in Mave's shadow, I was glad to see, and the tiny ceiling spots made her blond hair seem like a wispy halo around her head. She also had on a jacket that shone, a silvery satin baseball jacket. She jumped up when she saw me and came toward me in baby blue hightop sneakers.

She threw her arms around my neck. "God, I'm glad to see you."

"Pinkie," I said extricating myself, "why did you come over here?"

"I didn't know what else to do. Maurice told me to find you, but I couldn't. Then I thought about calling the police, but I didn't know what to tell them except that a hare-brained lawyer who doesn't know how to drive was out in a car trying to find his hare-brained girlfriend."

"Followed by his hare-brained secretary." She made a face at me. "What about this girl who got beat up?"

"Mave said she won't press charges. She won't even talk to the police."

"That figures."

We had to go around the cowboys and cowgirls who

were paired off straight down the center of the lounge doing a synchronized dance in which they seemed to be lazily kicking cowpies out of the way. At least it gave Mave a break.

She was squirting mixers into six drinks lined up on the side of the bar. She glanced over at me. "I called you first, Rafferty," she said in her Texas drawl.

A waitress took the drinks as she finished, then Mave moved in front of us, crossed her arms on the bar and leaned on them. Her large globes sort of cantilevered from the low-cut ruffled blouse she was wearing. She'd penciled in a beauty mark on the left one. It seemed to be on the verge of falling into her cleavage. She said, "I called the lawyer when I couldn't get you."

I nodded. "Who's on a rampage?"

"Nutley." I thought she was going to tell me it was Bubba. I felt a tiny burst of adrenaline hit my face. "The best I can understand it, one of the girls, Candy Malone, got upset because Rodney took all her money. Seems she threatened him and he beat her up."

"She *threatened* him?" I asked, astounded. "What in the world could she threaten Nutley with?"

"She said she was going to the Wildlife and Fisheries." Mave held both hands up to stop the question I was about to ask. "I don't know and I'll tell you what, Rafferty, I don't want to know. I like my job."

"I hear you," I said. "So what about Nita."

"Well, Nita showed up at Candy's place while Rodney was—" She stopped to shake her had. "He hurt her bad."

I panicked. "Nita?"

"No, no. The girl, Candy. He broke her jaw and she's got some head injuries. He knocked her unconscious, must have thought she was dead, she looked so bad. When she came around, he was gone and so was Nita. She called me and I took her over to JoEllen Smith hospital. That was about five. That's where I called you from. Then I had to get back here. I had this party." She waved her hand in the direction of the shuffling cowpokes.

"So this Candy Malone has no idea where Nita is, where Nutley would take her," I said.

"Nope, no idea."

I cursed. "What about Maurice?"

"I told him what I told you and I told him where Bubba keeps the boat."

"And where's Bubba?" I asked.

"Out on the boat, I guess."

Whenever you need them they've gone fishing. I could hear Pam's strident voice.

"Great," I said. I drummed with three fingers on the bar.

Mave stuck out a hand and put it on my drumming fingers, to make them stop.

"See," she said, "the reason I called, it's hard to say what Rodney might do. He's scared to death of Bubba."

35

Marshland Terror

Either the rumors Jackie had told me about Nutley had come true or he was doing a repeat performance, leaving the unconscious girl for dead. Candy Malone, the girl with the death wish, Nita had told me. And if Nutley thought Nita had witnessed a murder and he was trying to cover everything before Bubba got back . . .

"Call Delbert Dietz," I told Mave. "I'm going to La-fitte." I turned to leave but had another thought. "And call Aubrey Wohl, too. Tell him what's going on. Tell him," I added grimly, "I'm ready to go fishing. He'll know what I mean."

Pinkie followed me outside. We stood between two cars in the parking space in front of the Gemini.

"Go on home," I told her. "I'll call you after I find them."

"No way. I'm going with you."

"The hell you are!"

"The hell I'm not!" she fired right back at me. "Look,

Neal, you can pull the you're-just-a-kid routine and try to leave me here. I'll just get in my car and follow you.''

"How about the you're-a-pain-in-the-ass routine?"

"You're a pain in the ass, too!"

A couple decked in Western garb on the way to the party heard this exchange—the prostitutes down at the corner probably heard it as well—and snickered at us. For all they knew, I was a father come to rescue his rebellious daughter from the clutches of pimps and horny cowboys.

"Come on." I slid my hand across her slick jacket and tightened my fingers around the base of her neck. She swung her arm up and caught me on the bicep, flinging my hand away from her.

I walked the block to the Thunderbird at a furious clip, Pinkie's legs moving that much faster to keep up with me. She got in the car and nearly created sparks as she slammed the two pieces of the seatbelt together.

We drove to Lafitte in silence. By the time we got to the Intracoastal Canal Bridge, a fine mist was gathering on the windshield. For about three minutes on the Lafitte LaRose Highway rain teemed, and then the wind seemed to blow it away, back to a fine mist.

A half-moon showed sporadically through the heavy low-hanging clouds being pushed along by the wind. At the moment, though, it was obscured by a large mass so that I was having trouble locating the turnoff to Bubba's dock. All of a sudden we came upon the tail end of a dark-colored Mercedes-Benz.

"Neal!" Pinkie spotted it at the same time I did, and with a reflex reaction, reached over to grab my arm.

"I see it," I said.

The car might have been abandoned in a hurry. It was pulled off to the side, just barely, nosed down a grassy slope, all there was of any kind of shoulder. The way it looked, Maurice might have been run off the road, but more likely it was his idea of a park job.

It was a good hundred feet ahead to the turnoff. I

slowed down to a crawl to look for him, but it was so late I knew the chances of finding him meandering along the road were remote.

It could have meant anything, but with the couple of hours lead time he'd had, the car still being there seemed like a bad sign. I knew Pinkie was thinking the same thing from the way her body tensed, her hands clutching the dash.

I thought about parking away from the turnoff and approaching on foot, but the rain had started again, not pouring, but heavy enough to get us soaked if we walked too far. Instead I went past the turnoff and past the driveway leading to the garage where the refrigerated trucks were kept. I turned onto grass, bringing the car behind the oaks lining the driveway, hoping I wouldn't get stuck in mud. I drove until I was close enough to the water that I could see Bubba's dock. *My New Flame* was gone. This could have been cause for relief, but that's not what I felt.

What I was feeling was hard to define. Call it extreme uneasiness. Everything was contributing to a scenario that didn't promise to play well. The rain was coming down steadily now, the wind was up high enough to whistle faintly through the twisted oaks, their trunks tortured into those oddly writhing forms from weather exactly like this—good shrimping weather.

I surveyed the wooded area between us and the garage as best I could through the rain, in the dark. If there was anything out there, it was lurking in the dense shadows. I got the gun out of the glove compartment, the flashlight out of the compartment in the center console.

"There's a garage behind those trees," I said to Pinkie. "That's where we're going. Stay close. And don't talk."

We got out of the car and I waited until she came around the front of it before I started moving. She held on to the back of my jacket and, as fast as I could, training the flashlight on the ground and memorizing several feet ahead at a time before directing the beam into the trees and shrubs at the sides, I headed for the garage.

We stayed fairly dry because of the tree cover, and as it turned out it was the driest and warmest we'd be for quite a while. Because when we walked out into the clearing in front of the garage, one of the double doors was slightly ajar, and from inside I thought I could hear a drone, like a small motor makes, behind the sound of the rain on the corrugated metal of the garage. It made more sense to get wet than to dash into the garage. And then I realized what I was hearing was probably the refrigerator motor on one of the trucks.

I had to pull the door open a little wider to get in. I turned off the flashlight and crouched down; Pinkie, still clinging to my coat tail, followed me inside.

Once we were in I stopped to get my bearings and adjust to less light than there'd been outside, which hadn't been much. Finally more or less in front of us I could see the shape of a truck which had been backed into the garage, but the droning was coming from the left. Both trucks were there. I approached the nearest one and immediately could feel heat coming from the hood. I reached out—it was wet from the rain, but still warm enough that I knew it couldn't have been there very long.

Pinkie was tugging on my coat. I turned around and she slipped her arm around my waist. She was shaking, either from being chilled by the rain or from fright. Either would do. I stuck the flashlight in my coat pocket and held her close while I waited and listened and tried to feel if there was anyone else in there with us.

The rain beat on the tin roof. The motor droned. The longer we stood there, the noisier it got. The rain was picking up even more. There was no way of hearing anything or feeling anything with it clamoring on the rooftop and driving against the metal sides of the garage. All I felt was a desire to get to the truck to the left with its refrigeration turned on.

I patted Pinkie's shoulder and moved her arm, putting

her hand back at the bottom of my jacket to let her know we would be moving again. I took out the flashlight, my gun in my other hand aimed straight ahead, but before I turned it on, I took a couple of steps to the left and stopped. Still nothing. Another couple of steps would put us in the space between the two trucks. I started and as I went I snapped on the flashlight. The moment I did I caught a movement to my right just before a tremendous weight hit my gun hand and then my head. I heard Pinkie call out my name and I thought I saw the gun sliding under the truck behind me, and then I was swimming at the edge of unconsciousness, coming up for a moment, going down again.

The next thing I was aware of was someone pulling on me, dragging me, and my legs trying to move. I'd try to stand and get dragged down again. And then I felt the freezing rain on my face and it started snapping me to, so that I knew I was being dragged by the collars of my shirt and coat. I finally stopped trying to stand up and just let him drag me all the way down to the pier. By that time I was soaked to the bone.

As soon as he stopped I stood on legs that were shaking but gaining strength by the second from a hearty dose of adrenaline. Godzilla loomed above me, watching as I got up, one of his massive hands around Pinkie's throat. I knew with one quick movement he could break her neck.

I didn't know whether I should try to talk to him or not, but before I could make up my mind, he was shoving me toward a flatboat that was tied to the dock. That's when it dawned that we were on the rickety pier behind the garage, not on Bubba's dock. I think I would have given anything at that moment to see Bubba coming at us with his bullwhip.

Rodney let go of Pinkie and pushed her down in the boat on the middle seat. Then he practically threw me down next to her. There was no way to fight him; to try would be suicide. Rodney had no idea of his own strength or he would have killed Bubba by now.

He made us sit with our backs to him, so that when he started the boat we were facing into the wind and rain. He steered out into the marsh. Pinkie put her head down on her knees. I covered my face with my hands, but as the boat gathered speed I tried my best to see in front of us, the cold rain driving into my face like thin, sharp nails. First we seemed headed straight at one grassy bank, then he'd slice the boat away and seem to head into the other. I could feel panic deep within my chest, but it was nothing to what I felt when Nutley opened up the throttle and we rocketed through the dark narrow waterways, turning so fast from one cut into another that I thought Pinkie and I would be thrown from the boat. She had grabbed one of my legs, and I grabbed the seat of the boat. Every now and again we would emerge into an open pond where the water would be extremely choppy. As tight as I held on, I couldn't stop my body from lifting and slamming down on the metal seat, my spine hammering into my head with each slam. As painful as it was, I was much more concerned about us hitting something in the water. I found myself praying that the rain would stop and the cloud cover would break so the moon would come out. As if my seeing where we were going would make any difference.

Rodney twisted and turned and ran the boat through the marshy maze for what seemed like an eternity, but was actually only a quarter of an hour. I think I have never been so terrified in my entire life, going deeper and deeper into the marsh, knowing exactly what Nutley had in mind—to leave us in that place where everything looks the same, to kill us, drown us maybe, to let us die at the very edge of the earth.

He slowed the boat and maneuvered it up against the grass of a lump of mud that might not even be there after some big blow, maybe this one. Only I thought that and then realized that the rain had slackened, and although there was still a lot of wind, it wasn't as high as it had been. My ears were aching with cold.

Nutley stood up in the boat as though he were on concrete. He made a grunting sound and pushed on my back. Pinkie started to sit up, but he shoved her down. I assumed he wanted me to stand, so I did, but I wasn't up all the way before he chopped down on my shoulder to make me sit again. It felt as if I'd been hit with a piece of pipe.

I turned slightly to look up at him. He had his head cocked, his hair a wild black mass around it, his wedge-of-bone forehead so low over his eyes I couldn't see them. And then I heard it, too. The sound of another boat, a steady buzz getting deeper and louder as it came toward us.

With another grunt, Nutley sat in the back of the flatboat and we were moving again.

It was the shrimpers. The rain was being blown away, so the shrimpers were heading out into the channels and bays and passes to haul in the shrimp that would be swept along as the tide began to fall. I found myself thanking God for shrimpers.

But not for long because Nutley opened up again and my heart rose to my throat, threatening to choke me as we zoomed through the dark, speeding around curves, almost turned on our side, zephyring down the waterways. It wasn't until I saw the pier and the garage coming up fast in front of us that I was aware of the moon trying to peek from behind the clouds. I felt a great sense of relief, as though the moon were a friend, the pier and garage home.

The pier lurched strangely as I stepped up on it, but it was only my legs trying to believe they were on a surface that wasn't moving. I helped Pinkie up, her eyes gigantic in her small face, her body feeling small and too easily breakable in my arms as she grabbed me, hiding her face against my chest.

I was beginning to feel stable enough and strong enough after the blow to my head to think about trying to get Nutley. Only trying wouldn't be good enough. I would have one chance, just one, and if it didn't work, I'd be dead. And so would Pinkie, and then I cringed, wondering where Maurice and Nita were, hoping like hell they were sitting out on some mud lump, soon to be rescued by a shrimper, knowing full well the odds were against Nutley leaving them out there alive.

Nutley let us know with his all too articulate body language, in this case a rough shove on the back of my head, that he wanted us to walk. With periodic jabs to my back, he propelled us to the entrance of the garage and made a harsh sound in his throat that I knew with certainty meant he wanted me to open the door.

As soon as I did he thrust us inside. I pretended to lose my balance, and fell in front of the truck I thought my gun was under. It was, of course, hopeless that I would see it in the dark, but it was worth a try. Except when I got up, Nutley was in the doorway, holding Pinkie by the throat again. I lifted my hands to show I wasn't going to do anything.

He stepped inside and turned toward the second truck, but it was gone. His reaction frightened me almost as much as the boat ride. With a high-pitched scream, he threw Pinkie away from him. She fell on the dirt floor, crying out, more frightened than hurt. I held my hand out to her, but I did that without taking my eyes off Nutley. I couldn't see his face very well, but the way he was moving around, a jerky start to where the truck had been, then a jerky turn toward us, to the truck behind us, I was certain he was unpleasantly surprised the truck was gone, that somehow this was not part of his game plan. His game plan, in fact, seemed to have fallen apart, what with Pinkie and me still to be dealt with and this truck gone. I couldn't tell if he was panicked or frustrated. Whatever it was, it scared me plenty.

He was grunting again, pushing on us, directing us to the back of the truck, then kicking at our feet to make us get up into it. The door was open, but the ramp wasn't there, so as fast as I could I raised myself onto the bed, quickly turning and lifting Pinkie so he wouldn't hurt her.

He slid the door down and clunked its bolt into place. The mind is a strange thing, because the sound of that sliding door rolling down and the bolt clunking into place made me think of the garage door at Diana's parents' house rolling down and clunking into place. One roll, a clunk, and *finis*.

36

No Way to Die

It was pitch black, it stunk of fish, and we were locked inside. But it on was terra firma and Rodney Nutley wasn't locked inside with us.

Pinkie tripped and fell. I heard wood splintering.

"Are you all right?" I asked, groping in the dark for her. There were boxes everywhere.

"Yes. No." Her voice cracked. "I don't know." I found her and pulled her up.

Two soaked and dripping people hung on to each other. She was breathing deeply, trembling with cold, sniffling a bit.

"I'm not going to cry, Neal."

Like a blind man, I felt her face, felt the wet hair on her forehead, pushed it back, felt the curve of her head. "It's okay," I said. "Cry for both of us."

I made a space for us on the floor of the truck so we could sit. In the quiet I could hear the wind outside and the rain now tapping lightly on the garage roof. All

around us were those seafood crates, the kind I'd seen on
the truck before. I reached out for the one closest to me.
My fingers closed on it and contacted slime. The boxes
hadn't been cleaned yet; the truck had returned too
recently. I wiped my hand on my pants thinking it was
probably Rodney Nutley's job to clean them, but he was
busy at the moment.

Where the hell were the cops? It was well over an hour
since we'd left the Gemini. Surely Mave had done as I
asked and called Dietz. But what if she hadn't been able
to get Dietz and hadn't told anyone else in his office what
was going on? And what if Aubrey was out when she
called and she was back at the Gemini calmly waiting for
them to return her call? Even though I was cold and
clammy I felt myself break into a sweat.

I knew Aubrey was around, working the nightshift
somewhere in Westwego. It was still too early for him to
have taken off to go shrimping, and I knew he would
come immediately once he talked to Mave, even if Dietz
didn't consider any of us worth his rushing to Lafitte.

And what if no one came, no one but Rodney Nutley?
I picked up the seafood box and started feeling it all
over, the slime be damned. As I felt it I began to get a
much clearer image of what it looked like, how it was
constructed. The sides were made of fairly sturdy wooden
slats, the lightweight bottom a separate piece hooked to
the sides with wire. I could feel wire running around the
box itself, reinforcing it. I began to see it not as a box at
all anymore, but as a weapon.

Beside me, Pinkie sat close and I could tell by the way
tremors would hit her body now and again that she was
either crying or trying awfully hard not to. Or maybe she
was just cold, because when I stood up she said clearly,
"What are you doing?"

"What I'm doing," I said as I bent back the wire
attaching the bottom of the box to the sides, "is giving us
a chance against that goon when he comes back."

She got up, too, and I could hear her sneakers bump along the truck bed as she pushed boxes away from her.

"Neal, Maurice was in that other truck."

My head swung in the direction of her voice. "He was? How do you know?"

"I heard him. He called out when that guy hit you."

"Did you hear Nita?"

"No."

"Well, let's hope she was in there with him." At least they weren't out in the marsh somewhere. "My guess is Rodney doesn't know where they are as long as they're in that truck."

I went back to work. I turned the box upside down and stepped on the bottom with my foot. It made a harsh grating sound.

"What was that?" Pinkie asked.

"That was the bottom of the box coming out."

I lifted out my foot and went to pick up the box. It collapsed. I thought I'd broken it, but it had just folded up the way it was supposed to without the bottom in it.

Folded like that it was maybe a foot and a half by two and a half feet of wire-reinforced wooden slats. I began to take each slat and fold it up on the one ahead of it, then the two of them back on the third one and so on, accordion-like.

"Okay, Pinkie, see if you can stack the boxes up, starting about four feet from the door. Make a wall with them."

"Are we going to hide behind them?"

"That's what I want him to think."

I kept folding while Pinkie started stacking the boxes. Within minutes I had a pretty formidable club. I peeled wire off another box and wound it tight around the club to make sure it wouldn't come apart when I swung it. I struck the floor with it. It was solid.

The truck was six, maybe eight feet wide. I helped Pinkie with the boxes, our hands full of slime, our noses full of the stink of dead fish. We worked fast, stacking the boxes so there was a small opening on each side. Finished, the wall was three boxes high by three boxes deep. I took some more and stacked them to one side of the door, up to the roof of the truck, to give me something to hide behind when Nutley slid the door up. We made an identical stack on the other side. I counted on this order within the truck to give him a moment's worth of confusion.

Pinkie and I wedged ourselves between the wall of boxes and a stack next to the door, me cradling the club on my lap. I felt inside my coat pocket, took Pinkie's hand, and put the speedloader in it. With the bullets in, it had some weight to it. Then I told her what I wanted her to do.

That's when I heard the voice.

"Don't do that, Rodney," is what I thought I heard.

I strained to listen, wondering if I was hearing things through the wind and the flurries of rain like drum rolls now and again over the roof of the garage.

"Please don't do that." It was Nita. "You're hurting me, Rodney."

A terrible moment of silence, then Nita again—"Stop!"

There was some scuffling. I jumped up, nearly upsetting the stack of boxes at the side of the sliding door.

Nita let out a piercing "No!" I heard Nutley grunt.

More scuffling, a crash against the side of the garage, and the sounds began to come too fast—Nita's screams, Nutley's grunts, and my own voice yelling at Nutley to stop, my fists pounding the side of the truck, my feet kicking it, the whole truck rocking, and through it all those horrible, regular grunts, animal grunts, and then Nita wasn't screaming anymore, and beside me I heard a soft breathless humming.

Pinkie was rocking back and forth, humming tunelessly to herself, and when I bent down to her, I found her arms wrapped over her head, covering her ears. Humming and covering her ears so she wouldn't hear it.

There was nothing more to hear.

"Pinkie," I whispered and took her arms, moving them so she would hear me. She kept rocking. I shook her. "Pinkie!" I whispered again.

Outside the truck I heard Nutley moving around. I heard him at the back now, and I knew he was attaching the ramp, getting ready to open the truck door.

"He's coming!" I said urgently, trying to make Pinkie move, not sure if she could, but then she was getting to her feet, stumbling against me, finally standing up. I directed her across the truck, to her position, having no idea if she could follow through on our plan.

The truck shook as he stepped on the ramp. I went back to my side.

The club. Where the hell was the club? In my kicking and pounding I must have dropped it. I fell to my knees, feeling frantically along the floor, knocking the wall of boxes. One of the top boxes fell.

The bolt thunked. My hand found the club, and the jagged end of a piece of wire ripped one of my fingers to the bone. I hardly felt it.

Somehow I was standing where I was supposed to be, using the stack of seafood boxes as cover, club ready, as the door began its upward slide. I watched at the bottom and clearly saw Nutley's legs; it had been so pitch black inside the truck that even the dark garage was light.

I know it was a matter of a second or two, but the door lifting seemed to take forever. I wondered if Pinkie was going to be able to throw the speed loader.

The door was up and one of his big booted feet thudded on the floor of the truck. And the other one was coming up behind it. He hesitated. I was about to give up on Pinkie and swing the club when the speed loader hit Nutley in the face. He jerked his head in Pinkie's direction and I swung the club. It contacted just below his knees. The best I can remember, the sound that came out of him was halfway between a groan and a grunt. His body went forward, his face turned toward me. I raised the club and with every ounce of strength I had, I brought it down on his head. Then I hit him again.

He didn't utter a sound. He stayed upright for a second before he fell off to the left, away from me, his enormous hulk glancing off the side of the truck, then falling out. When he hit the ground the truck shook as hard as it had when he stepped into it.

Quickly, in case he was only stunned, I jumped off the truck after him, ready to hit him again and again, as many times as it took. But he wasn't moving. I knelt next to him and with a reticent hand I felt his throat for a pulse.

Pinkie came out from behind the wall inside the truck. "Is he dead?" she asked calmly, too calmly.

"Yes. He's dead."

"That's good," she said. I told her to wait in the truck. I stood up and as I moved to go around him, I stepped on one of Nutley's feet. The way it felt in its leather boot, the leather twisting around it under my foot, made me feel sick.

But that was nothing, nothing. I would have done a balancing act on his dead booted feet for two days if I hadn't had to find Nita.

She wasn't hard to find. She was over in a corner of the garage, and her pale skin in the little bit of moonlight seeping through the garage doors was like a beacon. She was lying there, her jeans around her ankles, her head thrown back as though she'd been gasping for air, and my guess was they'd find her trachea had been crushed, too.

This screaming siren sound was going off in my head. It went off until through it I heard Pinkie calling me, and then I wasn't sure if it had been in my head or if it was that bastard Dietz finally arriving. I found myself wanting to kill him—with my bare hands.

But there weren't any sirens. Everything was deathly quiet except for Pinkie calling my name out of the blackness on the other side of the garage.

"Just a minute," I heard myself say and my voice was normal even though my face was wet from tears. I didn't know if I was going to be able to stop them.

I took off my heavy sodden jacket and covered Nita's exposed body with it. I had to pull myself together, for Pinkie's sake, so I stood there drying my face with a wet shirt sleeve before going back to the truck to get her.

"Watch it," I told her, a strange thing to tell someone in the dark, and lifted her from the ramp, away from Nutley. I put my arm around her, keeping her on the side away from Nita. I just didn't want her to know yet.

"Where's Nita?" she asked.

"We have to go get help," I said, moving her toward the garage doors.

Outside I realized I was walking in the wrong direction, thinking the car was parked where it had been that first time I'd been here, but as I started to turn us around, I heard a noise. Someone was on the other side of the garage, the side closest to Bubba's dock. I put my hand over Pinkie's mouth, lightly, to let her know something was up, then I began to go forward again, alone.

If I'd heard him moving, then he'd heard me. I thought about my gun under the truck, but it was too late.

Aubrey and I practically ran each other down coming around the side of the garage.

He stepped back quickly, his gun aimed at me. Mine would have been aimed at him if I'd had it.

I held my hands palms up at my sides. I hardly knew what to say to him. "It's all over, Aubrey," is what I said.

He stared at me, at the pain that must have been showing on my face. The wind was blowing his hair around a bit, and felt as if it were going past my thin wet shirt straight through me. My body began to shake the same way the leaves on the oaks around us were shaking in that wind.

You would have thought Aubrey would have stopped pointing his gun at me by now, but he didn't.

"She accused me of burning down the Lizard, Neal."

For a split second I had no earthly idea what he was talking about. I said nothing.

"She thought I'd done it because I did the restaurant the same way. She was going to tell the organized crime people in the morning."

For his shrimp boat. He'd done the restaurant job for his shrimp boat.

"I didn't mean to hit her. She got wild."

She was going to throw him to the OCU to get Bubba, I was thinking. And then I was thinking everything at once—Mave's message that I was ready to go fishing had made Aubrey think I'd found him out, that I'd finally put it all together—his return to the scene of the crime, his intimacy with Jackie's house, his wanting to know if I was intimate with Jackie, if I knew where the bedroom was. Everybody loved Jackie.

He was saying, "She said Bubba always had to have a cop in his pocket. That's true. But it's not me anymore."

I spoke to him very softly, just so he could hear me above the wind. "So what are you going to do, Aubrey? Shoot me?"

"No, I guess not." He lowered his gun.

Right then a gunshot ripped through the sound of the wind and blew the side of Aubrey's face off.

I spun around. "Dietz!" I screamed. "Dietz, you son of a bitch!"

37

The Other Truck

Pinkie and I were speeding along the highway. I'd held the speedometer at a hundred or better ever since we'd gotten out of town and hit the wide open and empty interstate. We went out of Louisiana, through Missis- sippi, and were nearly out of Alabama into Florida when I spotted the other truck.

I edged alongside of it, dangerously close, shouting, "Pull over," through the open window, showing Clem Winkler my gun.

He slowed down and stopped on the highway's shoulder. I jumped out of the car and flung open the truck door, and held the gun on him.

"Wha' the . . ." he started.

"Get out," I told him and he knew I meant business. "Unlock that back door."

He scrambled around for the keys and went around to the back of the truck. As soon as he had the lock undone, I grabbed it, tossed it to the side, slid the bolt and threw up the back door.

It was icy outside but a blast of freezing air came from inside the truck. Maurice was curled on his side, his hands tucked inside his sleeves, out cold.

"Wha' the . . ." Winkler started again.

"Shut up!" I yelled at him.

I gave Pinkie the gun and jumped into the truck and went to work bringing Maurice around. His eyes fluttered a bit. It was as if he were doped from the cold. I talked to him and rubbed his face and got him sitting up.

"I'm never going to eat redfish again, Neal," he told me.

I told him I never was either.

He was standing outside, the crates of redfish in the truck behind him, focusing on my face. That's when he asked what I knew he would finally have to ask.

My face began to fall apart. He looked at Pinkie. Then he closed his eyes, his head lifted toward the nighttime sky, and his voice rose above the wind, crying out her name in two long, plaintive syllables that will play in my mind until I die.

38.

Epilogue

It was while dawn was breaking that I noticed the lacy foliage of the cypress trees down the river had turned brown, died. It had happened overnight, the result of that first frost a few days earlier, and it seemed to say it all.

But of course it didn't say it all. Nothing can. I can tell you, though, how at the inquiry it came down to my word against Dietz's that Aubrey Wohl was going to kill me. No, I said, Aubrey Wohl was going to expose Delbert Dietz and Bubba Brevna too, so Dietz murdered him. Internal Affairs, the OCU and anybody else who thought they had to said they'd look into all that.

I believe it was Diana who'd said maybe Brevna was fishing for something other than shrimp. And Larry Silva had said more than he realized when he told me that even the IRS couldn't audit fish. They couldn't count all the dead redfish either, the ones that got captured in the purse seine, but were too much for Brevna's boat, the ones that washed belly up on the barrier islands.

A few weeks later, after the killings were no longer headlines, there was a small article buried in the back of the paper. The headline read, REDFISH TRANSPORTING CASE DROPPED. No, believe it. A Florida court ruled against a state law that prohibited possession, selling, or shipping into Florida any food fish caught with a purse seine no matter where it was caught. The Florida court decided this law against purse seines was unconstitutional, so the Feds dropped their case against Brevna until the decision could be appealed. Tell that to all those white-bellied fish. Talk about that when you talk about national crazes for blackened redfish.

Since all this happened, commercial fishing of redfish has been banned in Louisiana. But there are other species of fish, and other kinds of nets. And there will always be pirates. What they can't profit from, they throw away. So dead redfish still wash up on the barrier islands. That's right, the ones that are now protected under the law.

It does no good to rage. But somebody has to do it.

Anyway, Larry Silva seems to be enjoying good health and Pam is definitely enjoying all his money. The best part is that Pam's little boy Jason thinks Larry is better than TV. Larry likes that.

And then there is Jeffrey Bonage who had the hiccups for two weeks, and that's all I intend to say about him.

Maurice. I can't really talk about Maurice yet. I'll just tell you what you already know—that he'll never be the same again any more than I will be—and let it go at that.

Of course, my theories about violence can always be expanded. My latest one is that witnessing an act of violence with another person, experiencing terror together, creates a bond closer than family.

I worried about Pinkie. She wasn't the same either, not that I expected her to be, but that quality I like to call youthful exuberance had left her. It made me sad that

Pinkie couldn't hold on to her exuberance a while longer, but it was replaced by a kind of quietness, a serenity I found extremely compelling and attractive. And, as always, youthful resilience counts for a lot.

It was Pinkie who held Maurice's law office together in the weeks that followed Nita's death, and it was Pinkie who found me a place to live when the new owners of the Euclid were threatening to move me out with the furniture.

The place was uptown, a large apartment on the second floor of a giant old cypress house that hadn't seen paint for many years. Trees grew up close around it, a low rusted wrought iron fence separated it from the rest of the neighborhood. It looked, in a word, haunted. There was a turret on it, and that turret, its rounded interior space, was part of my living room. There were also fourteen-foot ceilings, mantel pieces, and the smell of musk that becomes part of all these old New Orleans dwellings.

I recognized something about the place right away, a feeling of comfort, a smell of the past, a vision of the future with old photographs decorating the mantelpieces.

The night before the movers were due to arrive Pinkie and I built a fire in the living room fireplace. We sat on the floor, our backs against the wall, our shoulders touching with all that empty space around us, and watched the flames dance and spark and glow hotter, and for the first time in several weeks I began to believe that things were going to get better.